Advance Praise for *Julia & Rodrigo*

"In *Julia & Rodrigo* Mark Brazaitis takes *Romeo and Juliet* and wonders what becomes of impossible love when the lovers cannot simply die. Rendered in swift, elegant prose, his tale of a poor football star and the wealthy girl who loves him turns most painful after the forced parting. Anyone who has loved and lost will recognize the wounds of these doomed, gentle characters. What's most tragic, Brazaitis knows, is that in Julia's and Rodrigo's great love—like the bloody Guatemala Civil War that surrounds it—none can win, and all of it is so unnecessary."

—Tony D'Souza, author of *Whiteman, The Konkans,* and *Mule*

"This expressive, touching and at times wrenching novel tells the stories of two young people living in Guatemala during that country's civil war. Teenagers Julia Garcia and Rodrigo Rax meet at a school pageant and find that they are drawn to each other. Julia, the daughter of an engineer, lives in one of the few two-story houses in town. Rodrigo, who comes from less privilege, is a soccer star. But what begins as a love story soon becomes a struggle against circumstance. Julia and Rodrigo rise above old-fashioned customs of marriage and religious worship only to collide with events they cannot control. Ultimately, this finely crafted novel goes a long way toward answering the question of whether human free will can overcome fate, or God's will."

—Thaddeus Rutkowski, final judge of the contest and author of *Haywire, Tetched* and *Roughhouse*

"What a stunning novel! *Julia & Rodrigo* is ambitious, deeply felt, exquisitely written, masterfully structured, and informed by a wide-ranging knowledge of the culture and politics of Guatemala. Astonishingly, if one didn't know the gender and nationality of the author, a reader could never guess that it was written by a North American male—Mark Brazaitis so inhabits his two characters and the milieu in which they come of age. In many ways as tragic as *Romeo and Juliet,* his novel follows its own poignant, yet unsentimental story line to an inevitable, sorrowful, and yet hope-filled end. I read this novel in one sitting late into the night; I could not put it down. An instructive book for readers of all ages and a perfect accompaniment to high school and university courses on Latin America, as well as a compelling book club choice."

—Marnie Mueller, author of *Green Fires, The Climate of the Country,* and *My Mother's Island*

Books by Mark Brazaitis

The Incurables

The Other Language

An American Affair

Steal My Heart

The River of Lost Voices: Stories from Guatemala

Julia & Rodrigo

By Mark Brazaitis

Winner of the Gival Press Novel Award

Gival Press

Arlington, Virginia

Published by Gival Press, an imprint of Gival Press, LLC.

For information please write:

Gival Press, LLC
P. O. Box 3812
Arlington, VA 22203
www.givalpress.com

First edition
ISBN: 978-1-928589-85-3
eISBN: 978-1-928589-88-4
Library of Congress Control Number: 2013948199

Covert art: "Escena 8" by Luis González Palma.
Photo of Mark Brazaitis by Sheila Loftus.
Design by Ken Schellenberg

for Julie, Annabel and Rebecca

and, as always, for the people of Santa Cruz Verapaz, Guatemala

ONE

— 1 —

Julia hears him before she sees him. At the end of the Flor de Mayo pageant, as Ingrid Estrada strolls down the red-carpeted floor with her crown glittering in the gymnasium lights, he yells his displeasure: "Why do the blanquitas always win?" He follows with a chant: "Black! Black! Black!" His words seem to turn Ingrid Estrada even whiter.

Dark-skinned, although more a rich earth color than black, he is standing near the two open doors at the back of the gymnasium. Julia knows who he is. Rodrigo. Rodrigo Rax. She has known him most of her life—they are in the same class now at El Instituto Básico—but she has never heard him speak in such a firm, commanding voice. His voice is like a light shining on what else is attractive about him: his broad shoulders, his strong jaw, his large, expressive eyes.

Julia is sitting in an aisle seat, her body turned toward him. When his gaze moves from Ingrid Estrada to her, she holds her breath. The expression on Rodrigo's face turns from disgust to delight. Julia returns his smile, and he winks at her.

Rodrigo finishes his protest with exuberant laughter, and he and the heavyset man standing next to him depart into the night. As if trying to protect the audience from their return, Guillermo, the ticket taker, closes both doors behind them. They shut with a bang-bang, like two gunshots. But even as Julia watches Ingrid finish her walk back to the stage and accept kisses from the six judges, she hears the echo of Rodrigo's voice. It is hard to see Ingrid as she did a minute before, as a girl with flowing black hair and shining morning skin. She sees instead a girl who is so pale as to look ill; she sees her hair as a witch's cape. Ingrid waves goodbye, and the final applause is soft and brief. People are quick to leave the gymnasium, escaping into the cool night. The sky is bright with stars.

Julia walks under the roof of the municipalidad and past Santa Cruz's lone pay phone. She is about to step into the street when she sees Rodrigo across it, sitting on a stool at Tienda Esperanza, a white, wooden stand decorated with Coca-Cola emblems. Next to Rodrigo sits the man he was with in the gymnasium, Pedro Mendez, who appears often in her father's warnings of what most men, in their hearts, are like. Pedro is known to have fathered two children with women in town he never married.

Julia hides behind one of the municipalidad's thick columns, her head craning from behind it so she can observe them. Her heartbeat quickens from the excitement of spying.

"Ingrid Estrada isn't the whitest girl I know," Pedro says. "In the capital, I know dozens of gringas. Blond-haired gringas, red-haired gringas, even a gringa who dyes her hair pink and green."

"I don't like gringas," Rodrigo says. "I like Guatemaltecas. Dark eyes, dark hair, dark skin."

"Very patriotic," Pedro says.

Rodrigo and Pedro face each other on their stools. They are both drinking from bottles—beer, Julia guesses. She watches Rodrigo lift the bottle to his lips. She wonders how it tastes; she imagines it tasting like honey and something bitter.

Julia knows her father will be waiting for her. It is past ten o'clock, and her father wanted her home by nine-thirty.

"How long were you in the capital this time?" Rodrigo asks.

"Six, seven months," Pedro says. "Two days before I left, I was in Disco Tropical when a bunch of soldiers from the United States came. They didn't have their uniforms on, but they had crewcuts and they were gringos, so I knew who they were. One of the soldiers was talking to a certain muchacha. Her boyfriend didn't like it, so he sliced the soldier's neck. Blood everywhere, vos. People were slipping in blood."

"Did he die?"

"The newspaper said he was in the hospital. Critical condition." Pedro drinks from his bottle. "The soldier never imagined Disco Tropical would be his Vietnam." Pedro laughs and shakes his head and drinks.

"So the Americans are here to help fight the war?" Rodrigo asks.

"No, vos. Only to train and advise the army. To teach better ways to kill."

Rodrigo sips from his bottle before returning it to the counter. "What would you do if you were forced to join the army?" Rodrigo asks.

"I'd run away, vos. Once you're in the army, you're dead, even if you don't die. Your head, vos—it's never the same." Pedro pauses to drink. "And you, vos?"

"I guess I'd run, too." Rodrigo finishes what's in his bottle. They sit in silence for a while before Rodrigo turns on his stool and looks down the street. "I have to go," he says. "My mother is waiting."

Rodrigo shakes Pedro's hand, says goodnight and leaves his stool. Julia watches him walk down Avenida La Parroquia and reach the part of the road where the concrete ends. Because he is wearing a black T-shirt and black slacks, he easily merges with the darkness.

Pedro turns around on his stool to face the street, and Julia quickly moves her head behind the column. She hopes he hasn't seen her, but a moment later, he calls out, "Who are you looking for, señorita?" A few seconds later, he adds, "Come here, I have something to show you."

The streets are empty, and Julia fears Pedro will leave his stool, push her into the shadowed doorway of the municipalidad and do with her what he wants. But although she's afraid, she doesn't run. When, a minute later, she again ventures a look from behind the column, Pedro is gone. The light from within Tienda Esperanza glows on the empty stools. The woman behind the counter is standing against the back wall, her eyes closed.

Julia leaves her hiding place and looks down the street where Rodrigo lives. The moon hangs above the mountains beyond it. She imagines walking down the street to Rodrigo's house. She imagines listening at his bedroom window and overhearing his nighttime prayers. She imagines him speaking her name.

—

Returning to her house, Julia finds her father sitting on the couch in the living room. Although he has been sleeping, his head resting on his shoulder, he immediately opens his eyes and sits upright. He is thin, with a narrow face, and in his bearing there is the rigidity of a judge. "I was expecting you home earlier," he says.

"Yes, Papá. The pageant didn't end until a minute ago." She adds, "I came home as soon as it ended." She wishes she hadn't said this; her earnestness will make her father suspicious.

"Did Ingrid Estrada win?"

"How did you know?"

"I know all the candidates and I know all the judges. It was easy to predict what the decision would be."

Julia thought Alicia Güe, with her robust build and French haircut, would win.

"The pageant ended twenty minutes ago," he says. In the few minutes she has been in the room with him, neither of them has moved. Nevertheless, she feels he is closer to her now. She flushes, and the sensation is like having a fever.

Her father is waiting for her to explain where she was, and she knows she will have to tell him the truth. After she does, he will speak to her in hard words about boys like Pedro and Rodrigo. He will tell her that she is his first child and she needs to do what he says because he loves her and the world is cruel. He loves her and God loves her, and she can follow his word and God's word and be safe.

But before she begins her confession, her mother steps into the room carrying Angelica, Julia's three-year-old sister. Angelica is the family's miracle, the child no one thought her mother could have. Her mother and father tried everything to conceive a second child, including paying monthly visits to the capital to see doctors with degrees from the United States. But only after the family joined the Church of God, two blocks from their house, and, during cultos, clapped their hands and spoke in bursts of exultation when God moved them, did Julia's mother conceive. And it did seem to Julia like a miracle to see her mother, after years of sadness, filling with a child.

Her father, too, changed, becoming a lighter presence in their house. He laughed at what he usually frowned at—boys playing soccer at too late an hour in the street outside their door and the music with flamenco guitars and mournful, nostalgic voices that their neighbor, Don Adolfo, played too loudly on his radio. During the months of her mother's pregnancy, her father failed to monitor Julia's movements, and she played basketball in the rain and sat in the park until dusk, waiting until the last bus from the capital pulled into town and discharged its travelers. She imagined herself going the opposite direction on the bus, flying down the highway toward the city and its million people.

Her father turns to her mother. "How is she feeling?" he asks, and Julia's mother, whose long black hair is uncombed and covers her left eye, says, "She wakes every few minutes."

"Have you given her the medicine?"

"Yes."

Her father sighs. "It's only a cold. She will be all right."

Her mother carries Angelica back to the bedroom, where she will lie with her in the double bed and listen to Angelica's labored breathing until they both find sleep.

Julia's father turns to her again. "The streets are no place to be at night."

"Yes, Papá."

"I know what is best for you. You are sixteen and a woman, but you will always be my child. "

"I understand, Papá."

A minute passes before he allows a smile to cross his face. "What was the reaction when Ingrid Estrada was crowned Flor de Mayo? Did she receive the applause she deserved?"

Julia thinks about what Rodrigo shouted from the back of the gymnasium. Her father will no doubt hear about it, but she won't tell him because she might betray with a blush her newfound feelings toward her classmate. "She received great applause," she says.

"She wasn't the choice of the poor people or the indígenas," he says. "They say she looks too much like a conquistadora. But she is a fine girl, and she deserved to win."

Julia doesn't disagree with him; she never does. Her father stands and says, "It's late."

This is her signal, and she approaches him, kisses him on the cheek and goes quickly to her bedroom off the courtyard. Her room is tidy, with a single bed, an oak desk and a mahogany dresser. The room's white walls are bare. Before her family became Evangelical, she used to adorn her walls with calendars from the Catholic Church and pictures of Mexican television stars and Argentine soccer players. Her family no longer owns a television, and she no longer knows who the great soccer players outside of Guatemala are.

Julia's house is one of only three two-story houses in town, and every couple of years it receives a fresh coat of sky blue paint. Although the house contains amenities rare to see in Santa Cruz, including a refrigerator and an electric stove, it is, Julia believes, modest, with its unadorned walls, its clean tile floors and its small backyard lined with rose bushes where Julia sometimes watches Angelica chase butterflies and hummingbirds.

If her family is guilty of an extravagance, it is her father's Mercedes, one of no more than a dozen automobiles in town. Sometimes instead of taking the company bus to his job as an engineer at the Chixoy hydroelectric dam, he drives. It even has air conditioning.

Julia puts on a pink nightgown, one of four her father bought for her last month in Cobán, the large town north of Santa Cruz. She stares at herself in the mirror above her dresser, examining her skin. It is darker than her father's and mother's, but it is more cinnamon than black. Her hair is black, however, black and curly. She wonders if Rodrigo likes her skin and her curly, black hair.

What is he doing now? Is he in his bedroom, listening to music or reading or...or thinking of me? She wonders if his bedroom walls are as bare as hers. If so, it wouldn't be the fault of his religion, although her father might say Catholicism failed to keep Rodrigo's family together.

Rodrigo's father left town several years ago and hasn't been back. His mother sells lunches in the market. Rodrigo's brothers sell her leftover tamales and empanadas door-to-door in the afternoon, hauling them in gray buckets. Rodrigo works, too, at least sometimes, although she doesn't know what kind of work he does. She knows this: He is Santa Cruz's best soccer player, good enough, people say, to play professionally one day. She doesn't doubt it. She has seen him in El Instituto Básico's games against schools from San Cristóbal and San Juan Chamelco. If he does play professional soccer, she thinks, he'll have enough money to decorate his walls with whatever he wants.

In bed, Julia listens to the night sounds—the dripping from the pila in the courtyard, the rustling of chickens in the yard next door, the rushing of wind in the avocado tree behind her house—and she knows she won't fall asleep soon. Beneath her cool sheets and light wool blanket with blue horses, she lies still. Lately in the middle of the night she has found herself waking with her hands where they shouldn't be. She knows it is a sin to touch herself like this, even in her sleep. All the same, she can't help thinking how easy it would be to do it now, alone in the coolness of her bed.

She tries to concentrate on the night sounds, the dripping water, the chickens, the wind, but she finds herself thinking of Rodrigo and his voice. She thinks about how tall he stood in the back of the gymnasium. She thinks about what would happen if he followed her into the dark doorway of the muncipalidad or the woods behind their school, somewhere he could touch her in ways she cannot touch herself.

She lies still, her hands by her side. Tentatively, she speaks his name, a whisper, a dare.

— 2 —

Rodrigo is sitting at a round table in the house in Cobán, a red candle burning in front of him. Pedro is sitting next to him, close, as if to protect him. Pedro assures Rodrigo that this is what all boys do to become men. Smiling, he says, "And some boys keep becoming men all their lives." Pedro, eight years older than Rodrigo, laughs and tells Rodrigo to drink his beer.

Rodrigo notices the flecks of gray in Pedro's black hair. Although they've known each other since Rodrigo was twelve, when Pedro recruited him to deliver love letters to a schoolteacher in the village of Chitul, Pedro has taken more interest in him since his latest return from the capital.

The short woman who served them their beer whispers in Pedro's ear. Pedro stands and pats Rodrigo on the shoulder. "Old men first," he says. Rodrigo lifts his beer in a meek salute, and Pedro is gone. None of the men at the other tables speak. One by one, the short woman taps them on the shoulder and they stand and disappear.

Rodrigo imagines the short woman leading him to a door behind which he would find Julia García sitting by a window, the Bible or a book of poems in her hand. She would turn, their eyes would meet as they did in the gymnasium, and…

The short woman taps him on the shoulder. Rodrigo doesn't move until she says, "Come with me." He follows her down a hallway lined with doors. They reach the end of the hallway and the woman opens the door on the right. "Your friend paid," she says and leaves. Stepping into the room, Rodrigo notices the lamp on the vanity. It has no shade. Although the bulb is bigger and rounder than a fist, it isn't bright. He sees the girl, under covers in the bed in the near corner of the room, only when she says, "Buenas noches."

Her voice is lighter than he has imagined; he expected a voice to match the room's darkness. She points to the chair in front of the vanity, and he sits down. The girl, who must be only a little older than he is, has Asian-looking eyes. Rodrigo figures her friends call her Chinita.

She gets up from the bed. Her nightgown is sheer, with a faint flower pattern on it, and he can see her breasts beneath it. She is heavyset, and she sits on his knees gingerly. Rodrigo, however, does not feel her weight. He doesn't feel much at all besides the pounding of his heart.

She touches his hair and blows on it gently. She tells him he's handsome. He relaxes enough to feel her nipples against his chest, which she has made bare by unbuttoning his shirt. He leans to kiss her—this, he decides, is what is required of him—but he misses her mouth and kisses her on the chin. She doesn't seem to mind his failure, but makes sure his next attempt is accurate. After more kissing, she says, "What would you like?" He doesn't respond, unsure how he should respond. She smiles and says, "Okay." Removing her nightgown, she leads him to the bed.

Lying naked beside him, she takes off his trousers and underwear, then pulls him on top of her. But he is unable to enjoy her body; he is thinking of the way the room smells, like cloro, which his mother uses to kill cholera in the water in their pila. The girl moves under him, panting loudly. He can't think of anything but the smell. "Are you afraid of cholera?" he whispers.

The girl stops moving. "No," she says.

Rodrigo rolls off her. He retrieves his underwear from the foot of the bed and puts it on. "Why do you have cloro?" he asks.

"What?"

"Cloro. The smell here—it's cloro."

"We wash our clothes in the next room," says the girl, sitting cross-legged on the bed.

"When do you wash your clothes?"

"In the morning."

"Does everyone wash their clothes together?"

"Yes." The girl smiles as if remembering a particular scene. "It's fun to be all together. The girls tell jokes."

"What kind of jokes?"

"Oh. Just jokes."

"Tell me one."

"Well…Did you hear about the girl and her sweetheart, her novio?"

"No."

"Well, this girl died because of novio. She was walking down the street and this truck came and—no vio—and, wham, she was dead."

Rodrigo laughs. "That's funny."

"You tell me a joke," the girl says.

"I don't know one," Rodrigo says, although this isn't true. He just doesn't know any funny jokes. He asks the girl to tell him more jokes and she does, a series of them, each as funny as the first. He hopes he remembers them so he can share them with Julia. Or does Julia's religion prohibit her from listening to jokes? he wonders. Thinking of Julia makes him self-conscious again. What if Julia discovers he has been here?

I haven't done anything. Quickly, he puts on his clothes and says goodbye.

Pedro is standing outside the room, smoking. To impress him, Rodrigo yells into the room, "Hasta pronto, Chinita!"

As he and Pedro leave the house, Pedro asks him how it was and Rodrigo says, "Incréible, hombre!"

Later, after he and Pedro have said goodbye, Rodrigo thinks the girl was kind not to mock his failure. He wishes he had told her a joke.

— 3 —

Sitting by herself under a pine tree above the river, Julia sees Rodrigo approach her, climbing quickly up the hill. They were supposed to be studying English, but their teacher, Señora Tello, gave in to her students' demands for a día de campo. Señora Tello is standing on the riverbank, calling warnings to the handful of students who have discarded their blue and white uniforms and have waded into the water in their T-shirts and gym shorts.

Although Julia is tempted by the water's coolness, she thinks it would be immodest, perhaps even sinful, to do what Sandra Mo and Esmeralda Pop and María Caal are doing, even if they hide their bodies beneath the river's blue water. All the same, she can't help looking up from her Bible when they laugh or shout. She is reading the book of Isaiah, verse fifty-seven, when Rodrigo says, "You don't like to swim?" Staring up at his brown face and large, dark eyes, she finds herself blushing. A minute before, she had wished this would happen, and now she wonders if she spoke her wish aloud, if he heard her from the shore.

"I like to swim," she says. "My father taught me. Three times a year, the engineers at the dam in Chixoy have a día de campo and they swim with their families in the Chixoy River."

"Well, come on," Rodrigo says, waving toward the water.

She shakes her head. "There are too many people. And I don't have my swimming suit."

He nods toward the Bible in her hands and says, with a hint of a smile, "You're involved in something more important."

"I carry it with me everywhere," she says.

She doesn't tell him she likes to read only certain parts of the Bible. She likes to read the psalms because of the lovely flow of their words and she likes to read about Jesus' tribulations before his ascension to heaven because the sadness of His story sometimes makes her cry. She likes the way her tears feel, as if she is a part, however small, of Him and His suffering. "Do you go to church?" she asks him. Hermano Hector, the pastor of the Church of God, often exhorts members of his congregation to talk about their faith with their friends and neighbors.

Rodrigo shrugs. "Sometimes."

"It doesn't interest you?"

"Sometimes it does." He looks toward the river before looking back at her. "And sometimes it doesn't."

"But you do believe in God?"

"Of course."

"You might like to attend the culto my church is having this Friday night." She blushes, worried he'll see past her piety to what her heart desires. But she continues: "It will be under a tent on the town basketball court."

"Are you going?"

"Yes."

He smiles. "All right." He adds, "Should we go together? Should I come to your house?"

She would like this. But perhaps they wouldn't go to the culto after all. Perhaps they would climb the steps of the calvario and enter the temple and hold hands in front of the altar, the sweet smells of burning candles and dying flowers in the air. Before her family became Evangelical, Julia used to go with her mother to the calvario to put roses and birds of paradise in front of the crucifix and pray for the souls of their loved ones. Even now, when she knows better, when it's a sin, she goes sometimes to the calvario and sits with the icons, their faces more familiar to her than the faces of her classmates.

"Meet me at the service," she says.

"And we'll sit together?" he asks.

"Yes."

He continues to look at her, and she blushes again.

Someone from the riverbank calls him. It's Galindo, a tall, pale boy who usually sits with Rodrigo at the back of the classroom. Rodrigo doesn't turn around. He says to Julia, "Read me what you were reading."

She thinks he's joking. But after assessing his look, she realizes he isn't. She hears Galindo call him again.

"Read to me, please," Rodrigo says.

"Rodrigo, vos!" Galindo shouts. "Veníte!"

She waits to see if he will obey Galindo's third call. When he doesn't, she begins to read. She is conscious of how soft her voice is, how insufficient against the sounds coming from the river. She tries to speak louder, and she finds she is nervous, the Bible shaking in her palms. "The righteous man perishes, and no one lays it to heart; devout men are taken away, while no one understands." Thinking she might be losing his attention, she looks up. He hasn't moved. "Justice is far from us, and righteousness does not overtake us; we look for light, and behold, darkness, and for brightness, but we walk in gloom."

When she is finished, she doesn't look at him, but at the few small corn plants growing above the riverbank thirty meters west of where everyone is swimming.

"Rodrigo!"

Rodrigo turns and yells back, "In a minute, vos!" To Julia, he says, "I will see you at the culto." He begins to run down the hill but stops. She hasn't taken her eyes off him. He turns around. "But I'll see you in class first."

He continues his descent. By the riverbank, he removes his shirt, and the sunlight strikes his back. He stretches, lifting his hands toward the sky. She hears Galindo say, "You're not going in, vos. You don't know how to swim." But he does go in, diving, losing himself beneath the water. Seconds pass, and he is still under water. She thinks he is lost, drowned. She drops her Bible and stands up. Galindo shouts his name before frantically racing down the shoreline, following Rodrigo's body as it is carried down the river. In his pursuit, he tramples the corn plants.

Thirty meters downstream, Rodrigo pulls himself out of the river, coughing up water and laughing. Galindo offers him a hand, but Rodrigo shrugs off the help. Again, he stretches. Water falls off his arms and chest like illuminated jewels. His long, gray pants cling to his body like new skin. She hears Galindo say, "I thought you couldn't swim, vos."

Julia strains to hear Rodrigo's reply, but fails to catch his words. She hears only the deep, confident hum of his voice.

—

After his swim, Rodrigo lies on the grass above the riverbank and dries himself in the fading sunlight. Galindo sits beside him, his knees pressed against his chest. As always, Galindo looks uncomfortable, his limbs too long, out of proportion to his torso. "Why don't you lie down?" Rodrigo asks him.

Galindo unfurls his body across the grass. Galindo is taller than anyone Rodrigo knows, and spread on the grass, he is like a thin, enormous bird with featherless wings. "You were trying to impress Julia," Galindo says.

Rodrigo doesn't deny it. And he is pleased Julia invited him to a culto, although he doesn't know what he'll tell his mother. If he tells her he is serious about becoming an Evangelical, she will worry about losing him to a religion she mistrusts. He has heard her stories of families split apart over religion—about Doña Inez and her husband, Don Fernando, for instance, and how they live in the same house but never speak. But if he tells her he is going only because Julia invited him, she might accuse him of inventing interest in Julia's religion in order to impress her.

Galindo glances over Rodrigo's shoulder. "She's staring at you, vos," he says.

"Who?"

"You know who."

When, a moment later, Rodrigo turns to look, he is disappointed: Julia, sitting cross-legged where he left her, is leaning over her Bible. He wonders what passage she's reading. He'd like to hear her read to him again.

"You better watch yourself," Galindo says. "She'll ask you to go to a culto."

"She already did."

"And you're going?"

"Maybe."

"You'll have to listen to their terrible music and their terrible sermons. They'll ask you to repent your sins. They'll make you dance and speak in tongues." Galindo sighs. "I'd prefer listening to the Italian priest any day."

"No one can understand him."

"Who needs to? During his homily, I daydream about playing goalie for the national team."

From the school building, which sits on a hill fifty meters above them, the bell rings. They have one class left, history. "Come on, vos," Galindo says, standing. He offers Rodrigo his hand.

"I'm staying here."

"But Don Josue said we're having a quiz today."

"My pants are still wet. I'll come in a minute."

Galindo gives him a doubtful look. The other students have begun to trudge up the hill. They look like soldiers in a tired, drenched army. "All right," Galindo says, turning up the hill.

Sunlight is mixed with the darkness of the coming evening. Rodrigo walks to the river and stands among the trampled corn plants, watching the water pass. He looks behind him. No one is around, and he thinks how easily he could allow himself to fall into the river and sink beneath the water.

He wonders if Julia would come to his funeral. He wonders if she would cry.

— 4 —

The calvario door opens, surprising Julia, who is sitting in the front pew. No one has ever come to the calvario when Julia is here. The woman who enters is tall and wears blue jeans and a red blouse. Her black hair is combed over her forehead and tied in the back with a blue and gray cola. Her skin is as dark as the skin of people who live on the Caribbean Coast. She wears earrings, two gold hoops. Julia's first thought is to leave. The woman might know her father and tell him about seeing her here. But, on reflection, Julia feels certain the woman is a stranger.

The woman sits in the pew behind Julia. In the silence, Julia hears the woman's slow, even breathing. Amid the smells of flowers and candle wax, Julia detects another smell, of hair spray and lotion. Julia bows her head and closes her eyes and prays for the souls of her dead grandparents and uncle. She prays for her mother and her father and her sister. She prays for Rodrigo, although the image her mind lingers over is him beside the river, his hair wet, his bare back glowing in the sunlight.

When she is finished praying, she stands and, without looking at the woman, slips outside into the late afternoon. On the concrete steps ten meters below her are five children circled around a toad. They giggle and shout, and one of them, a ten-year-old boy, tries to jab the toad with a stick. An older girl grabs the boy's wrist. The boy wails a protest. Behind her, Julia hears the calvario door open. "Buenas tardes."

Julia knows it's the dark-skinned woman. She has a strong accent, the accent, Julia suspects, of the Caribbean Coast. When Julia turns around and returns the greeting, the woman says, "My name is Alejandra." She offers her hand and Julia shakes it. Julia tells the woman her name.

"Do you live in town?" Alejandra asks, and Julia nods.

"I moved here ten days ago," Alejandra says. "I'm a volunteer with Casas Para El Pueblo."

"Have you come from the Caribbean Coast?" Julia asks. "From Livingston?"

Alejandra frowns. "No, I'm from the United States—from Ohio."

Julia blushes, fearing Alejandra must think her small-minded and unworldly.

"You can see the whole town from here," Alejandra says, spreading her arms. She is pretty, with bold, wide eyes and a pleasing redness in her cheeks. "How many people live here?"

"I don't know," Julia says. "I think two thousand."

"It's a nice size."

"It's very small."

"I lived in the capital before I came here," Alejandra says. "I didn't like it. Too big, you know? I prefer it here. It's tranquilo."

"Some people say it's triste."

"It's too beautiful to be sad."

Julia looks out across her town, at the large, white Catholic Church in its center, at the park across from the church, at the block houses, painted yellow, blue and green. "I think you're right," she says. "It isn't sad."

They continue to look until Julia says, "What is your work here?"

"I'm helping people build houses. Poor people. Campesinos."

"Are you a Mormon?" Julia asks. "I've heard about Mormons building houses."

"No," Alejandra says. "I'm Catholic, like you."

Julia blushes. "I used to be Catholic."

A puzzled look crosses Alejandra's face. "But you were praying here," she says, gesturing behind her to the calvario.

"My family converted," Julia says quickly, "and I'm Evangelical now."

"Oh," Alejandra says. "But you come here sometimes."

"Yes." This is all Julia wants to say on the subject. "Where do you live?"

Alejandra tells her she is living in a room in Doña Flor Cabrera's house. "Come visit me sometime," Alejandra says. "I don't know many people in town."

They say goodbye, and Julia watches Alejandra walk up the dirt path to Doña Flor's house above the calvario. The children are gone; they have left the toad in the center of a step. Julia walks down to it. Gently, she picks it up, moves to the edge of the step and releases it in the tall grass.

— 5 —

"Where are you going?" Rodrigo's mother asks him.

"Outside."

"At this hour?"

His mother leaves her seat on the red couch in their living room to follow him. Rodrigo's two brothers are on the living room floor, huddled over a portable radio, arguing about which station to play. Rodrigo's mother trails him into the dirt court-yard. In front of them are clothes drying on a pair of laundry lines. Rodrigo cannot remember when he or his brothers last wore new clothes. For his mother, he is sure, it was even longer ago. *The next time I have work, I'll buy her a new blue dress, like Julia's.* Rodrigo notices the blue corte and white güipil hanging at the end of the line closest to him. They belong to his aunt Aura, his father's sister, who lives in an adjoining house and works as a teacher in the village of Najquitob. Although indígena, Rodrigo's father never believed in following Maya customs. He didn't understand why his sister continued to wear a güipil and corte or why she volunteered to record Maya folktales from the town's ancianos in order to preserve them in the town's library. At best, he said, no one wants to help an indígena succeed; at worst, he said, there are people—people with guns—who want all indígenas dead.

His father scorned his heritage, which is why, Rodrigo supposes, he chose to marry a ladina, however poor his mother's family. His mother's family came to Alta Verapaz from the capital two decades before Rodrigo's birth to help build the hydroelectric dam in Chixoy, but after the dam was built, there wasn't much work for them. His father's family owned a pharmacy, but before his father left Santa Cruz forever, he sold the pharmacy to Don Marcos, the richest man in town. Wherever his father went, he took the money with him.

"I don't like you going into the streets at night," Rodrigo's mother says.

"I'll be all right, Mother."

"Too much can happen, Rodrigo. Soldiers could come and make you join the army."

"I'd run from them."

"You can't run from a rifle."

Rodrigo waves his hand. "You haven't seen me run, Mother. You should see me on the soccer field. No one can catch me."

"Are you meeting Pedro? Are you going drinking with Pedro?"

Rodrigo laughs, thinking about how in a few minutes, when he's at the culto, he will be surrounded by hundreds of people who have renounced drinking as a sin. "I won't be drinking. I promise." He approaches her and puts his arm around her shoulder. Above her, the half moon looks like a feather frozen in the sky. And his mother, in a too-large red dress that once must have fit her, is feather light. "I'll be safe where I'm going."

She looks up at him. She has straight black hair that reaches the middle of her back and large, somber eyes.

"I promise, Mother. I promise."

He hears his brothers shout from inside the house, and already his mother is gone, trusting him to the night.

———

At the culto, Julia is sitting in the second row of fold-up chairs. Rodrigo is sitting next to her, looking alternately at his hands and at her. Julia tries to keep her eyes on Hermano Hector, who stands on a wooden stage in front of a microphone. His large, red lips come close to it, as if it's food he is ready to devour. He is a heavy man with a lizard's eyes and a booming, melodic voice. "Can a man be lonely in the kingdom of God?"

The three hundred people under the canvas tent shout, "No!" Another fifty people stand outside the tent, peering in like the hungry at a bakery window.

"When a man is lonely, should he run to houses of prostitution and the unloving arms of wicked women?"

"No!"

"Should he run to cantinas and the slow poison of whiskey and boh and rum?"

"No!"

"Should he run to the capital and the seduction of bright lights and easy money?"

"No!"

"Should he run to Jesus?"

"Yes!"

"Should he run to Jesus?"

"Yes!"

"Brothers and sisters, I ask you one more time… should… he… run… to… Jesus?"

"Yes!"

Hermano Hector steps aside. Behind him, on a higher part of the stage, a bald man begins playing an electric piano. Dancing starts on the grass in front of the stage. Men and women sway with their eyes closed, their hands lifted toward heaven. Julia catches Rodrigo looking at her. He smiles, nodding toward the dancers. She offers no gesture in response. Instead, she closes her eyes and holds out her arms, palms up. Knowing it is a sin to think about Rodrigo, to feel delight in his nearness, she tries to feel the spirit of God moving through her. She tries to feel the warm touch of His grace on her body. She tries to clear every earthly thought from her mind, every memory, every desire.

I am a sinner. She knows the thought should worry her, should cause her to fall to her knees or dance, shaking the sinfulness from her soul. But she doesn't move. She doesn't want to leave Rodrigo's side. So she allows the music to inhabit her; she trembles with the vibrations of the piano. *Please, please, please,* she whispers, but she doesn't know to whom she is directing her prayer or for what she is asking.

When the culto ends, Julia finds herself alone on one of the basketball court's foul lines. Her father is on the wooden stage, speaking to Hermano Hector, their backs to her. Her mother left the culto early to put Angélica to bed. Julia doesn't know where Rodrigo is. One moment he was beside her, the next he was gone. She wonders if he didn't like what he heard and left in disgust.

Rodrigo isn't the right boy for her anyway, she thinks. She tabulates their differences: *He is Catholic, I am Evangelical; he is indígena—or his father is—and I am ladina; his family is poor and mine is…* But these seem meek objections when weighed against the wild emotion in her heart. She steps outside the tent and looks up at the sky, radiant with stars.

"I was worried you'd be gone."

Julia turns to find Rodrigo so close to her someone seeing them might think they were locked in an embrace. She doesn't shy from the closeness. The opposite: She tilts her head up, an invitation, and he places his lips on hers.

If their first kiss thrills Julia, it also terrifies her. In her mind, she sees her father turn around, sees the anger climb to his face. But she holds still. Only when Rodrigo pulls back, to catch his breath, perhaps, perhaps to savor with his eyes the lips he kissed, does she glance inside the tent at her father. His back remains turned toward her, and her relief is immense.

She feels Rodrigo's lips in her hair. "Everything about you is beautiful," he whispers, and as he takes his first step home, Julia's father calls her name.

— 6 —

After lunch one Saturday, Rodrigo walks the dusty back road out of Santa Cruz. He passes the Hotel Mundo, whose white mini-houses, four rooms in each, are spread under pine trees on the edge of the two-lane Cobán highway. He crosses the highway and walks another five minutes to the soccer field in the village of Chixajau. He drops the soccer ball he has been carrying. Immediately, he lifts it into the air with his right foot. He keeps it bouncing between his feet for a minute. At last, he gives it a good kick, sending the ball to midfield. He chases after it, feeling the wind on his face and in his hair. He dribbles toward the far goal, imagining himself eluding one defender, then another.

The goal, which has no net, is twenty meters in front of him, and he stops, taps the ball to his right, sweeps his foot down on it and sends the ball soaring toward the upper right-hand corner. The ball nicks the bottom of the crossbar and bounces into the cornfield behind the field.

After he retrieves the ball, he runs up and down the field ten times. As he is resting in the middle of the field, he notices a crowd of children watching him from the dusty road. There are six boys and two girls, and they stand quietly, like witnesses to a ceremony. He kicks the ball directly above him, and when it falls, he meets it with his head, sending it five meters in front of him. He does this a few times, picking spots where he wants the ball to land.

One of the boys, thin, long-faced and with small, dark eyes, leaves the safety of the road to step onto the edge of the field. The other children hang back, murmuring in Kekchí. Rodrigo thinks they are warning the boy to go no further. He knows he could scare the boy—he could scare all the children—by rushing toward him like a maniac. As children of Chixajau, they live only a ten-minute walk from Santa Cruz, but if they have been to town, he guesses, it has only been to help their mothers sell vegetables in the market. If they speak Spanish, it is only the little they've learned in school. He is nearly as strange to them as a foreigner would be.

"Here," Rodrigo says, and he shoots a pass to the boy, a slow pass that comes to a stop against the boy's feet. For a moment, the boy looks frightened. He takes a few steps backward before charging the ball and sending a strong kick toward Rodrigo. Rodrigo knows how athletic some of the children from the villages are. Soccer is their only diversion, and so they play all day. "Tell your compañeros to come play," he says to the boy, although he doubts the boy will understand him.

But the boy turns around and shouts to the rest of the children in Kekchí. The other boys come running hard onto the field; the girls follow at a suspicious pace. Rodrigo divides the teams—himself against the eight children.

When Rodrigo has the ball, he doesn't send it flying down the field, where he could race after it. Instead he dribbles in the middle of the field, the children hounding him. This way, he must keep the ball close to his body, protecting it from the wild legs of his pursuers. He finds he can keep possession of the ball for no more than a minute before having it swiped.

When the children have the ball, they shout crazily, everyone wanting to receive a pass. Rodrigo chases down the weak passes easily and returns with the ball to mid-field, where he dances with it.

After half an hour of play, he begins to tire, and he kicks the ball high into the air, races up the field to retrieve it and shoots on goal from thirty meters. The ball blazes past the head of a girl standing, terrified, in front of the goal and disappears into the cornfield behind her. "I win!" Rodrigo declares, laughing and panting. He lies on his back in the grass, suddenly exhausted. The children surround him, worry in their faces, as if he might have died.

"Next time," Rodrigo says, "I want at least one of you on my team."

— 7 —

Julia stands within the branches of bougainvillea on the stone steps behind the telegraph office in Purulhá, a town thirty kilometers south of Santa Cruz. She wears her red and blue basketball uniform, damp from sweat after the recent game, damp from the humidity. Fifty meters behind her to the east, a pair of mountains begin their long climb to the sky. The bougainvillea rustles, and Rodrigo embraces her before she has a chance to be startled. He is dressed in his soccer uniform: red jersey, blue shorts. She is far shorter than he is, and he bends to kiss her. His lips are wet and warm.

They have kissed before, of course, after the culto and, later, in moments stolen before and after school, in secret places they've discovered around town, but Rodrigo's kisses have been careful, restrained. Now, far from Santa Cruz, he devours her, running his hands in her hair and across her body. She feels his stiffness below his waist, and she feels the way her body tingles and softens and yearns. She knows how easy it would be to lose herself.

"Rodrigo, por favor," she says.

He responds with heat, "I love you."

"Yes," she says. "But we can't." He covers her lips with his so she can't speak. She allows him this deep, entangled kiss before pulling back and saying, "When we're married."

He grins and kisses her again, lightly. Deeper in the branches of bougainvillea, she sees a pair of hummingbirds dance and disappear, brief flashes of green and motion. She puts a hand on Rodrigo's chest and feels how solid it is. Above his lip, she notices a faint growth of hair.

Somewhere in the distance, she hears Rodrigo's name shouted. Before she can urge him to leave, he kisses her again and slides out of the shelter of bougainvillea. She hears his cleats tapping against the concrete. The tapping grows softer until it is lost in other sounds: trucks on the highway, birds calling, marimba music on a radio.

She waits for a minute in the embrace of pink flowers, ashamed of her desire, thrilled by her desire. In her backpack at her feet, she has a Bible. She opens the bag and removes the Bible, pressing it to her chest. Its leather cover feels warm. She holds her head up and marches out of the bougainvillea and toward the soccer field.

In the concrete stands, Julia concentrates on the game. Rodrigo receives a pass near the center of the field. He begins a quick dance toward the goal, moving left, right, left. Twenty meters from the goal, he stops suddenly, and his defender overruns him. Julia can feel the anticipation rise in her. Before she can stand up, it is over. Rodrigo crushes the ball with his left foot and sends the ball flying into the top right corner of the goal.

In celebration, Rodrigo races with his arms extended toward the sky. His teammates chase him, finally catching him near midfield. They leap on him, bringing him down into the grass.

When his teammates release him, Rodrigo spots Julia in the cheering crowd and waves, two quick strikes of his hand across the air. It is like he is blessing her.

— 8 —

Two days later, Rodrigo sits upright in a chair in Julia's living room. It is a kind of chair he is familiar with, the kind students in industriales class at El Instituto Básico make out of cheap pinewood. He made such a chair last year, and the chair he is sitting on now suffers from the same problem: It wobbles. The third person to sit on his chair was one of his aunt's suitors, Don Teodoro, who was so enormous Rodrigo's youngest brother thought he was hiding a soccer ball beneath his shirt. When Don Teodoro sat on the chair, it did more than wobble. It quivered, it quaked and, as Don Teodoro bellowed a protest, it collapsed into a pile of sticks. Fearing a fate like Don Teodoro's, Rodrigo leans forward and keeps most of his weight on his feet. He wonders if Señor Garcia, who is sitting across from him on a couch, purposely put him in this chair to make him feel uncomfortable.

Rodrigo is here to ask Señor García's permission to be Julia's novio, but first they discuss Rodrigo's studies and his mother and brothers. They talk about the rain and how, with each year, there seems to be less of it. This, Señor García says, is because of the vanishing forests. He blames the families who climb high into mountains to cut down trees to use in their cooking fires. Rodrigo knows who else is responsible for the disappearing trees and the balding mountains. In his last job in town, Pedro worked as a scout for a lumber mill. He would hike into the mountains around Santa

Cruz to find a suitable forest and would alert the men at the mill. Pedro told him he saw entire forests disappear in a week.

Sitting erect on the couch, Señor García looks like an emperor on a throne. He leans forward, and Rodrigo sees how sharp his face is—his flat cheeks, his pointed chin, his knife-blade nose—and how dark and small his eyes are. "I know what you've come to ask," Señor García says abruptly. "Julia and I have discussed it. I have shared with her my concerns."

Before coming here, Rodrigo thought about what he would say and how he would say it. But when he opens his mouth, he finds it hard to speak. He begins twice before, too quickly, saying, "I will treat Julia with respect, I will respect whatever restrictions you place on our relationship, I...I..."

This is all Rodrigo can remember of his prepared speech. In frustration, he leans back in the chair, and, a moment later, feels a sickening, creaking sound. The chair's seat shifts violently to his left. Before he can catch his balance, he is on the floor, his bottom aching. The chair is now a collection of wood, with nails poking everywhere. Rodrigo flushes with embarrassment and begins an apology, but Señor García is chuckling. His amusement softens his face.

"Did you know that Julia made that chair?" Señor García says, standing and going to the far right corner of the living and pulling from it another chair, its wood darker, its frame solid. "She made it last year. She said the boys in industriales were all making chairs and she said she'd rather make a chair than the paper flowers the girls in hogar were supposed to make. I told her she had to make the flowers, it was required, but she could also make the chair. I had Professor Fernandez come here and show her how to do it. I never trusted myself to sit in it. But I thought you, her novio, would have better luck."

He smiles and Rodrigo smiles back. Rodrigo didn't fail to notice the word he used. Novio. He is Julia's boyfriend. Her father's word makes it official. He didn't need his speech after all.

Señor García places the new chair in front of the couch and gestures for Rodrigo to sit in it. Señor García returns to his seat and says, "I understand the hardship your family faces. In a family without a father, there is a special burden on the oldest son." He pauses; his eyes don't move from Rodrigo's face. "I ordinarily would not allow Julia to become the novia of someone in such a situation. She could only distract him from his family responsibilities. But I see your seriousness and sincerity, Rodrigo. And I see promise in how you have taken an interest in our faith."

Señor García stands and offers Rodrigo his hand. Quickly, Rodrigo stands to shake it. He notices how small Señor Garcia's hand is. "You can visit her two nights a week here, in this room," he says. "My wife or I will always be in an adjoining room."

"Yes, señor."

When Señor García speaks again, his tone is easier. "I have heard about how well you play soccer. People who know the game tell me you could be the best player ever in this town."

A grin fills Rodrigo's face.

"The men who told me about you have also seen your uncle Tomás play. He was your father's brother, wasn't he?"

"Yes."

"The best indígena soccer player in the country, some people said."

"I've heard people say so."

"Didn't he go to Mexico to play?"

"He did."

"And was he successful?"

"He was."

"What is he doing now?"

"He is coaching a team in one of the Mexican leagues."

In truth, Rodrigo doesn't know what happened to his uncle. His father used to receive a letter or two from him every year, but this was a long time ago. His uncle's career lasted only four years. He suffered several injuries and, gradually, he lost his speed. One of his last letters told of him quitting soccer and wanting to become a coach, but when Rodrigo's father left Santa Cruz, his uncle's letters stopped coming.

"I saw your uncle play several times," Señor García says. "If you are as good as he is, you have a great talent. And if you are better…" Señor García smiles and gestures to Rodrigo's left. "Well, if you are better I will want you to autograph that broken chair."

— 9 —

Alejandra lives in a room with a private entrance on a wing of Doña Flor's house. She smiles when she sees Julia on her doorstep. "Pase adelante," she says in her accented Spanish, and Julia follows her inside. On the near end of the room is a three-burner stove connected to a gas tank. Above it, hanging on nails, are three blue coffee mugs. Alejandra directs Julia to sit on a wooden stool near a fold-up table against the back wall. "Café?" she asks.

"Gracias."

Alejandra turns on one of the burners and places a red kettle on it. The flame curls around it like a yellow hand.

Above her bed, Alejandra has hung a güipil from Santiago Atitlán. Red and blue birds are embroidered around the neck. Beside the güipil is a small jade crucifix.

Soon the kettle whistles, and Alejandra fills two mugs with hot water and instant coffee and brings them to the table. She sits at the opposite end of the table from Julia. Julia again regards her dark, smooth skin and round, wide eyes. If Alejandra had been in the Flor de Mayo pageant, she would have been Rodrigo's choice. Alejandra is wearing the same gold earrings she wore the day Julia met her. "It isn't the best coffee," Alejandra says. "Of course, the very best coffee goes to the States."

Julia sips her coffee. She finds it no different than the coffee her mother makes. "I think it's fine," she says.

"But I bet you haven't tasted your country's best coffee."

"Once my mother brought home coffee from Antigua. She said it was grown on one of the volcanoes. She opened the bag and let me smell the beans. They smelled as good as anything I've ever smelled—better than chocolate and roses."

"Now I know what to bring you when I go to Antigua," Alejandra says.

Alejandra asks Julia about her studies, and Julia tells her she will be graduating from El Instituto Básico in October and studying at Colegio Verapaz, a private high school in Cobán, beginning in January. "My father wants me to be a lawyer or a doctor," Julia says.

"Your father is ambitious."

"Yes, he is."

"Are you?"

"I am the same." Julia doesn't know if she is ambitious. It feels nice to say so, however. Until she met Rodrigo, she wanted to live in the capital and do what she'd only read or heard about—walk the long avenues in zona uno, visit the Presidential Palace, see an opera or ballet in the Teatro Nacional. She didn't know what kind of job she would want, although she had thought of several: teacher, journalist, owner of a five-star hotel.

Julia looks around the room. In addition to the bed, table and stove, Alejandra has a dresser, on top of which are two framed photographs and a tape player. Alejandra sees where she is looking. "Would you like to listen to music?"

"I can't."

"Why?"

"For Evangelicals, it's sinful."

For a moment, Alejandra doesn't respond. "Do you believe it's sinful?"

"It's a distraction."

"A distraction from what?"

"From thinking about God."

"I see. Are you supposed to think about God all the time?"

"I don't know," Julia says. "I think so."

"And couldn't God be present in music?" Alejandra asks.

"He is—in the music we sing at cultos."

"And in no other music?"

Julia considers this. "Maybe in the songs my sister sings. She's three years old, and she sings songs she makes up about frogs. They're beautiful." And she laughs because it's true.

Julia looks around the room again. "Are you lonely here?"

"No," Alejandra says. "I have friends."

"A novio?"

"He lives in Puerto Barrios."

"Is he Guatemalan?"

Alejandra goes to her dresser. She removes one of the pictures. It's of a tall, blond-haired gringo standing on a beach and wearing sunglasses. "His name is Ben," Alejandra says.

"He's handsome," Julia says. She hands the picture back to Alejandra. "When he isn't with you, are you lonely?"

"I have my music," Alejandra says, smiling. "For me, listening to music isn't sinful."

"Is all of your music in English?"

"Most of it. But I have a couple of tapes in Spanish."

Julia finishes her coffee. She feels bold and free in Alejandra's room. It's as if she stepped across a border and into another country. "Can we listen to one of your tapes?"

Alejandra looks puzzled. "I thought you said…"

"We are in your house," Julia says. "You can do what you like in your house. I am your guest."

"All right." Alejandra returns to her dresser and puts in a tape. A guitar plays, followed by a woman's high, mournful voice. They listen for a minute.

"It's pretty," Julia says.

Alejandra says the songs on the tape are from Mexico but are sung by a woman who lives in San Antonio, Texas. Alejandra brings Julia more coffee and sits down again.

"Does your boyfriend come to visit you?" Julia asks.

"He has been here, yes."

"And he stays with you here?"

Alejandra nods.

"Doña Flor doesn't say anything to you?" Julia asks.

"Doña Flor isn't my mother." Alejandra smiles. "I'm twenty-four years old."

"But if you are unmarried, you are still a part of your father's house."

"In your country, this is true. In mine, it isn't."

Julia knows she would be lonely living in a room by herself, even if Rodrigo came to visit her. "How long will you stay in Santa Cruz?" Julia asks.

"My project lasts a year."

"And afterwards?"

"I'll go back to the States."

"To marry your boyfriend?"

"Maybe. But I don't think so."

"Why not?"

"Because there's more we want to do with our lives before we settle down."

Julia doesn't understand. She thinks Alejandra's boyfriend must be, as her father would say, a muchacho malo. A user.

"Do you have a boyfriend?" Alejandra asks.

Julia nods.

"Do you plan to marry him?"

"Some day, yes—if my father consents."

"How old are you?"

"Sixteen."

"You're very young." With a smile, Alejandra asks, "You're certain you love him?"

"Of course."

"What do you love about him?"

"He's handsome," Julia says quickly and blushes.

"I would expect so," Alejandra says. "What else?"

Julia wants to tell her how Rodrigo speaks of the children in the village of Chix-ajau in the same affectionate way he speaks of his brothers. She wants to tell her how she saw him once with his mother in front of the market and how he put his arm around her shoulder and leaned toward her and whispered in her ear, as if to console her. And she wants to tell her what he said from the back of the gymnasium during the Flor de Mayo pageant, his bold protest of Ingrid Estrada's undeserved victory. Instead, she says, "He is kind, and he isn't afraid to speak what he believes."

"He sounds like Ben," Alejandra says. She smiles and her eyes seem to grow even wider. Julia would like to have eyes as large and radiant as Alejandra's. She wonders why Alejandra's boyfriend will not marry her.

The next song plays, and Julia thinks she knows it. She must have heard it on busses or on radios playing from tiendas around town.

If you spurn me because I'm poor

I understand.

I offer you no riches.

I offer you my heart.

She wonders if Alejandra's boyfriend is too poor for her to marry. She wonders if Alejandra will enjoy his kisses and his affection now, but will marry a richer man when she returns to the United States. She thinks it would be cruel of Alejandra to play with a boy's sentiments only to leave him because his heart isn't sufficient.

Alejandra says, "I love this song."

Julia sees a sad look in Alejandra's eyes, and now Julia wonders if Alejandra is poor and her boyfriend rich and if this is why they won't marry.

— 10 —

The soccer practice ended an hour ago, but Rodrigo is still on the field. So is Galindo, standing between the goal posts, gamely defending the net from Rodrigo's blistering shots. Rodrigo started shooting balls from a distance of fifteen meters; now he is at least twenty-five meters from the goal. Nevertheless, his shots usually find a home in the net, eluding Galindo's long arms.

"Last shot," Rodrigo declares, and he hears Galindo sigh. Evening came with a red sky over San Cristóbal, the nearest town to the west, and now the sky is dark gray. Stars have begun to appear. Rodrigo can see little save the outlines of the goal and Galindo's tall, pale frame standing guard in front of it.

Boom. Rodrigo's foot strikes the ball and it flies past Galindo into the bottom, left-hand corner. Galindo doesn't move.

"You didn't try!" Rodrigo chides.

"I couldn't see it, vos." Galindo turns to retrieve the ball from the net. "I saw only a flash—like lighting."

"You're lucky I didn't shoot it right at you. You'd be dead, vos."

"At least I wouldn't have to be your goalie anymore."

Galindo trudges up to Rodrigo and hands him the ball and they turn to walk home. Rodrigo tells him what Julia's father said about his uncle Tomás, about how men would gather in the stands of Santa Cruz's stadium in the evening merely to watch him dribble up and down the field alone. "He'd dribble by moonlight, vos," Rodrigo says. "He knew he was a great player, but he knew he could be even greater. To be the greatest, he had to practice longer and harder than anyone else."

They pass in front of Señor Caal's auto body shop, a rusted Malibu sitting under the aluminum roof of the open-air garage. A pair of German shepherds race up to the chain-link fence and bark. Galindo jumps back and Rodrigo laughs. Galindo kicks the fence, and the dogs retreat before continuing their barking. They turn left on Calle Martí and pass Doña María's tienda, where students from El Instituto Básico buy their school supplies. They pass the gymnasium, its yellow paint looking gray in the darkness. Beyond the gymnasium is Avenida La Parroquia, where they stop.

"Have you seen the norteamericana who lives in town?" Galindo asks.

Rodrigo shakes his head.

"She's a negra," Galindo says. "Very pretty. Her eyes, vos. They're gigantic."

"Do you know her?"

"No, vos. I've only seen her. They say she allows muchachos into her house. I heard Marcos goes to see her at night."

"Don Marcos?"

"No, Marquitos. Marcos de la Cruz."

"What does he do at her house?"

"What do you think?"

Rodrigo shakes his head. "Lies."

"I heard she'll let whatever boy who knocks into her house. And she'll give him a beer if he asks for it. And she'll do more…if he asks for it."

"Lies," Rodrigo says again.

"Do you want to visit her? After dinner, we'll go, vos. What do you think?"

"I don't know. Where does she live?"

Galindo tells him. "I'll come to your house," he says. "I'll come in an hour."

"If you want, vos."

Two hours later, Rodrigo and Galindo are climbing the stairs of the calvario. They stop on the landing in front of the temple to allow Galindo to catch his breath. Rodrigo remembers how during Semana Santa he used to build sawdust alfombras here, using bougainvillea flowers and pine needles to adorn them with hearts and crosses. When the procession came from the calvario and the purple-robed men carried the statue of Christ across his carpet, destroying the work he'd spent hours on, he'd felt both proud and sad. He was happy to have his carpet be the first the statue crossed, but sad to see it ruined so soon.

"She lives up here," Galindo says, and they climb beyond the calvario to Alejandra's room in Doña Flor's house.

"What are you going to do?" Rodrigo asks.

"Knock on her door."

"No, vos. No."

"What do you mean?"

"It's mala honda, vos. She's a woman alone."

"She'll invite us in, I swear."

"You don't know her."

Galindo releases a small groan. "Come on, vos."

Rodrigo shakes his head. "You go ahead, if you want to."

"Okay, vos," Galindo says. "I will."

Rodrigo walks to the right of Alejandra's door and around the side. Here there is a window. The curtains are open, and Rodrigo can see Alejandra sitting at a fold-up table at the end of her room, reading. Her eyes are as large as Galindo said, and her skin is dark, darker than his own, and beautiful.

Rodrigo hears knocking. Alejandra looks up from her book. The knocking resumes, and Alejandra puts down her book and goes to her door. Rodrigo is surprised Galindo had the courage. In embarrassment, he wants to flee, but he can't seem to move. When Alejandra opens the door, she takes a step back, as if surprised or frightened by her visitor. No doubt she isn't used to seeing someone as tall as Galindo in Guatemala. Rodrigo can't hear what is being said. He can't see Alejandra's face. He can only see Galindo filling the doorframe.

They talk for what to Rodrigo seems like a long time, and Rodrigo wonders whether she'll invite him in, offer him beer, offer him more. He feels a rush of jealousy, of regret, but he smells something—roses—and it reminds him of Julia and her backyard bordered by rose bushes.

Alejandra closes her door and locks it. She stands in the middle of her room for a moment before approaching the window, the window into which Rodrigo is looking. Rodrigo crouches. On the ground in front of him, he notices a small rose bush with a single red flower. When, a moment later, he stands again, the curtains have been drawn.

Rodrigo finds Galindo on the landing in front of the calvario. "What'd she say, vos?" he asks.

Galindo shrugs. "She said I should come talk to her during the day." He turns to face Rodrigo. "See—she invited me back." Galindo crosses his arms across his chest.

"She had a man in her room," Rodrigo says.

"Who?"

"Marquitos."

"Are you serious, vos?"

"Didn't you see him in her bed? He was lounging there, smoking a cigarette."

"Liar."

"I saw it through the window."

"No, vos. You're lying." Galindo looks at Rodrigo. "You aren't lying?"

Rodrigo can't help himself. He breaks into laughter. "Vos, you need a novia. I'll have to take you to Cobán and buy you one." He pats Galindo on the back and, laughing, they walk down the calvario steps and onto the lighted street.

— 11 —

Even after he is praised in a sports column in *La Presa Libre* as the best amateur player in Alta Verpaz and receives telegrams of interest from professional teams from as far away as Puerto Barrios and Quetzaltenango, Rodrigo returns to the field in Chixajau to practice. One day, Pedro comes with him, walking in black leather shoes down the road, which is muddy from a recent rain. When they reach the field, Rodrigo invites Pedro to play a game of keep away. "Okay, vos," Pedro says. "You tell me how to play."

With sticks, Rodrigo creates a circle in the center of the field. "Both of us stand in the circle," Rodrigo explains. "One of us has the ball, the other tries to get it. You're allowed to go out of the circle as long as the ball stays in. If you keep the ball for a minute, you win."

Pedro laughs. "Look at the shoes I'm wearing, vos. And you're wearing cleats."

"I'll take them off," Rodrigo says. "We'll play barefoot."

Pedro considers Rodrigo's proposal before removing his blue windbreaker, folding it and placing it outside the circle. He removes his shoes and black socks, putting them beside his jacket. Rodrigo, meanwhile, strips off his cleats, and after stuffing his socks into them, hurls them toward one of the goals. They fall onto the field with thuds.

Rodrigo jumps up and down, feeling his blood move. Pedro stands licking his new mustache, the soccer ball cradled between his feet. "My ball first," Pedro says.

"Are you ready?" Rodrigo asks.

"Sure," Pedro says, and no more than five seconds later, Rodrigo has stolen the ball. Already, Pedro is breathing heavily. "Mierda," he curses between breaths.

Now it is Rodrigo's turn with the ball, and he dances. Pedro jabs his left foot to kick the ball away, but Rodrigo flips the ball into the air, corrals it and slips past his friend. Pedro tries rushing at Rodrigo, but Rodrigo puts the ball between Pedro's legs and races around him to retrieve it. Pedro is like a beaten boxer. His head droops and his breathing is quick and heavy.

"How much time left?" Rodrigo asks.

Pedro checks his watch. "Twenty seconds," he says. He approaches Rodrigo carefully, his knees bent, his arms spread. Rodrigo is dancing, the ball bouncing from one foot to the other. "There's no escape," Pedro says.

"Right, vos," Rodrigo says. "Except I am a magician. I am like…" He hesitates a moment on the name. "I am like Houdini!" Pedro takes another step toward Rodrigo, and Rodrigo slips around him, stepping outside the circle but keeping the ball inside.

"Out," Pedro calls.

"No, vos," he says. "The ball was in."

"Liar," Pedro says, his face flushed red.

If he were anywhere else, Rodrigo would not feel he could taunt Pedro like this. But with the grass between his toes and the ball in his command, he feels strong, ferocious, indomitable. "I won," Rodrigo says.

Pedro doesn't bother to check his watch. "Okay, vos," he says. "If you say so."

Rodrigo kicks the ball to him. "Your turn again."

This time, Rodrigo lets Pedro dribble the ball for twenty seconds before he steals it. "Mierda," Pedro says.

Rodrigo retreats with the ball, and Pedro stalks after him. Rodrigo decides he'll let Pedro come within a ball's length of him before eluding him.

Pedro does come close, and Rodrigo steps left, steps right, then races right, the ball safely in front of him. As he is about to burst free, he feels Pedro grab his shoulder, and a moment later, he finds himself being pulled down. He falls heavily, his left cheek hitting first. He smells the grass, and the grass is rough against his skin. It takes Rodrigo a moment to comprehend what has happened, and when he does, he enunciates his complaint, his accusation, with bitterness: "You could have injured me, vos. What if you'd hurt me bad enough so I couldn't play?"

Pedro, above him, is gasping for breath; even so, he is smiling, large white teeth between wet lips. "It was a kiss, vos," he says, "no more dangerous than a kiss."

— 12 —

On a subsequent visit to Alejandra's room, Julia finds her friend wearing a T-shirt and shorts. She isn't wearing shoes or socks and her hair is uncombed, spread above her head like thick black feathers. Two empty Gallo bottles sit on the table.

"Where is he?" Julia whispers from the doorway, looking around the room. Alejandra promised she would introduce her to her boyfriend.

"He's gone," Alejandra says, sighing. "He had to go back a day early. He needs to be in Puerto Barrios tomorrow morning for a meeting. He caught the last bus." She waves in the direction of the Cobán highway. "I was hoping you'd come at two, when you said you would."

"I had to help my mother at the market," Julia says with disappointment. "Are you sad he's gone?"

"No," Alejandra says. "I'll see him next weekend. I'll visit him in Puerto Barrios." She pauses. "Come in," she says.

The bed is unmade. The blanket, with its depiction of two brown volcanoes, is bunched at the end of the bed, and a corner of the fitted sheet has come undone. Alejandra sees where Julia is looking, and she quickly makes the bed.

"Sit down."

Julia sits on a stool in front of the fold-up table. Alejandra pulls from beneath the pillow a pair of men's underwear. She holds the underwear in front of her with both hands, examining it. Alejandra looks at Julia, who looks alternately at the underwear and at Alejandra's eyes. Quickly, Alejandra folds the underwear and tucks it under the pillow. "You're going to think I'm a bad influence," she says.

A moment later, Julia asks, "Will he be cold?"

"Cold? Who?"

"Ben. Without his…" She points toward the pillow. "It's cold this evening."

"Oh." Alejandra, catching Julia's joke, laughs. "He deserves to be cold—for leaving early." Alejandra goes to her stove and lights the burner below the kettle. To the left of the stove is a mirror, and Alejandra stands in front of it, brushing her hair. She uses hard, deep strokes.

"You and Ben don't want to get married?" Julia asks. She has asked this question several times but has never been satisfied with Alejandra's answer.

Alejandra carves the brush into her hair. "Maybe we do," she says, an answer she hasn't given before. She stops brushing. "But in the United States, it isn't easy. He's white and I'm black, and if his parents knew about us, they might not be happy. And if my parents knew about us, they might not be happy." She pauses. "But that's only part of it. I'm Catholic, you know, and Ben's Jewish. If we were to get married, he'd want me to become Jewish, too."

"But if you love him…"

"I also love my religion." Alejandra pauses. "What if you loved someone who wanted you to become something you weren't?" Alejandra asks her. "What would you do?"

When, four years ago, her father told her about the culto he planned to bring the family to, she said, "All right, Papá." She didn't think much about it, even after they were sitting in the hard pews, listening to Hermano Hector tell them how they could be reborn, his voice louder and more impassioned than any priest's voice she'd ever heard. They'd gone to the Church of God for fourteen consecutive days. A month later, when her mother knew she was carrying Angelica, they'd gone to be baptized in the river below El Instituto Básico. A pair of indígena women, on their way to the market in Santa Cruz, stood on the bridge above them, watching as Hermano Hector dunked her father and her mother in the water. Then it was Julia's turn, and she found the water cold, and when Hermano Hector dunked her, water rushed down her throat.

Twenty people from the church had come to see them baptized and, standing on the shore, they applauded. After coughing up the water she'd swallowed and after listening to their applause, she felt better. She felt the presence of God or thought she did, even as she heard the pair of indígena women on the bridge giggling.

She thinks about Rodrigo, who has accompanied her to six cultos now. At the last culto, Hermano Hector spoke with him about becoming saved. "I am considering it" was all Rodrigo said.

"Well?" Alejandra asks. "What would you do?"

"I don't know," Julia says.

The kettle whistles, and Alejandra makes two cups of coffee. She sits next to Julia at the table. After a minute, Julia says, "We are friends, right?"

"Yes," Alejandra says. "Of course."

"We have confianza."

"Yes, we do."

"Con confianza, I ask…" Julia stops, blushing.

"Go ahead."

"I ask…are you afraid of becoming pregnant?"

Alejandra takes a sip of her coffee. "There are ways to prevent it."

"Pills?"

"Some women use pills."

"Do you use pills?"

"No, Ben uses…you have heard of condoms?"

Julia hesitates. "Yes."

"Ben uses condoms. Do you know how they work?"

Julia is curious. "No." She hesitates again. "Do you have one here?"

Alejandra goes to her dresser and, from the top drawer, removes a small, square blue-and-white packet. Alejandra looks at Julia closely. "Are you sure you want me to show you?" she asks. "You won't be offended?"

"No," Julia says.

"This is what they come in." Alejandra tears open the side of the packet. "And this is how you open it."

When she pulls out what's inside, it looks to Julia like an eye socket absent an eye. "The boy…?" Julia begins. "The boy wears it on his…?"

"Like this." Alejandra looks around her room. She goes to her dresser and brings from it a thin white candle. "Imagine this is his…how do you say it?…pene. When he is aroused, it fits like this." She holds the candle in her left hand. With her right hand, she unfolds the condom over the candle.

Julia says, "And now the candle's flame will not burn."

"What?" Alejandra smiles. "Yes, the fire is under control." Alejandra laughs. "Sometimes you surprise me, Julia."

"I do?"

"You surprise me with your jokes. I don't expect them."

"Next time, I will give you a warning."

"Thank you. Do you want more coffee?"

"Yes, a little more please."

From the stove, Alejandra says, "Remember: you are young. You and your boyfriend should wait before having relacciones."

"And you?" Julia says. "You are also young."

Alejandra turns around quickly. "Compared with you, I'm an anciana." With the coffee made, she walks back to the table like an old woman, stooped and shuffling. She holds out a cup to Julia with a trembling hand.

— 13 —

Every day for weeks, Rodrigo asks Julia to come with him to the soccer field in Chixajau. At last, she agrees, but she doesn't want people to see them walking out of town together. She says she'll meet him at the entrance to the Hotel Mundo.

He arrives at the hotel before she does, and he passes the time by whistling at the green parrot who sits on the lowest branch of an orange tree next to the hotel's office, a small block building thirty meters from the main hotel building, and speaking with Hidalia, who sits behind the counter.

Plump, with robust cheeks and rabbit teeth, Hidalia is a year older than Rodrigo. They attended El Instituto Básico together, but Hidalia didn't go on to colegio. Rodrigo asks her if she likes working at the hotel, and she says it's all right. "Sometimes no one comes, so I sit here, waiting," she says. "If I wanted to, I could use the phone." She points to the phone on the desk behind her. "But I don't have anyone to call." She smiles at Rodrigo. "Do you want to call someone?"

Rodrigo wonders if Pedro has a phone where he works, but even if he does, Rodrigo wouldn't know the number.

Hidalia asks him what professional team he's going to play for when he turns eighteen, and when he answers, "Cobán, I hope," she says, "Yes, it's better to stay local." She rubs her hands together. "But it would be fun to go far away, wouldn't it? To go to the other side of the country? You could play for San Marcos. Or for Tecún Umán—you'd almost be in Mexico!"

"You're right," Rodrigo says, although he would want to play so far from home only if Julia came with him.

Hidalia gives him another smile, a softer smile. "You should come here again," she says. "You could use the phone. Or I could get you something from the restaurant. I could pretend it was for me, and you could sit here in the office and eat it." She taps her fingers against the wood counter, moving them closer to Rodrigo's hand. "It's good food," Hidalia says. "The chef is from Argentina."

In a loud, crackling voice, the parrot says, "Argentina." The sound startles Rodrigo. Hidalia laughs.

"Is it strange sitting with this parrot all day?" he asks her.

She thinks about it. "I'm used to it. Sometimes I talk to him." She shrugs. "You could say we are friends."

When Julia comes, walking quickly, Hidalia frowns. "Goodbye," Rodrigo says. Only the parrot replies, with a crackling "Adios."

Julia doesn't speak to him until they have crossed the Cobán highway. "Hidalia will tell everyone in town about what we're doing," she says.

"She doesn't have any friends," Rodrigo says. He moves the soccer ball from his right arm to his left so he can hold Julia's hand. "She'll only tell the parrot."

"And the parrot will tell the world." Julia laughs, and Rodrigo knows he is forgiven. Even if the sky is threatening rain—clouds have gathered over mountains to the east—he feels an elation he associates with sunny days.

By the time they reach the field in Chixajau, the first drops have fallen. Julia says, "We should go back." Rodrigo says, "It's only a light rain, hardly a chipi-chipi." Shrugging, she joins him in the center of the field, and they kick the ball back and forth. Some of the girls in town play soccer, but Julia is a basketball player and she kicks the ball tentatively. He moves toward her to instruct her, but when he stands behind her, about to demonstrate, he can't help himself. He wraps his arms around her and kisses her neck. She doesn't resist. Slowly, he leans back, pulling her with him. She says, "What are you doing?"

A moment later, he has fallen to the grass, Julia on top of him. "It's wet here," she says, but he senses little complaint in her voice. He cradles her head in the crook of his arm, keeping it protected from the grass. He dips his face to hers and kisses her. "I thought we were going to play," she says.

He doesn't answer; he kisses her again. A minute later, she whispers, "Rodrigo, stop."

"Why?"

"Look."

He turns to where she is looking. Children from the village are staring at them from the road. One of the boys waves. Julia stands quickly, brushing the grass from her pants and blouse. The boy charges onto the field, trailed by other boys. "Can we play with you?" the boy asks. Rodrigo kicks the ball to him, and all the boys cheer.

But as the boys begin to play, the rain falls fast and hard. The girls, who have been watching from the road, race toward their houses. "We need to go," Julia says, and Rodrigo calls to one of the boys to pass him the ball.

The rain is falling harder now, and Rodrigo takes Julia's hand, and they sprint for the cover of an avocado tree on the other side of the field. The tree is tall, perhaps five stories, and offers a haven beneath its thick leaves. Rodrigo thinks the boys may join them, but they have run in the other direction.

In the dry privacy under the tree, Rodrigo kisses Julia again. With the rain comes a cold wind, and Rodrigo pulls Julia to him, warming himself with her body. With his hands, he finds the soft flesh above her waist. His hands are hungry to touch more. She pulls back. "Please, Rodrigo."

"Okay," he says, kissing her on the forehead.

She falls into his arms again, and he kisses her hair. "You will marry me, Julia, won't you?" he asks.

"Yes," she says.

"Tomorrow? Will you marry me tomorrow?"

"When I am eighteen," she says.

"In two years? It's an eternity."

"It's only a year and a-half. My father will not let me marry any earlier. You will come to my house and ask my father for his permission."

"Do I have your permission?"

She doesn't hesitate: "Yes."

"And if your father doesn't give his permission? I'm Catholic, and I know he wants you to marry an Evangelical. A rich Evangelical."

They listen to the rain strike the large leaves. "You could become Evangelical," she says.

"I will, if you want."

"But you must feel it."

"Do you feel it?" he asks. "You were born Catholic."

"I was," she acknowledges. "But when my mother became pregnant with Angelica, I was made to...I was given another life."

"But if I never feel it, will it matter to you?"

Even holding Julia in his arms, Rodrigo is worried she is slipping away. He feels the coldness around him, the wet wind, the rain. The cornfield across the soccer field is barely visible in the downpour. Everything is disappearing in front of him, receding into grayness. Everything is leaving. Julia will leave him here, under the tree, with the rain finding its way past the leaves, the cold coming colder.

But an instant later, he feels Julia pull closer to him. He is surprised by the force of her embrace. "Do you know Alejandra, the norteamericana?" Julia asks.

"The negra?"

"She loves a muchacho who is of a different religion, and she doesn't think they will be able to marry. When I think of it, it makes me sad."

Rodrigo says nothing; he feels her face against his chest, her arms around his back.

"And I have something else to tell you, Rodrigo."

He looks down at her. "What is it?" he asks.

"Sometimes I go to the calvario to pray."

"Because the doors of your church are locked?"

"It isn't because of this."

"So why?" he asks.

"I don't know," she says. "It's something I feel I need to do. I worry I am betraying my religion—Hermano Hector would say I am, and my father would agree—but I go anyway." She sighs and moves into him again. She whispers now, as if to his heart: "So it doesn't matter about your religion, Rodrigo. I love you, all right? I love you."

As Julia and Rodrigo walk home—the rain having, for the moment, ceased—Julia thinks about what she almost told him: *I was made to change my religion.* This wasn't the first time she'd had this thought, but it was as close as she has come to speaking it. If her sister is the miracle child, the one in whom God revealed Himself to her father and mother, who is she? Was her birth, blessed by their old religion and its priests, something less than miraculous, something unremarkable?

One morning, several weeks after Angelica's birth, Julia returned home from the market, and stepping into the living room, saw her parents on the couch and Angelica asleep in her mother's lap. Her father's arm was wrapped around her mother's shoulders, his lips were against her neck. Immediately her father pulled back and stood, but from the moment she saw the three of them, she thought they were perfect, their own family trinity. She felt like an intruder.

She looks at Rodrigo, who has been talking about soccer ever since they left the shelter of the avocado tree. If her father hadn't permitted him to become her novio, what would she have done? And if one day her father doesn't permit them to marry, what will she do?

They have arrived at the Hotel Mundo, where Hidalia, imprisoned in her booth, gives them a bored wave. The parrot is more enthusiastic. "Hola," it says. This is where Rodrigo will leave her so she can walk back into town alone, her reputation intact.

"Tell me one more time," Rodrigo says, his eyes large and pleading.

"Tell you what?" Julia asks.

"That you love me."

"I do," Julia says.

"Say 'I love you.'"

But before Julia can speak even the first word, the parrot squawks the entire phrase.

— 14 —

Waiting below Alejandra's doorstep, Rodrigo rehearses the lines he'll say to her. He'll tell her his friend Galindo is thoughtless sometimes. He'll tell her Galindo made a mistake in thinking norteamericanas have different customs than Guatemalans and she wouldn't be offended by him turning up at her door. He'll tell her this won't happen again, with anyone. Rodrigo imagines Alejandra hiring him to stand guard outside her door, turning back unwanted visitors. He allows himself to feel the power of his invented position. He imagines a gun in his pocket, a knife tied to his belt. Would he wear a helmet, like a soldier? Here the fantasy ends, and he laughs at its foolishness. He would never want to wear a soldier's helmet.

By the time he sees Alejandra on the steps above the calvario, Rodrigo has forgotten why he's here. "Buenas tardes," she says, her words labored because she's out of breath.

"Buenas tardes," Rodrigo replies.

There is a silence, which lasts several seconds, before Alejandra says, "May I help you?"

Rodrigo is facing west, where the early-evening sky is layered in blues and oranges and pinks. "I'm Julia's novio." It's all he can think of to say.

"Rodrigo," she says, smiling. "I have heard so much about you." She adds, with another smile, "All your secrets."

Rodrigo's thoughts flash to the house in Cobán, the single candle, "Chinita." He has thought of Chinita—what, he wonders, was her real name?—often. Sometimes he regrets not doing more with her than listening to her jokes, and he wonders, with a mixture of fear and anticipation, when Pedro will invite him on a similar adventure.

"Would you like coffee?" Alejandra asks. "We'll drink it on the stoop."

"Yes, thank you," he says, and she goes into her room and he stares at the sky to the west, its colors brilliant but already fading. A few minutes later, she is outside again, with two cups of coffee. He finds it stronger than anything his mother ever makes him, and less sweat. After a few more sips he likes the coffee better, even if it is bitter.

Rodrigo wonders if Julia will come soon. As they were walking back from Chixajau yesterday, she said she would be seeing Alejandra this afternoon. He hoped to surprise her.

Alejandra spares him having to initiate conversation by asking him about soccer. He tells her about his hopes of playing professionally. "Everyone thinks I have a great chance, but I worry they are dreaming as much as I am. What if I am invited to join a professional team—the Cobán Imperials, let's say—and I am, in the end, not as good as what they expected?"

He begins to dismiss his doubts, hurrying to cover up what he sees now as a confession of his weakness, his lack of faith in himself, but Alejandra stops him to say, "The most successful people, in whatever profession, are often the people who doubt their talents the most."

This sounds like something she made up to appease him. "But of course there are thousands of people who never tried to do what they most wanted because they were afraid to fail," she says.

"I don't understand," he says. "If you want something, of course you do what you can to have it. And if you fail, you are where you were before."

"So if you were to fail as a soccer player, where would you be?" she asks him.

"I would be here, in Santa Cruz."

"Where would you work?"

"I would drive a logging truck. Or I would work at Caminos Rurales and help build roads to villages. Or if I had enough money, I could open a store or a movie theater. We could use a movie theater."

Alejandra says she thought Santa Cruz had a movie theater, and Rodrigo laughs. "At Don Armando's pharmacy? On Friday nights, he shows movies on the back wall, which is cracked like an egg."

"Now I know why I haven't been to the movies," Alejandra says.

Rodrigo is a sip from finishing his coffee. He wonders if she'll offer him more. There is only a small strip of red light in the sky to the west, and he knows it would be rude of him to stay past dark. "Was it your ambition to come here?" Rodrigo asks. "Is this what you most wanted?"

"For a long time, I wanted to live outside the United States, doing work I thought would help people." She turns to him, her smile bright in the growing darkness. "But before this, I wanted to be a singer."

"Like Madonna?" he asks.

Alejandra laughs. "Opera. I wanted to sing opera."

"But you aren't fat," Rodrigo says.

Alejandra laughs again. "Maybe that's why I didn't think I could succeed."

"You could try again."

"I could."

"Now. This minute."

Alejandra laughs.

"En serio," Rodrigo says.

"I'd scare you. I'd scare the whole town."

"Please. A few notes," Rodrigo says, employing the same voice he does when he asks Julia for one more kiss. He thinks he has Alejandra convinced, but they are interrupted by the sound of someone coming up the steps from the calvario. "Oh. Discúlpeme, Alejandra," Julia says when she's standing in front of the two of them. "You have company."

It is clear to Rodrigo that Julia doesn't recognize him in the darkness. He might be Alejandra's lover. Stealing a glance at Alejandra, he thinks they look suited to each other, more so, perhaps, than he and Julia. But it is strange to think of himself as the novio of anyone besides Julia, and quickly he stands and moves toward her. By now, she sees who he is, and her surprise becomes pleasure.

After Rodrigo leaves, Julia knows she doesn't have much time left to spend with Alejandra. She knows her father is settling into his chair in their living room, alternately looking at his watch and looking at the darkness outside the window. He will think she has been with Rodrigo. But before saying goodbye to Alejandra, Julia wants to know what she thinks of Rodrigo.

Alejandra doesn't answer immediately, and in her hesitation, Julia reads disapproval. Alejandra's disapproval would bear nearly the weight of her father's. Julia prepares to defend Rodrigo, although unlike with her father, she cannot imagine on what fronts the attacks would come. "I liked him before I met him, because you told me how much you liked him," Alejandra says. "And I like him as much now. If you are looking for my blessing, you have it. You have it with everything you do, Julia García."

— 15 —

"That's all?" Rodrigo asks. "Just 'I love you'?"

"That's all," Pedro says.

They are sitting on stools in front of Tienda Esperanza across from the municipalidad. Rodrigo is drinking a Coke; Pedro is drinking a Gallo beer. It is evening, and on the street behind them, busses discharge colegio students home from Cobán and San Cristóbal.

Rodrigo makes Pedro explain it again: They go into Cantina Paz, have a few beers each, maybe share an eighth of whiskey. When they finish enough alcohol to satisfy the cantina's owner, Don Federico, he will signal them, and Pedro will go first into the little room behind the cantina where the woman has her mattress. The woman, Pedro explains, is Don Federico's special feria surprise, his way of competing with all the makeshift cantinas set up especially for the feria.

"If it's like last year," Pedro says, "she'll have on a güipil from Santa Cruz. She isn't from around here and she isn't indígena, but she wears the güipil anyway. I don't know why.

"And after I go, it's your turn," Pedro says. "And remember, all you have to do to get her to spread is say, 'I love you.'"

"And if I don't say it?" Rodrigo asks.

"I don't know," Pedro says. "Maybe she'll play cards with you or sing you a lullaby."

"'I love you,'" Rodrigo says.

"Right," Pedro says. "And you will love her. She's magnificent."

Rodrigo doesn't like the feria as much as he used to. He remembers when people would come from the capital with a Ferris wheel and men from the villages who owned horses would offer rides for five centavos. But the people from the capital have stopped bringing the Ferris wheel and Don Sebastian had his horse stolen during a feria a few years before, so no one comes with horses anymore. Now the feria is dominated by cantinas, room-sized tents and wooden shacks with a few tables and coolers full of Gallo and Venado. At the last feria, Rodrigo's mother counted nineteen cantinas and complained about the number of bolos passed out in the street. This year, she is not permitting Rodrigo's younger brothers to go to the feria. "The Evangelicals are right," she told Rodrigo. "Bolos are a plague."

"I don't know," Rodrigo tells Pedro.

"What don't you know?"

"I don't know if I should."

"Why?"

"Because of Julia. We're novios, you know."

"But is she sleeping with you, vos?"

"No," Rodrigo says quickly.

Pedro finishes his beer. "Listen, vos, men are supposed to have more than one woman. In the daytime, you have Julia. At night, you have freedom." Pedro frowns. "Besides, Julia is cold."

"What do you mean?"

"You go with her to those cultos, vos. You see how wrapped up in God she is."

Rodrigo doesn't reply. He knows Julia isn't cold. She can be as serious as Christ when she's in church, but when the sermon is over and the people have spilled into the street, she makes jokes about the way the preacher spits when he speaks. "If Hermano Hector had gone on much longer," she said after the latest culto, "he would have had to build us an ark."

Rodrigo might see her jokes as disrespect, small criticisms of a faith in which she doesn't entirely believe. But he knows this isn't her intention; if Julia goes to cultos and yet prays at the calvario, it is because her devotion is such that neither of the two religions offers her enough time with Him. Rodrigo would like to feel even a small portion of the connection with God Julia feels. But if he feels closer to Him at cultos than at other times, it is only because he is next to Julia. And whatever the private rules of her worship at the calvario, Julia is strict about following the teachings of the Church of God. When one afternoon Rodrigo mentioned the feria, Julia told him she hadn't been to the feria in four years, ever since her family became Evangelical.

Pedro says, "The only reason her father let you be her novio is because he thinks you're going to be a famous soccer player. If you didn't play soccer and had asked his permission to be Julia's novio, he would have laughed in your face. Or he might have done worse—he might have run you over with his Mercedes."

Conceding to the truth of Pedro's words, Rodrigo doesn't reply.

Pedro tells Rodrigo he'll meet him in the park at ten o'clock on the last night of the feria and they'll go to Don Federico's cantina. "Okay, vos?"

Rodrigo hesitates. "Okay."

— 16 —

Julia hears her father speaking with Don Carlos in the living room. Don Carlos is a foreman at the electrical plant in Chixoy, where Julia's father works, and is also a member of the Church of God. Don Carlos' daughter, Alma, studies with Julia at El Instituto Básico.

It is late, and Julia is sitting at her desk in her room, reading a book of poems by Pablo Neruda. She is supposed to write a report about the poems, due the following week, but she finds herself re-reading the same poem, mouthing its words: "Tonight I can write the saddest lines." With her door open to allow in the cool night air, she hears her father: "I saw the woman, the black norteamericana, a few days ago walking to a village. I offered her a ride. She said she preferred to walk."

"She's from the United States? I thought she was from Belize or Honduras. What is she doing here?"

"I think she works with campesinos."

Julia wonders why they would be talking about Alejandra.

"My daughter visited her yesterday," Don Carlos says. "But she didn't tell me what the woman had given her. I found it in her room."

A dog barks in the yard next door, and this sets off a round of dog barks. Every dog in town seems to respond. When the dogs are quiet, Julia hears Don Carlos say, "I told Alma she is forbidden to see this woman. She will listen to me, I'm sure of it. But I worry about other girls whose parents are less vigilant."

"Someone should talk to her. Someone should tell her about our town. If she is determined to encourage our children toward sin, she can't stay."

"I understand men come to see her at night."

"What men?"

"Don Gerardo's son, Marcos, is one. And his cousin, Oswaldo."

"Does she live alone?"

"She lives in a room in Doña Flor's house. But you know Doña Flor, ever since her husband disappeared…"

Neither man speaks for a while. Julia is no longer reading the poem, although one of its lines comes to her, as if spoken by someone outside her door: "Love is so short, forgetting so long."

Julia's father says, "We must talk to her."

Julia feels nervous, uneasy; she's worried her father will discover her visits with Alejandra. Cowered by his voice, Alejandra will confess everything they've done and said to each other. Julia wonders if after her father talks to her, Alejandra will want to see her again. Perhaps she will only want to see Marcos and Oswaldo, and when Julia comes knocking, she won't open the door.

The two men discuss the feria, which will begin the next day. Julia's father tells Don Carlos he won't let either of his daughters leave the house during the feria, even to go to a tienda or the park. "There's too much sin in the street," he says.

She hears Don Carlos chuckle. "But you will go to the feria, won't you?"

"No."

"Not even to play one game of La Lotería?"

"No, not even one game."

"I remember when you won six games in a single night. You carried home flower vases, and you gave three to your mother and three to Sabina."

Julia's father laughs. "It was only a day or two before I proposed to Sabina, and I decided my luck at La Lotería was a good sign. It seemed I had been blessed and I could look forward to a long, happy marriage."

"And you were right."

"Yes, I was."

Julia has never heard her father tell the story of winning at La Lotería. She has never heard him speak of how he wooed her mother. But this is where the story stops, and before long, the two men say goodnight. Julia hears her father close the front door as Don Carlos leaves. She hears him click off the light in the living room and walk to his bedroom.

All is quite now, even the dogs. She looks again at the Neruda poem, but can't concentrate. The words fall over each other: "In the distance…tonight…my soul is not satisfied…it has lost her." She puts down the book and goes to her bed and lies on top of it. She stares at the ceiling. Over the three days of the feria, she knows she'll have a hard time escaping her parents' sight. She wonders how she can warn Alejandra about her father.

— 17 —

During the days of the feria, Julia helps her mother with housework. She dunks clothes and sheets in the basin of the pila and runs soap over them and pours palanganas of water over them until the soap is gone. She hangs the clothes and sheets on the line in their courtyard to dry. For the last year, Julia's father has talked about buying machines for washing and drying. But she has also heard him praise the smell of clothes and sheets left to dry in the sun.

Julia clips roses from the garden and puts them in vases, perhaps the same vases her father won her mother long ago at La Lotería, and sets the vases on the tables in the living room and dining room. In the afternoons, she sits on her bed, the book of Neruda poems on her lap, and reads the poems aloud. And all the time, she thinks about Alejandra. She hopes Alejandra left town during the feria.

During the nights of the feria, Julia and her family attend cultos at the Church of God. The singing in their church and Hermano Hector's amplified sermons are enough to shelter them from the sounds of the feria on the street. When they leave the church, however, the streets are alive with strange music and firecrackers and the sound of bottles breaking. Julia's father leads his family in a quick march back to their house. After entering their house, they kneel in the living room and say another prayer to wipe away the sin of their encounter, however brief, with the feria.

On the morning of the feria's last day, her father leaves the house early to go on an errand to Cobán and her mother calls her from outside her bedroom door. Julia doesn't answer. Her mother calls again, saying, "Julia, I need to go to the market. I'd like you to look after Angelica. I'll only be gone a minute."

When Julia again doesn't respond, her mother asks, "Are you sleeping?" Julia thinks her mother will open her door and discover her sitting at her desk. But her mother doesn't open the door, and a minute later, Julia hears her leave the house with Angelica.

At last alone, Julia escapes her house by the back door. She runs past the avocado tree at the edge of their property and continues under a canopy of pine trees. She follows a path halfway up the hill on the north side of town until she is above Doña Flor's house. Seeing no one around, she descends to Alejandra's door. When no one answers her knock, she tries again.

She hears a voice behind her: "She left."

Julia turns to find Doña Flor, who is wearing a brown dress and an orchid in her hair. Doña Flor is fifty years old, but with the heavy lines in her face, which seem to Julia as deep as the ditches farmers carve on hills to stop soil from eroding, she looks seventy.

"Where did she go?" Julia asks.

"To Puerto Barrios."

"When will she be back?"

"She isn't coming back."

"Why?"

"She wasn't wanted here."

"Who didn't want her?" As soon as she asks the question, Julia fears the answer.

Doña Flor smiles. It's a crooked smile, and it highlights the wrinkles around her lips. "No one likes when a señorita lives by herself."

"When did she leave?"

Doña Flor doesn't answer. Instead, she says, "Do you want to see her room?" She steps up to the door, and Julia moves aside. Doña Flor removes a key from a pocket in her dress. "Pase adelante," she says, and they step into the room.

The three-burner stove is gone, but the gas tank remains. On the sink in the right-hand corner is a purple toothbrush. Julia notices a scattering of black hair around the basin. She pulls a strand between her fingers until it breaks. On the fold-up table, Julia finds one of Alejandra's blue coffee mugs. It is half filled with coffee. She wants to drink it, to see if she can taste Alejandra in it, but she is conscious of Doña Flor looking at her. The bed has been stripped; only the thin foam mattress remains. The dresser top is barren save a single photograph without a frame. In the photograph, Alejandra, alone and leaning against a palm tree, is wearing a white blouse. Beneath her blouse, Julia can see the outlines of her breasts. On the back of the photograph, she finds words in Spanish in large, neat handwriting: "Don't forget me." Beneath the words is Alejandra's signature.

Julia turns to ask Doña Flor if she can keep the picture, but Doña Flor is no longer in the room. Julia finds her outside, standing in the pale mid-morning sunlight and staring down at the calvario and, below it, Calle Tres de Mayo, which is filled with feria games and cantinas set up under canvas tents. Busses and cars have been diverted off the street; they have to loop around town on the poor dirt roads. A bus appears to be stuck in front of Hugo Tul's carpintería.

When Julia steps beside Doña Flor, she thinks the old woman is laughing. But when she sees her face, she knows she was wrong. "The way her room looks," Doña Flor says, "reminds me of when the army came for Mario—everything scattered, nothing in order."

"What did she say to you when she left?"

"She told me where she was going. She told me she wasn't coming back. That is all."

Julia begins to ask another question, but Doña Flor continues, "I heard the men come to talk with her. I heard the threats they made. I heard shouting. I should have gone to help her, but I was too frightened. I was thinking about Mario."

She bows her head. "I was in the house the night the soldiers came for Mario. I left by the back door. I ran into the woods. When I returned, he was gone."

"What did the men say to Alejandra?" Julia asks.

Doña Flor lifts her head to look at the scene below. Julia can see boys wielding guns in front of a shooting gallery. Someone must have struck a target because she hears a snippet of a happy, careless song.

"What did the men say?" Julia repeats.

"Perhaps," Doña Flor says, "you should ask your father."

— 18 —

On the first night of the feria, Rodrigo plays La Lotería, covering the devil, the drum and the skeleton on his card, but he doesn't win. He doesn't play again because he's saving his money to buy liquor with Pedro. He stands in the long grass outside the Lotería booth and watches Doña Elena win five straight games and collect five vases, each a different color. She stacks them next to each other on the wooden table in front of her in a horizontal rainbow.

On the second night, he counts the bolos. Don Sebastian sits slumped against the wall of the abandoned house with Bayer: El Mejor Para Su Salud painted in pastels on the front. Don Reginaldo sleeps with his guitar in a doorway. Don Lico hasn't even reached a safe place to become unconscious. He lies in front of the El Pistolero shooting gallery. People aiming at the gorilla need to rest a foot on his back in order to have a clear shot.

On the third night, Rodrigo meets Pedro in the park. They walk down the street toward Don Federico's cantina but stop at the first booth. A girl who looks like a gypsy, with black hair left long in back and cut straight above her eyebrows, is picking ten centavo pieces from beside iron rings on a table. An old man stands next to her, holding a light bulb above the table. A wire connects the bulb to a nearby electrical pole. The object of the game, the old man explains to Pedro and Rodrigo, is to throw a ten centavo piece into the center of one of the rings. If your coin lands in the middle of a ring, you get fifty centavos plus your coin back.

Pedro spends three quetzals, winning only once. He gets change for another quetzal. He flips a ten centavo piece. It lands outside a ring. He throws another. No luck.

A bolo Rodrigo doesn't know stumbles next to him. "Play for me," says the bolo, his breath hot with Venado. Rodrigo shakes his head, but the bolo insists, waving a quetzal in front of Rodrigo's face and grabbing him on the shoulder. "Come on, play for me, mi hijo."

Rodrigo takes the quetzal and changes it with the gypsy girl. He throws the first ten centavo piece. It lands in a ring. He throws the next, and it, too, lands in a ring. Rodrigo has turned the bolo's quetzal into two. "Here," Rodrigo says, offering the bolo the coins, "you won."

"Keep playing," the bolo says.

Rodrigo throws again. Again he wins.

Pedro tugs on his shirt. "Ready?" he asks.

Rodrigo hands the bolo his money. "Gracias, boy," the bolo says. "I can buy another drink now." Following Pedro, Rodrigo feels elevated by his luck, as if blessed or carried by a dream.

In Cantina Paz, Pedro and Rodrigo order beer and an eighth of whiskey. Pedro drinks his beer quickly and calls out to Don Federico to bring him another. When Don Federico doesn't bring Pedro his beer quickly enough, Pedro drinks Rodrigo's.

Don Federico puts down a beer for Pedro. "Another whiskey," Pedro says, finishing the bottle. As Don Federico is walking away, he adds, "No, two more."

Pedro drinks both bottles of whiskey and begins a third beer.

"I'm feeling..." Pedro begins.

"What?" Rodrigo asks.

"Very tired." He closes his eyes, opens them slowly. They're pink on the edges. "Sorry, vos."

Pedro lowers his head on the table. A few seconds later, he begins to snore. Rodrigo thinks he's joking. "Come on, Pedro," he says. "Pedro? Puchica, vos, what happened to you?"

Pedro doesn't respond. Rodrigo pulls the beer from Pedro's hand. Pedro doesn't move.

Well, Rodrigo thinks, standing, *it's better this way*. Rodrigo is nervous about seeing the woman, if there is a woman. He has thought about her, fantasized about her, every night since Pedro mentioned her, wondering if it can really be so easy. Just "I love you." But every time he thinks about her, he also thinks of Julia and feels ashamed.

He leaves money for his beer on the table and takes a step toward the door. Don Federico calls him. "If you would like," Don Federico says, "you may pass inside here." He indicates the door at the back of the cantina.

———

Julia spreads her arms to touch both sides of her bed and listens to the sounds of the feria's last night. They are louder than the three previous nights. She hears a woman shout: "You can't play without paying." She hears a man's reply: "I gave you all my money. Give me a free one! Please! Puchica!" She hears the pop-pop-popping of guns at the shooting gallery and brief explosions of music. She hears the churning of the Lotería balls and the barker's high, excited voice announcing what ball he pulled: "El diablo, el diablo! No es San Pablo, es el diablo!" She hears close by, as if from the under the avocado tree behind her house, the unintelligible whispers of a man and woman.

Julia came to bed two hours ago, but she hasn't been able to sleep. She keeps thinking about Alejandra. She wonders if Alejandra knows it was her father who came to talk with her, to chase her from town. She has tried to picture her father in Alejandra's room, standing by the stove or sitting in a chair at her table, but the thought of him there seems beyond imagining, as impossible as seeing him on his knees in front of the icons in the calvario.

She knows her father was wrong to do what he did, and she fears—no, she is sadly certain—she won't have the courage to tell him this. No matter what Alejandra did, no matter what she gave to Alma, she didn't deserve to be threatened; she didn't deserve to be forced to leave Santa Cruz. *She was all alone here,* Julia thinks. *She liked our town. And she was my friend.*

She wonders what words her father used. She wonders if Don Carlos, who used to be in the army, shook his fists at her, as Julia saw him do to his wife once, in the market. When, at last, she thinks of Rodrigo instead of Alejandra or her father, she is relieved. She knows she would be less troubled tonight if she had seen him in the last four days. She wonders if it was he whose shots set off the most recent music at the shooting gallery or if it was he who won the latest prize at La Lotería by covering his card with the black man, the sword and the sky.

—

Entering the back room, Rodrigo has to adjust his eyes to the new light. The room is lit by two candles, standing perhaps three meters apart in the center of the room. There is a mattress on the floor between the two candles; a woman is sitting on it, her back to the wall. She is wearing the Santa Cruz güipil, white with a black pattern around the neck. A blanket covers her waist. Her bare feet stick out from beneath the blanket.

"Buenas noches," Rodrigo mumbles. The woman points to a chair a few feet from the door. Rodrigo sits. "Don Federico showed me in," he says.

"Good," the woman says.

"How do you know him?"

"He's my cousin."

Rodrigo can't tell how old the woman is; because of the poor lighting, he can't see her face well. More distinct is the shadow of her tangled hair on the wall behind her. He thinks of Julia and her precise curls, and he wonders if she's sleeping. He feels confident that she is, and assuring himself of this, he's relieved.

"I have a lot of cousins," the woman says. "All over the country."

"Do you travel to all the ferias?"

"Most of them. Puerto Barrios last week."

"And next week?"

"I don't worry about next week."

She smiles and pulls down the blanket a little, revealing her bare stomach.

"I've never been to Puerto Barrios," Rodrigo says. "I don't travel much. Just to the towns around here."

The woman doesn't reply. She moves her right hand under the blanket. Rodrigo can see where she places it. She begins to move her hand, and he watches the blanket rise and fall softly.

"I guess this is a small feria compared to the ferias in other towns," Rodrigo says. "I'm sure the feria in Puerto Barrios is bigger. Do they have a Ferris wheel at the bigger ferias?"

Again the woman doesn't answer. Rodrigo says, "When I was younger, I mean young, there used to be a Ferris wheel here. A few years ago. Do they have a Ferris wheel at the bigger ferias?" he asks again.

"I don't know," the woman says. "I never look." She smiles, a smile that rides high into her cheeks. "Why, do you miss your Ferris wheel?"

Rodrigo knows the woman is mocking him, but he sees her hand again, moving faster beneath the blanket; she breathes heavily. He can't help himself: what she does excites him. The woman begins to moan softly. He feels his own breath grow more labored, the air suddenly heavy, and his body grow warm. The woman moves one hand under her güipil to caress her breast. Inspired, he stands and approaches her.

She stops moaning, sits up higher against the wall and covers her stomach with the blanket. She looks at him with hard eyes. Rodrigo stands tall and foolish in the center of the room. He is conscious of his penis pressing against his trousers, and he knows she can see it. He can't go back to his seat, he realizes, without looking cowardly and foolish. But he dreads saying the words to her.

After a while, she smiles—a gentler smile, he decides, although he has a feeling it's not completely free of scorn—and begins moving her hands again, one on her breast, the other beneath the blanket. A moment later, laughing, she changes hands, her right now below the blanket and her left rubbing her breast. Finally, she places both her hands below the blanket and whispers soft, unintelligible words.

Rodrigo wishes he could sink into the floor, escape without retreating like a magician, but he also can't help wanting to throw off her blanket and involve himself in what's beneath it. He feels his head grow light with a sensation more compelling and pleasant than drunkenness. He sighs, dreading what he is about to say, but the words escape his mouth with the urgency of a battle cry: "I love you."

"Come here," she replies, lifting the blanket from her body.

—

Rodrigo wakes up when he hears a bottle break in the street outside his bedroom. "Damn bolo," he says. He can hear faint sounds from the cantinas, the last of the feria music. Rodrigo sits up and leans against the wall. He thinks of the woman, whose back was against the wall when he walked into her room. The parallel disturbs him, but he doesn't change his position. He rubs his eyes. "Did I really say, 'I love you'?" he asks himself. He tries to convince himself he hasn't. Or that he has, but too softly for the woman to have heard. Then he recalls distinctly how his words sounded—wild and loud—and how she responded.

Rodrigo shakes his head and puts his palms against his eyes. He can't believe he said "I love you." He wonders who will forgive him; he knows he won't be able to tell anyone—not Pedro, and of course not Julia. He can't escape the thought that he has done something irrevocable and wrong. He wonders how he can save himself.

He closes his eyes and feels the woman again, her body dry, and her tongue too damp and long. Tired of her intrusion into his mouth, Rodrigo kissed her forehead, and it was salty from sweat, a pleasant taste, and her hair smelled faintly of smoke from a wood fire. But there was no fire in the room. "Why did her hair smell of smoke?" he asks himself, imagining damnation, hell.

Rodrigo opens his eyes and murmurs: "I'll follow her. I'll follow her to all those ferias, to every last one, to every one until she does love me and I love her. I'm younger than she is, maybe fifteen years younger. But she can love me. And I can love her. She was cruel to me, and then I…then we…but I know that once she knows me, she'll be kind, and I'll love her. Of course I'll love her. My words will be true. It will just take time."

Rodrigo allows himself to fall back on his bed. "I'll follow her all over the country. And maybe in a few months or a year, she really will love me and I'll love her. I'll have to say goodbye to Julia, and this will be sad and terrible, but I'll have to do it to save myself."

He envisions himself riding in a beat-up pick-up truck, the kind all the feria vendors have. Maybe he'll ride with the gypsy girl and the old man. Maybe he'll work with them, make a little money with the iron rings. But always he'll seek the cantina woman, to be with her. And one day, they will love each other.

Yes, he thinks, falling into a deep, forgiving sleep, a sleep that will last until noon, *I will love her. And that will put everything right.*

TWO

— 1 —

It is Rodrigo's eighteenth birthday when he receives the telegram from the Cobán Imperials. He reads it three times, each time without understanding anything except this: He is a professional soccer player. There is no one in his house with whom to share the news. His brothers are at school, his mother is in the market. He is supposed to be getting ready to go to Colegio Verapaz, in Cobán, but he hasn't attended classes in several weeks. If he does take the bus to Cobán before classes start in the afternoon, it is only to accompany Julia. Now he'll be able to quit school, although this isn't what makes him dance around his house pretending chairs and tables are stoned-legged opponents and the back door is the goalmouth.

He looks at his watch and realizes he is late to meet Julia at the bus stop in the park. He dashes outside, his hair wild from his celebration. He races up his street, picking up speed as the dirt gives way to concrete. The bus across Calle Principal is painted like a rainbow, and Rodrigo thinks this is right: He has been delivered a pot of gold.

He is about to cross the street when he notices Julia sitting on the bus, beside an open back window. She is looking straight ahead, as if expecting him to walk any second down the aisle. "Here, Julia!" he shouts as the bus starts moving. "I'm here!"

He fails to look both ways before crossing the street, but he's lucky. No cars are coming, and soon he is jogging next to the bus beneath Julia's window. "Right here, Julia! I'm right here."

The bus rumbles over a speed bump and its groaning prevents Julia from hearing him. As the bus picks up speed, he is worried he'll have to wait until she returns in the evening to tell her his news. But he keeps pace with the bus, and at last she notices him, her face brightening. She calls his name, but he knows he doesn't have much time left before the bus will reach the steep downhill slope of the road and roar off to the Cobán highway.

"I'm a professional!" he says, holding up the telegram. "Paid to play!" He falls a step behind. "Marry me, Julia. You will, won't you?"

She waves, but whether in affirmation of his proposal, in celebration of his professional status, or only in goodbye, he isn't sure. He stops and watches the bus wind down the last stretch of Calle Principal, meet the Cobán highway, and disappear.

—2—

If not for his soccer career and the money he earns from it, Rodrigo knows Julia's father would never allow him to marry her. Most boys with his education work in lumberyards or pick coffee beans on one of the plantations outside of town. But Rodrigo's soccer talents put him in a class apart from even the most educated. His class is the elite of childhood dream and adult envy.

Rodrigo is standing in front of his mirror, combing his hair. For the occasion of his discussion with Señor García, he is wearing a blue suit with a crisp white shirt and a red tie with light gold figures of eagles. The tie belonged to his uncle, who left it with a few shirts and an old pair of soccer cleats when he went to Mexico. The cleats fit Rodrigo perfectly, but he never wears them. Instead, he keeps them on top of his dresser like a shrine.

There is a knock at his bedroom door, and, thinking it's one of his brothers, he says, "Go away, vos." But it's his mother, and she lets herself into his room and stands against the far wall. Rodrigo gazes at her reflection in his mirror. "I thought it was Augusto or Mario," he says to the mirror.

"I know."

He puts his comb down and straightens his tie.

"What will Señor García say, Rodrigo?"

Rodrigo picks up his comb again and flicks it above his right ear. "He'll say 'Yes.'"

"Are you certain?"

Rodrigo puts the comb down, but picks it up again and flicks it above his left ear. "It doesn't matter. I'll marry Julia whether he says yes or no."

"You would marry her without her father's permission?"

"Yes."

"But you would not be able to marry in her church," she says.

He runs his hands down his suit coat and turns around. "It doesn't matter." He gazes at his mother, whose black hair flows around her narrow face. She is wearing a new blue dress with black outlines of hearts around the neck. A tiny rosary is lodged between her breasts. Her cheeks are red from the sun or the stove.

"It looks as if you are the one who is preparing to speak to Señor García," he says.

Her lips rise in a hint of a smile. "I don't envy you this interview. In his presence, I am sure I would have no words to speak."

"And I wouldn't have much to say to him either if he wasn't so interested in the Imperials. He wants to know everything—about the length of our practices, the fields we play on, the way we are treated by other teams' fans."

"And I thought he didn't like you."

"He doesn't. But he loves soccer."

Slowly, she moves from the corner and stands beside him. They stare at themselves in his mirror. His mother is only as tall as his shoulders, the same height as Julia. He feels an urge to put his arm around her and draw her close. He wonders if his mother misses the feel of a man's embrace, his warmth, the low tone of his voice. His father has been absent for more than a decade, and he is certain his mother has been with no man since. She manages with her God and her sons and her strength. *But how often is she lonely?* Rodrigo realizes how little he knows of what his mother wants and dreams.

He puts his arms on her shoulder and pulls her to him. At first, she resists, but she soon relaxes and leans into him. He thinks he should speak, but when he imagines the words he might say, they are less convincing than his embrace. So he holds her tighter.

—

Julia is sitting at her desk, reviewing a trigonometry problem. She is in her last year of colegio. During her first year, she found studying at Colegio Verapaz more difficult than she'd expected. The classes were harder than at El Instituto Básico; the students, who came from as far away as Lanquín and Purulhá, were smarter and more diligent about their work. She had teachers who had been educated in the capital and expected their students to know what someone in ancient Greece had said about triangles and what politicians in the capital were proposing to end the civil war.

She is more at ease now. In her second year, she decided to study accounting after discovering she liked numbers, their precision, their certainty. After she graduates in late September, she could easily find work at a cardamom exporting business or coffee finca in Cobán. She won't have to, however; Rodrigo makes more money than anyone she knows. They will marry in October. Rodrigo is speaking to her father about it now.

Someone knocks on the door. Before she can say "Pase adelante," her father enters. He leans against the doorframe. He always seems especially tall here, his hair brushing against the top of the frame. Julia drops her pencil and stands. "Yes, Papá?"

"Rodrigo has spoken to me."

She bows her head. When her father doesn't say anything, she looks up. He gazes at her for a moment. "I gave him my permission," he says.

She wants to smile, to break into laughter, but she knows such behavior wouldn't be appropriate. She knows the occasion of this conversation requires solemnity. Instead of smiling, she bows her head again, staring at the calculator on her desk as her father moves across the room and sits on her bed. She looks up and notices the red razor cut on his neck and the unshaved hairs below his nose. The top two buttons on his white shirt are undone. "This is what you want, isn't it, Julia?" he asks.

"Yes," she says, perhaps too quickly.

She's afraid he's disappointed. After a pause, he says, "For a long time, you and I have talked about you attending college in the capital. If you marry in October, this won't be possible. We are a family without sons, and some people see this as bad fortune. But I have always said you could do what a son could do. Some of the dreams I had for you are the same dreams I would have for a son. Do you understand?"

"Yes, Papá."

"Many fathers would be pleased to have Rodrigo as a son-in-law." He pauses, and Julia wants to ask him, "Are you not pleased, Papá?" She knows he hasn't finished, so she waits.

"I would be happier if Rodrigo were of our faith," he says. "I know he has tried to be. And I know he continues to accompany you to cultos. This is admirable. But he hasn't been saved in our faith, and I doubt he ever will be." He sighs. "And I would be happier if Rodrigo had finished colegio. He says when his soccer career is over, he will return to school to finish his degree. It's obvious he would say anything to receive my permission to marry you."

He pats a place next to him on the bed and she sits beside him. "I won't call him a liar," he says. "I think his love for you deludes him into thinking he can do anything." He stares out the window above Julia's desk. Outside, clothes hang on the line. A breeze fills her mother's yellow dress.

"To win your grandfather's permission to marry your mother, I, too, said everything I thought would impress him," he says. "I told him I planned to work in a bank. The first bank in Alta Verapaz, Banco del Norte, had opened a few weeks before and everyone was talking about it. What did I know? I was nineteen."

Julia glances at her father. His eyes are fixed on her mother's dress, dancing in the wind. After a moment, he looks at her. "If Rodrigo is smart," he says, "he will be in a position to provide for his family long after he finishes with soccer."

"God willing," Julia adds.

Her father nods. "Do you believe he will be true to what he will promise you on the altar?"

"Yes, Papá."

"A soccer player like Rodrigo will have temptations. At times, he might find it easy to forget he is a husband."

Julia doesn't say anything. She has heard Rodrigo's name spoken with the names of other girls, but when she mentioned the girls to him—casually, so he wouldn't suspect why she was interested—nothing changed in his expression; nothing changed in the urgency with which he wrapped her in his arms.

Her father stands. "You will finish colegio," he says. "Your wedding will be two weeks after your graduation, in October."

He bends down and embraces her, his head resting on top of hers. He holds her like this for a long time. She feels his breath in her hair. She feels his body tremble and she wonders if he is crying.

When he leaves, he leaves quickly, the door snapping shut behind him.

—

Julia's mother comes to her as she did often before Angelica was born. She enters her room after Julia has turned off the light and lies next to Julia above the sheet and blanket. For a minute, she says nothing. Julia hears her mother's soft, even breaths. It is such a peaceful sound that Julia finds herself drifting into sleep.

Her mother's voice rouses her: "I remember when you were seven years old and your father and I took you to the ruins of Quiriguá. We spent all morning in the ruins, touring the great altars. We had a tour guide—your father wanted answers to all his questions—and afterward, your father quizzed you on what you'd seen. And you did well on the quiz. You had learned." Her mother laughs. "And that afternoon, below our hotel room in Morales, we saw a train come by. You stood by the window, and you were fascinated. For months afterward when someone asked you about your trip to the ruins, you only wanted to talk about the train."

"I remember the train," Julia says. "I don't remember the ruins."

"It was filled with bananas, do you remember?" her mother asks.

"The train cars seemed about to burst with bananas," Julia replies. "And I re-member the three men in the caboose. There was a crowd of children following the train and the men threw bananas to the children like candy."

"One of the men was very tall and the other two were very short. They looked like a circus act."

"It was fun to imagine all the places the train would pass before it reached its destination."

"Even if it was only going to Puerto Barrios to put the bananas in a cargo ship."

"Was it only going to Puerto Barrios? You told me it was going all the way to the North Pole. You told me about the mountains it would have to climb in Mexico and the long bridge it would have to cross over a certain waterfall on the border of Canada and the United States."

"I think I wanted to entertain you."

"So the train was only going to Puerto Barrios?"

"I think so. But, who knows, maybe it was going to the North Pole." Her mother sighs. "Your father didn't pay attention to the train. He stayed in his chair. He was tired. He'd hiked around the ruins and he'd asked a lot of questions of the tour guide. It was you and I who stood by the window."

Julia feels her mother's face come closer. She can smell her mother, a smell of detergent and avocados and tortillas. She cannot remember a time her mother didn't smell like this.

"If someone asked me, I would say our trip to Quirigua happened only a few months ago, at most two years ago," her mother says. "And now—look—you will soon be a bride."

Her mother touches her forearm. "Your father hoped you would study in the capital and meet a nice, ambitious muchacho there."

"I know he doesn't want me to marry Rodrigo."

"I don't think it is Rodrigo alone who is the obstacle." She pauses. "I think your father, too, would have said he visited the ruins of Quirigua with his seven-year-old daughter only a few weeks ago."

Julia feels her mother's fingers tighten around her arm before withdrawing. Her mother begins another story, a longer story about another trip they took. Julia falls asleep before she hears its end.

— 3 —

Rodrigo cares for the instruments of his talent the way vain men care for their hair. Sitting with Julia on the couch in her living room one evening, her father in an adjacent room, he makes her laugh with tales of the ablutions he performs in the name of soccer. Before leaving to go to Cobán to practice, he explains, he strips to his underwear and plunges his legs into his mother's pila and wiggles his toes in the freezing water. Rodrigo does this, he tells Julia, to toughen his feet. "And during my bus ride to Cobán, I never put my feet on the floor."

"Why?"

"I worry about the vibrations from the motor," he says, smiling. "The floor always shakes—it's like a little earthquake—and I don't want my ankles twisted under the seat in front of me."

"So you keep your feet off the floor the whole ride?" She asks this jokingly, but his reply is serious: "I lean back and wrap my arms around my knees and close my eyes. It's like I'm meditating."

Rodrigo demonstrates on her couch, and Julia laughs, but softly, so her father doesn't hear.

Rodrigo puts his feet on the floor. He kisses Julia loudly, so her father hears.

—

It is Saturday, and the Imperials are playing Antigua in Cobán's El Estadio Imperial. Julia sits in the row of seats reserved for the players' wives and fiancées. This is the second time since her engagement to Rodrigo that she has sat here, and instead of the curious stares and doubtful nods she received the first time from the wives and fiancées, she is welcomed with familiar words and friendly smiles. She sits next to a tall, round-faced woman whose cheeks are enflamed with crimson blush. Her name is Gloria and she is the wife of the goalie, Frederico Briones.

Gloria wears gold bracelets around her wrists. Her fingernails are painted the same color red as her cheeks. As an Evangelical, Julia is supposed to shun such adornments, but in her blue cotton dress, she feels simple and unstylish.

The game begins, and the crowd roars when Frederico makes a diving stop. Julia turns to Gloria, expecting to share her pleasure in the great play. Gloria, however, is examining the palm of her right hand, as if trying to read her own fortune.

The sun emerges between two mountain-sized clouds, and for a minute, the field is covered with glaring white light. The players seem disoriented, shielding their eyes, all save Rodrigo, who steals the ball from an Antigua forward and races down the middle of the field. Julia blocks the sun by cupping her hands over her forehead. The sun reflects off Rodrigo's hair and the black, laminated number three on the back of his red jersey. In a moment, he is twenty meters from the goal, and he cocks his leg and sends a hard kick straight at the goalie. The goalie, crouching, throws up his hands to stop the ball, but it smacks off them and bounces back toward Rodrigo. Two Antigua fullbacks are about to converge on the ball when Rodrigo slices between them and sends another shot toward the goal. This time, the ball eludes the goalie and smashes into the bottom right-hand corner of the net.

Julia is the first person in the stadium to stand. And hers is the first shout. A half second later, everyone in the stadium fills the air with cheers. Rodrigo is tackled by his teammates near the Antigua goal.

The sun slides behind the second mountainous cloud, and the field is again easy to see, drab and comprehensible in the muted light. The game resumes, with the ball staying near midfield, the two teams trading it over the same limited ground.

A thin, indígena woman comes down the aisle, selling mango slices; Gloria buys two bags. She offers one to Julia, and Julia accepts, although she doesn't like the fleshiness of mangoes. Julia watches Gloria eat her mangoes. There is no way to eat them gracefully, and juice soon covers her chin, which makes her seem younger and somehow happier. Julia eats her mangoes with care, keeping them in the plastic bag and pushing the edge of a slice toward her mouth, clipping it with her teeth. Despite her caution, her chin, too, is soon damp with mango juice.

"Would you like a napkin?" Gloria says, offering a cloth napkin from her purse.

Julia wipes her chin clean. Gloria opens her hand and accepts the napkin back. With the same napkin, she wipes her own chin.

At halftime, the players run into a tunnel toward their locker rooms. Julia follows Gloria to the bathroom. As they wait in line, Gloria says, "Look around. After the game, a dozen of these muchachas will be waiting behind the fence at the players' exit. Some will want your novio; some will be happy to go with whatever player looks at them first. On days you don't come to the games, you'll wonder who's blowing kisses to Rodrigo."

Most of the girls around them are wearing as much make-up as Gloria. A trio of girls stands in front of the sinks, staring in the mirrors, combing their hair. One of the girls has used cloro to dye yellow streaks into her black hair.

"You have probably heard about my Frederico and what a mujeriego he is," Gloria says. "And, yes, what he does used to bother me. The first time he didn't come home after a game, I thought the army had recruited him. I even visited the zona in Cobán and asked the captain if I could please have my husband back. But the captain said the army wouldn't take my husband. The Imperials, he said, needed him more. He told me to ask for him at Las Serenitas. I didn't know what Las Serenitas was. The captain had to explain." She laughs, but with bitterness. "The next time Frederico didn't come home, I could only hope the army had taken him."

It is Gloria's turn in the stall. Around Julia, there is talk of the players but not of the game. She hears Rodrigo's name spoken and repeated and spoken again at the far end of the bathroom. Julia catches a glimpse of herself in the mirror above the sinks. A blue cola, which matches her dress, keeps her curly hair in place. She notices a blemish below her right eye. Her loose-fitting dress hangs like a shell over her body, obscuring her breasts. If she were to stand outside the players' exit, she wonders if any of them would notice her.

After they have returned to their seats, Gloria says, "Frederico and I have three children. He is teaching our son to be a goalkeeper. With the two girls, he looks around the barrio, wondering what boys might be interested in them, wondering how he can scare them off. The girls are only ten and eight years old, and already he is worried they will become like some of the girls who wait outside the players' exit."

When the same indígena woman who sold them the mangoes returns with bags of cashews, Julia buys two and gives one to Gloria. Julia loves the subtle, meaty flavor. She likes how they leave a smudge of oil on her fingertips. Within a minute, she has devoured all the cashews in her bag.

The game drags, the score remaining 1-0 in favor of the Imperials. Late in the game, Rodrigo makes another breakaway drive toward the Antigua end, but his shot sails over the crossbar. The crowd, which had stood during his run, sits down with disappointed sighs. But the Imperials don't need the extra goal. The game ends, and the crowd files contentedly out of the stadium. Julia asks Gloria if she plans to meet her husband by the players' exit, and Gloria shakes her head. "I'll wait for him at home," Gloria says. "Maybe he'll even come."

They walk down to the ground level and Gloria says goodbye to Julia and leaves by the nearest gate. Julia walks around the interior of the stadium to the opposite side. She finds the players' exit, a gate in a chain-link fence, and stands a few meters to the left of it. In addition to the wives and fiancées of the players, familiar from the section of the stadium where she was sitting, Julia sees in the crowd muchachas her age and younger, wearing crimson lipstick and vivid blush. The girl with streaks of blond in her hair is here. Julia notices a long, thin scar, as if from a knife cut, behind her right ear. She wonders what caused the scar and guesses a childhood accident with a machete. But as she looks more closely at the girl, she notices a redness around her left eye, which her make-up fails to disguise, and a bruise the size of a ten-centavo coin at the edge of her lips.

She remembers the Imperial players as they were before the game, spread on the field, their jersey numbers flashing in the sunlight. Controlling the ball between their nimble feet, they seemed as graceful and gentle as dancers. But she doesn't know them off the field; she barely knows their names. What cruelty are they capable of?

She knows only the threat of violence from men. She knows the way her father, in anger, will lift his hand at her or her mother or Angelica, his hand poised above them in menace before he remembers himself and God and puts it down. She knows the way Rodrigo, in play or in emphasis, sometimes pulls her especially close to him, so close she can barely breathe and, to extricate herself, can only beg, "Please, Rodrigo, please." And she hasn't forgotten, and never will forget, how her father and Don Carlos pounded on Alejandra's door and spoke to her with the fire of their outrage and ignorance.

She cannot keep her eyes off the blond-haired girl's wounds, and they remind her of the photographs her political science teacher brought to class in her second year of colegio. The photographs showed men and women without arms and eyes. She remembers this photograph especially: a girl of perhaps eight with only three fingers on each hand and no right ear. She was looking directly into the camera. She seemed stunned, as if amazed she was alive. When they'd finished looking at the photographs, one student asked, "Which side in the war did this?" After a pause, the teacher replied, "Does it matter?"

Their teacher said he thought the war would be over before long, perhaps in another three years, perhaps in ten, but the wounds of the war wouldn't heal for a hundred years. "It will be up to your generation," he said, "to determine who is to blame for all this suffering and what will be done to prevent such devastation in the future." He had exact numbers of the dead and the disappeared, although Julia can't remember them now. They were in the tens of thousands.

The next week, the professor had been replaced, and everyone knew why.

Julia steps back, losing her place near the players' exit. She finds herself retreating to a small hill twenty meters from the gate. She stands on top of it, watching.

The first player to leave is one who hasn't played. He is wearing his uniform and carrying a black and red Imperials duffel bag. He is ignored as he opens the gate and walks past the crowd gathered around the fence. Five minutes pass before the next player reaches the gate. He is greeted with applause. The player is Rodrigo. He is wearing black slacks and a long-sleeved red shirt and his hair is slicked back. He, too, carries an Imperials duffel bag. Julia hears a muchacha call his name. Rodrigo scans the crowd before opening the gate and stepping into the crush of people. From her perch on the hill, Julia watches him look around, and she feels both cruel and satisfied, knowing he is looking for her. The muchacha with the blond hair reaches for him, but he moves past her.

She is about to shout Rodrigo's name when he looks up and sees her. His smile comes quickly, and he climbs the hill with the ease of someone stepping onto a curb. "You're hiding here," he says, dropping his bag in the grass beside her. As he embraces her, as her nose fills with the clean scent of his soap, she is certain he will always find her, no matter how well she hides herself, no matter what the obstacles she scatters in his path. He will find her because he loves her; he has no choice in this—neither of them does.

— 4 —

At halftime of the Imperials' game against Escuintla in El Estadio Imperial, it begins to rain. The rain is a chipi-chipi, but it's damp enough to cause the players to lose their footing. They carve out strips of mud with their cleats.

With only a few minutes left in the game and the score 0-0, Rodrigo controls the ball in the right corner of the field, jukes left, then moves right. The fullback covering him slips. Rodrigo is almost out of bounds, but he stops inches from the sideline and, in the same motion, kicks the ball, launching a pass into the sky. Rodrigo watches the ball ascend. Although the ball is beyond his control now, he is confident of what will happen.

The ball falls onto Mateo Rey's toes and springs from them into the net. There is a moment of silence, as if no one in the stadium believes what has happened. Then the crowd erupts with cheers and shouts. Rodrigo joins his teammates as they pile on top of Mateo Rey. A spray of mud finds his mouth, and he chews the earth happily.

After the game, Rodrigo steps out of the players' tunnel. The rain has turned into a gray, cool covering, as if a cloud has settled over Cobán. He sees Julia on the field, on the near sideline. He has secured special passes for her and her father. Julia is looking at her feet, doubtless worried about the mud ruining her shoes. He begins to jog toward her, but he sees her father, wearing a black leather jacket, striding in her direction from the other side of the field. Rodrigo walks casually now, and he reaches Julia at the same time Señor García does.

Julia's father acknowledges Rodrigo with a nod. "An emotional game," Señor García says, and Rodrigo detects a smile on his lips. "And a beautiful pass. I don't think I've ever..." But whatever compliment he was going to give Rodrigo, he keeps private. Instead, he says, "I'll drive the two of you home."

"No, thank you, Don Eduardo," Rodrigo says. "I'm going to take Julia to Pollo Campero. To celebrate."

Señor García seems about to say something—a refusal, no doubt—but instead he looks over Rodrigo's shoulder. Perhaps he is thinking about how in four months, after the wedding, he will have no say in his daughter's life. Presently, he turns to Julia and says, "I will see you at home."

"Yes, Papá."

"In two hours, no more."

"Yes, Papá."

Señor García extends his hand to Rodrigo and Rodrigo shakes it. Rodrigo is, as always, surprised at how small Señor García's hand is. Señor García turns quickly in the grass and walks toward the gate at the east end of the field. When he is nearly out of sight, Julia embraces Rodrigo, hiding herself in his chest. Rodrigo, however, is still following her father with his eyes. Rodrigo imagines him as one of the soccer players he defeated today, one of the players who, at game's end, trudged off the field, mumbling excuses, contemplating revenge.

As sometimes happens, Cobán is without running water, and Rodrigo has been unable to shower. He wears a white shirt and crisp slacks, but he smells of the field, of sweat and grass. He says to Julia, "Don't get too close to me."

"Why?"

He waves his hand under his nose. "No water today."

"Oh," she says. "I don't care."

But when she moves to hug him again, she draws back quickly.

"It's the perfume of victory," he jokes.

"If this is the perfume of victory," she says, "what does defeat smell like?"

"I wouldn't know," Rodrigo says and laughs.

After they eat chicken legs and drink chocolate milkshakes at Pollo Campero, Rodrigo and Julia stand with a dozen other people at the grassy bus stop across from Tienda Santa María, which is closed for siesta. It begins to rain again, a quick, hard rain. Everyone save Rodrigo and Julia races to stand under the tienda's aluminum awning.

Rodrigo and Julia stand in the grass without umbrellas, and Rodrigo talks again about the game, his voice rising above the patter of rain. In his telling, he makes it seem as if they both played, as if Julia scored on his sky-touching pass. "It was like I wasn't lifting the ball with my foot," Rodrigo says, holding her shoulder in his palm, "but with my mind, like a magician. I didn't even feel it hit my foot, but I heard a sound in my ear like wings flapping." He bends down and presses her big right toe. "Here," he says. "I kicked it here and the ball flew for me like an angel."

"Like this?" she asks, kicking.

"Good," he says, "but kick harder."

She kicks again. "Right?"

The people standing under the awning stare at them. The rain comes harder now. "Watch me," he says, and he kicks. As he kicks, he feels himself slide, slip. An instant later, he is on his back, his shirt filled already with mud and water.

"Are you all right?" she says, alarmed.

"I will be," he says, "as soon as you kiss me."

So she does.

— 5 —

When sitting at her desk in her bedroom or under the pine trees behind Colegio Verapaz or in the stands at El Estadio Imperial, Julia finds herself thinking about how much time is left before she will become Rodrigo's wife. When she steps into tiendas to buy soap or tomatoes, her eyes move to the calendars on the walls. She counts the days.

Rodrigo showed her the house he plans to rent in Cobán after they are married. It is a six-room, concrete block house, painted white and blue and located half a kilometer from the stadium. In the front yard are twenty-two rose bushes. An old woman, the grandmother of one of Rodrigo's teammates, lives in the house, but she will be leaving soon to live with her son in the capital.

Often Julia tries to picture what her life will be like with Rodrigo. Some parts are clear. She knows what sitting in El Estadio Imperial is like, what eating mangoes and cashews with Gloria is like. It is easy enough to imagine the chores she'll perform in her new home, the meals she'll make him—spaghetti, carne asada, chicken caldo and, during holidays, tamales with chipilín and carne de cierdo. She can even guess what it will be like the first night with him when he comes to her in their bed, when they will share more than kisses and caresses.

What she cannot foresee, what she puzzles over during her days of waiting, is what it will be like to wake up the morning after her wedding, to have Rodrigo beside her, suddenly her husband. She wonders how they will greet each. Will they cling to each other, unfamiliar travelers in a new place? Or will they have settled into their roles so swiftly that they merely say "Buenas días" and rise and meet the day?

— 6 —

Early one Sunday morning, Julia is in her bedroom when she hears a knock at the front door. Her father is gone; it is her mother who answers. Julia hears her greet Rodrigo and invite him in. Her mother does not call her, as she thought she would.

Julia brushes her hair, gazing at the mirror above her desk, before putting down her brush and walking toward the living room. She stops at the threshold after hearing her mother's voice. In it is a lightness Julia rarely hears. "I'm sorry I can't go to see your games," her mother says. "I have Angelica to look after. But I listen to the games on the radio. The announcer likes your name. When you score a goal, he spends the longest time pronouncing it. Rod-riiiii-go R-aaaaa-x." Her mother laughs, and Rodrigo tells her that the announcer is a former Imperial whose voice was always more powerful than his shot.

"Well, I love his voice, as I'm sure your mother does. Or does she see all of your games in person?"

"She has come to two or three. But she has to look after my brothers. And she has work around the house. She does listen on the radio. I think she does. My brothers do. When I come home, they tell me exactly what happened, as if I wasn't there."

There is a pause in the conversation, and here, Julia thinks, is when her mother will call her. But she says, "You probably don't know the name Juan Ramón, do you?"

"No."

"He played soccer with your uncle. He was the town's second best player after him. And like your uncle, Juan Ramón was going to be famous, an international futbolista.

"He was offered a chance to play in Argentina, and of course he accepted. But after he left, people in town didn't hear from him. They made up stories. Some said he was leading the Argentine league in goals. Some said he never made it to Argentina but was kidnapped on a train in Peru by the Shining Path. Other people said the Argentines were jealous of him and sat him on the bench to keep him humble. To this day, people have their theories."

"What was the truth?" Rodrigo asks.

"No one knows." Her mother pauses before saying, "I think if he came back to Santa Cruz, no one would recognize him. He would not be what they imagined."

"He would be older."

"Yes, but it wouldn't matter if he looked exactly the same. In his absence, he has become what people want him to be."

If Rodrigo responds to this, it isn't with words. A moment later, her mother says, "I'll call Julia." She steps out of the living room's open rear door and finds Julia standing to the side of the threshold. A flash of embarrassment crosses her mother's face before she says, "Rodrigo is here."

Rodrigo has brought a soccer ball, and he asks her to go play with him on the field in Chixajau. "But aren't you worried about injuring yourself?" Julia asks. "You told me the grass is too tall, the field too rough."

He shrugs and says, "I had a dream last night about the field—I dreamed you and I were playing on it in the dark—and when I woke up, I wanted to see it with you."

"But it isn't dark," Julia says, smiling. "Perhaps we should wait until dusk."

"With pleasure," Rodrigo says with a grin.

They leave Julia's house and walk out of town on the road past the Hotel Mundo. Hidalia is sleeping in the booth at the hotel entrance. The hotel's parrot, pacing on the low branch of the nearby orange tree, squawks Hidalia's name. Julia suspects he has been repeating Hidalia's name all morning.

"He's lonely," Julia says.

"No," Rodrigo says, "he's in love."

The field is more overgrown than Julia remembers. Only in the center of the field and in areas around the rotting wood goal posts is the grass less than ankle high. Rodrigo stands in front of the near goal and kicks the ball to Julia. "Take a penalty kick," he says.

"Against you?" she asks. When he doesn't respond, she says, "You aren't a goalie."

"Today I am. Go on. Kick."

She places the ball in front of her, ten meters or so from him. She backs up; he crouches, ready to make a play. She takes a few swift steps toward the ball and kicks. Her kick lacks power, and Rodrigo easily stops the shot, trapping the ball between his feet. "Come closer," he says, sending the ball back to her. She sets up the ball another meter in. She kicks again, harder this time; the result is the same.

"Closer," Rodrigo says.

This time, she aims for the top left-hand corner. Her foot obeys her and the ball soars, clips the crossbar and falls into the weeds behind the goalpost. "Goal!" Rodrigo shouts. He sounds both enthusiastic and relieved.

"You weren't trying to stop my shot," she says.

"I was," he says. "It was a good kick."

"I was too close to you."

"Shhh." He puts a finger to his lips. "It was a good goal."

Usually, he will not tolerate having lost, even in small games against her, and will complain about forces out of his control—weather or the height of the grass or the tilt of the playing field—having influenced the result. Today, he seems only too glad to lose to her.

"Come here," he says, and she comes to him and they embrace under the rotting wood crossbeam. "Sometimes I think I've been too fortunate," he says, holding her close. She feels his heart kick against his chest, against hers. "Sometimes I think God will resent my good fortune."

"But God is responsible for it. It's a sign of His blessing."

"Maybe." Rodrigo shrugs. "I don't know." He looks hesitant, lost. "Do you still pray for me, Julia?"

"Of course," she says. "Every day."

"You pray for me when you go to cultos and when you go to the calvario?"

"Yes," she says, blushing. He has asked her more than once why she continues to go to the calvario if she is Evangelical, and her answer is the same: she doesn't know, except she likes the solitude of the calvario. It is this; but it's more: She goes because she has made it her place. It reminds her of her childhood and her grandparents and the great, solemn marches during Semana Santa. These memories are good and comforting, however unacceptable they might be to the believers of her new faith. And this: the calvario reminds her of Alejandra.

Lately, as her wedding date with Rodrigo has drawn closer, she has wondered what Alejandra would think of her, at eighteen, marrying. *You're too young,* Alejandra might say. *You're only a child.* Or: *Become what you wanted to become—a lawyer, a doctor, a traveler to parts of the world you've only imagined—before you marry.* But Alejandra met Rodrigo only once, and she never could have known how at times he holds on to her as if she were a deep-planted tree and he, in the middle of a hurricane, had only her to cling to. Or how, at other times, most times, he is the tree, ever fixed and tall and unbending, and she finds in his presence a peace and happiness she doesn't know anywhere else.

Behind Rodrigo is a cloud, broken like a thin carpet pulled apart. He takes her hand and leads her under the avocado tree behind the goalpost. He covers her face with kisses. He kisses her neck. He runs his hands across her body, touching her thighs and shoulders and chest. She shivers and grows warm.

He pulls her down to the roots at the base of the tree. She returns his kisses, deep kisses, and touches him where she hasn't touched him before. She thinks how easily she could let herself go. They are almost married; in a few months, their desires will be sanctioned, their coupling expected and praised. Feeling herself grow warmer and more excited, she thinks she might accede to what he wants.

He withdraws his hands from her body. "Did you hear that?" he whispers.

"Hear what?" she asks. But now she does. It is a noise like a pack of animals. She thinks of jaguars and tigrillos and deer.

"Where is it coming from?" she asks.

Rodrigo points to the left of the soccer field. "Come here," he says, and he leads her, crawling, behind the tree trunk. He peers from behind it. After a moment, he whispers, "Soldiers."

Above the top of the weeds in front of her, she sees two dozen soldiers march across the soccer field and onto the dirt road. They turn right toward town. They do not talk. The only sound is the jangling of their guns and the thud of their boots against the ground. The soldiers' appearance has spared her from giving herself up to her desires, to a sinful capitulation to pleasure. She whispers thanks to God. She vows to repent fully later, in church, her arms spread and her palms open.

She turns to Rodrigo, expecting him to continue kissing her and seeing what more he can touch. But he is looking at where the soldiers have gone, murmuring something she can't understand.

— 7 —

Outside the market, Rodrigo sees an old woman he remembers from years ago, from before he was in school, perhaps from before he could even walk. Years ago, she was old, and when his mother would buy tortillas from her, she would fish the tortillas out of her basket and hold them in a hand so small and withered it looked reptilian, a toad's hand. He never liked buying tortillas from her, but his mother insisted because, she said, "las ancianas make the best tortillas." It was true: Her tortillas, both yellow and blue, were delicious. The memory compels Rodrigo to walk up to her.

She is wearing a white güipil and a blue corte, the traditional clothes of Santa Cruz, although he knows she must live in one of the villages. He wonders if she remembers him, and as he steps up to her—she is sitting on a stool, her basket of tortillas, covered by a blue-and-white cloth, at her feet—he is tempted to ask. But he doesn't need to. Her face, with lines so deep they might have been made by a knife, rises into a smile, revealing a mouth entirely empty of teeth. "You have grown tall and strong," she says.

"Thanks to your tortillas," he tells her, hoping his smile hides his disquiet over her decay.

She continues to look at him, waiting on his order. He hears a groan from the pullman bus from the capital as it climbs up the hill into town, and he turns his head in its direction before returning his gaze to the old woman. Her güipil hangs on her like it might on a clothesline, as if propped up by little more than air.

"Are you from Pambach?" he asks her.

"Yes," she says, nodding. "Pambach."

"How is Pambach?" Three years earlier, the army came to Pambach, a village two-and-a-half hours by foot from Santa Cruz, on a rumor guerrillas were in the area. Helicopters descended. All men of a certain age in the village, on accusation of being guerrillas, were hauled off by the army. Most have never returned. This, anyway, is what Rodrigo has heard.

To Rodrigo's question, the woman replies, "Quiet." Under her breath, she adds, "And sad. Yes, sad." She tries to smile. "How many tortillas?"

"Twenty," he says.

She counts them twice, her fingers trembling. He thanks her and turns back to the street, where the pullman has stopped in front of Doña Josefina's tienda. He stares at it until it pulls away. Standing on the curb across the street is a man he doesn't at first recognize. When he does, at last, recognize Pedro, he turns back to the old woman, preferring to hide from his friend, back after so long from the capital. But it is too late. "Rodrigo!"

Rodrigo waits until Pedro calls again before he turns around. There are two black leather suitcases at Pedro's feet. Pedro spreads both his arms and turns his hands up, palms to the sky, and Rodrigo knows what the gesture implies: *Why aren't you happy to see me?* Slowly, Rodrigo walks across the street.

Pedro, who wears black slacks and a black, button-down shirt, embraces him, slapping him twice on the back, and Rodrigo returns the greeting. Pedro smells like aftershave and busses. "You never came to see me, vos," Pedro says. "You left me in the capital with only half a million women to keep me company."

"I wanted to visit you," Rodrigo says. "But my mother..." Rodrigo doesn't finish the thought.

"You mean Julia, don't you? The little Evangelica? She doesn't want her novio loose in the big city with the devil."

"It isn't Julia," Rodrigo protests.

"It better be Julia," Pedro says. "Otherwise, you're a faithless friend."

"Soccer," Rodrigo says, offering another excuse.

"I know, vos. I've been reading about you in the papers. The sports editor of *La Prensa Libre* thinks you'll make the national team."

Rodrigo can't help but grin.

"I should have told him he's super loco, but every man deserves his delusions." After saying this, Pedro throws a soft punch against Rodrigo's shoulder.

"I didn't think you were coming back," Rodrigo says. "What happened to your job at the nightclub?"

"Nothing. I could have kept it."

"But you came back. You missed it here?"

"Sure, vos. A sad little town like Santa Cruz. I missed the roosters crowing and the street dogs howling."

At first, Rodrigo doesn't catch Pedro's sarcasm. There is something nice, Rodrigo thinks, about Santa Cruz's peacefulness. But at last understanding Pedro's overtone, Rodrigo asks, "So why did you come back?"

Pedro grins. There is a flash of silver from his back teeth. "I was becoming like the quetzal—at risk of extinction—thanks to my appetite for women with boyfriends and husbands." He laughs and again slaps Rodrigo on the shoulder. "Should we celebrate my return with a drink?"

Rodrigo feels the tortillas growing cool in his hand. "I have to go home," he says.

"Family man," Pedro says. "The soccer star is also a good son. Call the newspapers."

"I'll see you soon," Rodrigo says.

"Of course you will," Pedro says.

—

As a soccer player, Rodrigo earns more than he knows how to spend well, and after every practice, waiting in the Cobán terminal for the bus to Santa Cruz, he usually buys his mother and brothers a recuerdo or two. When he sees something especially nice, he buys it for Julia's sister. Today, he buys his mother a ceramic bear with "Te Amo" written across its chest and his brothers a deck of playing cards with portraits of Jesus on the back.

When the bus doesn't come, he opens the pack of cards. He inspects each one and is surprised to find one without Jesus' portrait. On the back of the three of hearts is nothing but white space. He shuffles the cards and flips through them again, thinking he might have been mistaken about the white card. He finds it at the bottom of the pile.

He thinks he should walk back to the market and return the cards, but before he can do so, the bus comes. After finding a place in the back of the bus, he opens the window, and as the bus passes the garita at the edge of Cobán and begins its climb past coffee fields, he holds the white card in the air, wondering if the wind will be strong enough to wrest it from his fingers. But even after the bus turns onto Calle Tres de Mayo and heads into Santa Cruz, the card remains where it is.

When he goes home, he tapes an old wallet-sized photograph of his father to the blank back of the card. But he doesn't like the way his father stares with his somber, dark eyes, so he removes the photograph and replaces it with one of himself dribbling a soccer ball. But he doesn't like this photograph either, so he removes it and returns the blank card to the deck.

His brothers like his gift, and they quickly find the blank card, which they call an albino and try to pass off to each other in games they invent on the living room floor.

—

Rodrigo and his mother sit at the dinner table after his brothers have left to listen to the radio. His mother, across from him, watches him finish his beans. This is his third helping—his mother has scooped every bean from the pot to give him this last serving—but even so, he's still hungry. The kitchen is dark—the light bulb above the table is dim to the point of expiring and the fire in the corner is hardly more than a faint orange radiance—but he sees his mother's eyes clearly. "Why are you so sad?" he asks her. She shakes her head and looks away, hiding her face behind the curtain of her black hair.

Rodrigo knows his mother is suspicious of Julia, worried about her Evangelism and its preachers who consider Catholics little better than non-believers. This evening, after he came home and presented her with the ceramic bear, she asked what he had bought for Julia. When he said, "I don't need to buy her anything—she has the best gift of all" and, with mock bravado, pounded his chest, she looked at him with a pout. She placed a finger across her heart and said, "Only give half, mi hijo." Such advice seems to Rodrigo unduly cautious; he loves Julia, and she loves him, and to give her only half his heart would be to insult their love.

He supposes his mother is jealous of Julia and worried about losing her oldest son to a woman she doesn't trust. And he supposes she is worried about how she'll support herself and his brothers. He'll continue to give her money, of course, although she must know the sum will decrease as soon as he and Julia have their own family. His mother makes only ten quetzals a day tending the counter in Don Marcos's pharmacy, which used to belong to Rodrigo's father. His brothers, even young as they are, will have to work odd jobs during the long break from school between October and January, and their wages as cattle tenders or asparagus pickers will be half what his mother earns. All the same, they will never be poor—Rodrigo won't allow this—and he is sure his mother knows this.

He wants to ask her again why she is sad, but she stands and removes the tortillas from the basket on the table and takes them to the courtyard to feed to the dogs. Rodrigo goes outside to comfort her, reassure her, but she's gone. The two dogs, sleek and gray in the moonlight, growl over a tortilla.

At Julia's house, he finds the mood happier. Julia's father greets Rodrigo at the door with a smile, a handshake and two swift strikes on the back. If Rodrigo didn't know better, he would have thought Señor García was drunk. Rodrigo sees Julia's mother in the doorframe of the adjoining room. She is taller and thinner than Julia, and her hair is longer and straighter. She says hello, moving her fingers in greeting as if they were playing a stringed instrument, and disappears.

"Julia went to a friend's house to work on a school project," her father says. "She'll be back in half an hour."

Señor García offers Rodrigo a seat on the couch in the living room. Rodrigo is surprised when Señor García chooses to sit next to him rather than in the chair in the corner. Against the wall to their right is a glass cabinet with family photographs and framed diplomas. To their left is a bookshelf with two Bibles and a dozen children's books, most of them illustrations of Bible stories.

"How is the team?" Señor García asks. Rodrigo tells him about the recent fight between the two robust brothers who play fullback. "They were wrestling after practice," he says. "Playing around. But a second later, they weren't playing anymore. They started throwing punches. But before anyone could stop them, they began laughing and hugging each other."

He tells Señor García about Frederico, the goalie, a long-haired man of thirty who would rather be a singer in a merengue band but is one of the best in the league at his position. "He brought a karaoke machine to practice the other day," Rodrigo says. "He said his Japanese girlfriend gave it to him and…." Rodrigo stops, wondering if Señor García knows Frederico is married.

"Go on," Señor García says.

"The electricity wasn't working, so he had to sing without music. He held the microphone and sang an old sailing song from Puerto Barrios."

"Do you remember the words?"

"Some of them."

"Let's hear."

Rodrigo looks at him cautiously.

"Come on, Rodrigo, I'm an old man—I've heard everything."

"I only remember the chorus."

"All right. How does it go?"

Rodrigo doesn't sing so much as whisper: "And an English girl and a Spanish girl and a mermaid from the sea…"

Señor García joins in: "…they are what I worship as my holy trinity." Señor García laughs, and although Rodrigo knows he should join his merriment, he is too surprised at how easily Señor García sang the words, as if he'd been practicing.

"I lived in Puerto Barrios for two years when I was a boy," he says. "I used to walk up and down the docks, watching the men load bananas onto the boats. I heard some of their songs. This song was very popular."

Señor García talks about how he used to play soccer as a colegio student in Cobán. He speaks of the music of his foot meeting the ball, the shouts of crowds, the wonder and relief of the ball avoiding a goalie's outstretched arms and settling into the net.

"Do you play anymore?" Rodrigo asks him.

Señor García mentions an amateur team composed of men from the electrical plant where he works. "When they are missing a player, I will, on occasion, agree to play," he says. "But when I do something, I prefer to do it well, and I could never play soccer well. You, on the other hand…" He looks at Rodrigo with what seems like either envy or pride. "I heard talk of you making the national team."

"Coach Hernandez has spoken to me about it," Rodrigo says. "He thinks I'll be ready in two years."

"When you play on the national team, you must be sure to get to know the team's patrones," Señor García says. "You will play soccer for a decade, perhaps a few years more, but one day you won't be able to play and you will need a profession. If you have made friends with these men, you will be able to assume a position in one of their companies or perhaps, with their help, start a business of your own."

Rodrigo nods, pretending to be interested. A moment later, Julia comes in, her face showing surprise at seeing Rodrigo and her father sitting together. "Our scholar," Señor García announces. Señor García stands, and Rodrigo follows his lead. Julia pushes the door closed and leans against it. "Buenas noches," she says. They return her greeting.

Señor García turns to Rodrigo and says, "The pass you made against Escuintla…" His smile is soft. "I have dreamed about it twice." He gives a brief, tentative kick. "It was," he says, "perfect." He pauses to glance at Julia, still standing against the baby blue door. "There is too much imperfection in the world, too much waste. Sometimes we need reminders of the divine, even if they come only on a soccer field."

He steps toward Julia and gives her a brief hug and a kiss on the head. He turns back to Rodrigo, his look less friendly. "Sailors sing because it's all they can do, in a boat, in the middle of the ocean," he says. "But soccer players are on land, and perhaps their songs are more history than fantasy."

Rodrigo is, for a moment, puzzled by Señor García's comment. But as Señor García moves toward the next room, Rodrigo says, "It isn't my song."

Señor García stops and turns around slowly. "What is your song, Rodrigo?"

Rodrigo looks at Julia, who is alternately looking at her father and at him. "It's…" he begins, but he fails to come up with a title. He knows the song, though; it's slow and a little mournful but utterly sincere.

Presently Señor García is gone, having retreated into the adjacent room, the dining room, where Rodrigo imagines him settling over a cup of coffee, the Bible open in front of him. Slowly, like a cat, Julia approaches Rodrigo. She hurries the last two steps and embraces him quickly and tightly before pulling away and sitting at one end of the couch. From somewhere in the distance, in the house next to Julia's, he guesses, he hears a radio crackle and an announcer's voice say, "Two guerrillas and a soldier died today in a skirmish near Playa Grande."

"Where were you?" Rodrigo asks.

"At Lorena's house," Julia replies. "We have a presentation tomorrow in Spanish class. We'll be discussing *One Hundred Years of Solitude*."

Even the last word, soledad, sounds cheerful and comforting coming from her.

"I saw your friend Pedro," Julia says.

"He's back from the capital."

"He was gone a long time this time. What was he doing there? I've forgotten."

"Working." Rodrigo is reluctant to be more specific, and Julia does not ask.

At her end of the couch, Julia is too far from him. He whispers, "Move closer."

Smiling, she asks, "Why?"

"Don't you love me?"

They have had this exchange before, and Julia plays her teasing part: "I love the sun and the moon and all the oceans of the earth. And, above all, I love this end of the couch."

"So I guess I'll have to come to you."

"But only if you love me."

He moves over to her and pulls her into him as if he wants to make her part of his body. He spends an hour with her. It seems like minutes.

Returning home, Rodrigo whistles the song he would call his. He always hears it playing in El Dragón, the cantina at the end of Calle Tres de Mayo. He knows that the words are sad, but when he whistles the song's notes now, his whistling is like a bird's in the morning.

His spirits are high until he slips into his bed and cannot sleep. The moonlight is bright through the gaps between the tin roof and his walls and it seems to cover everything in his room—the soccer posters on the far wall, his chest of drawers, his cleats in the corner—with a substance like flour. Turning over and burying his head in his pillow, he remembers how his mother seemed tonight, how resigned and sad. He tries to comfort himself with thoughts of Julia and soccer, but he can only picture his mother.

He rolls onto his back. The ghostly light in his room reminds him of the story his mother often told him when he was a boy. It was the story of La Llorona, an indígena princess who became the mistress of the conquistador Cortés. For days and years and centuries after her illegitimate son dies, La Llorona haunts the streets of certain towns—Santa Cruz is one—looking for him. Sometimes she'll peek behind the doors of cantinas, hoping to find her son inside; sometimes she'll search for him in the park. If she doesn't find her son—and she never does—she'll grab whatever boy she sees and carry him off to wherever ghosts go when the night ends. "At night," his mother told him, "the only place for a boy is home."

Rodrigo long ago stopped believing such stories—his mother also told him stories about the serpent below Santa Cruz's Catholic church and El Sombrerón, the midget who seduces señoritas with his sad guitar—but tonight he pictures La Llorona as real, and when he closes his eyes, he half believes he can hear her weeping.

— 8 —

In the right-hand corner of the soccer field in Chiquimula is a patch of grass a few centimeters taller than the rest. It's what Rodrigo first notices when he and his teammates race onto the field. As Rodrigo and his teammates stretch, he sees the referee standing behind the far goal. He jogs up to the referee, a short man who hasn't shaved, and points out the unmown patch. The referee doesn't see it at first, so Rodrigo leads him over to it. With apologies, the referee says he'll have someone trim the grass with a machete.

Satisfied with the response, Rodrigo runs back to his teammates. They stretch for another five minutes, then take shots on goal, filling the net with their practice balls.

When Rodrigo sets up on the wing as the game starts, he notices the patch of grass, untouched. He wants to say something to the referee, but Mateo Rey kicks the ball to him and the game begins.

———

The radio crackles from the living room. The announcer's steady shouting rises above the static. Julia is in her room, staring at her unopened economics book. Her door is open a few centimeters, enough for her to hear the broadcast. She listens for Rodrigo's name, catches it every few moments. The announcer loves his name, loves to enunciate it slowly, extending the second syllable. Rodrigo told her that the announcer is trying to make him known by his first name alone, like Pele and Romario and certain women singers from Mexico and the United States.

Her father shuffles between the living room and the courtyard. She is unsure what he is doing and suspects he is in motion only because he does not like to be idle. Idleness is a sin, even if it's the idleness of listening to a soccer game on the radio. And yet she sees how he returns to the living room to listen.

———

Rodrigo dribbles to the corner. He stops before the unmown patch of grass and allows the opposing fullback to steal the ball from him. Moments later, he gets the ball back and dribbles again toward the corner. He slides a pass across the middle. Mateo Rey traps the ball and shoots, but the goalie dives and stops the shot.

The goalie kicks the ball to midfield, where four players leap for it. The ball bounces off Mateo Rey's head toward Rodrigo. He controls it and dribbles toward the corner. A fullback is in front of him. Because of his large nose and fat lips, Rodrigo thinks he looks like a clown, and he wants to make him act like one.

Rodrigo jukes left, dances right, then dribbles past the clown and cuts toward the goal. But as he's about to shoot, his right foot catches on something. Pain slices up his leg like a machete jammed in the middle of his foot. He falls, his ankle caught in the high grass. On the ground, he feels light-headed and thirsty, and he's conscious of a burning pain running up his leg. His teammates rush toward him. "I'm fine," he tells them, even as he feels his ankle swell.

The team doctor, Edvin Escobar, a pale man with a heavy leather case, charges onto the field and removes Rodrigo's cleat. Rodrigo sees what is wrong: his ankle isn't in its usual place, connected hard to his leg and foot. "Bad?" he asks the doctor.

The doctor mutters. Rodrigo catches only the word "serious."

"I'm fine," Rodrigo protests, trying to encourage himself even as the pain persists. The doctor isn't listening. He makes room for the two heavyset men carrying a stretcher. Rodrigo tells them he merely wants to be helped to his feet. "I can walk," he says.

One man takes him by the shoulder, the other by the knees. They lift him onto the stretcher. He falls back against the canvas. Sunlight shoots into his eyes and he turns aside, gazing into the stands. He thinks he spots Julia, but he remembers where she is: in Santa Cruz, a hundred kilometers from this dusty, dry place lacking the blessing of mountains or rain.

"I can walk," he tells the men again, but they have already carried him below the stands and into the team's locker room. Doctor Escobar stands above him again. "I'll have to call for an ambulance," he says. "You'll need a cast."

"Give me some ice, and I'll be fine," Rodrigo says. But the doctor isn't listening. A moment later, Rodrigo is alone in the damp, quiet locker room. He pulls himself to a sitting position and gazes at his foot. It is like something apart from him, the swollen foot of an ogre in a fairy tale.

———

The announcer's voice stops. A second passes. Another second of empty air. Julia hears her father pause from his pacing outside her door. She hears the announcer's voice again: "Rodrigo is down! Rod-riiiii-go is holding his ankle! Oh, Rodrigo, what happened? This is terrible. The young star of the Imperials is hurt! Rodrigo's face shows pain. It shows misery! Terrible! Terrible!"

Julia closes her eyes, wondering if when she opens them she will have found herself to be imagining, dreaming. She tries it. And, indeed, when her eyes are again open, the announcer is describing the game as he always does, with exaggerated shouts of enthusiasm. She hears no mention of Rodrigo until ten minutes later when the announcer says, "It's obvious the Imperials miss their young star, Rod-riii-go Rax. Without him, they demonstrate no daring, no enthusiasm."

At this, she rises from her desk and walks into the living room. Her father is sitting in the chair next to the radio, cupping his long, thin chin in his palms. His eyes are closed.

"Papá?" she asks.

He opens his eyes slowly, as if being woken gently from a dream.

"What happened, Papá?"

"Rodrigo is injured."

"How serious is it?"

"I don't know."

She glances to her left and catches her reflection in the glass door of the cabinet housing pictures of her father's parents and grandparents. Her curly black hair surrounds a face on which nothing is distinct—neither eyes nor lips nor nose. She looks back at her father. "What will happen?" Julia asks.

"I'm sure he will be all right," her father says. He leans forward, as if to rise. She thinks he might be coming to console her. But he continues to sit. "The announcers always exaggerate. All he needs is a little ice on his ankle. He'll return in the second half and score three goals."

"What if he isn't all right?"

He sits upright. His body, as thin as it is, is too big for the chair. She knows why the chair seems small; she is used to seeing her mother in it, sewing.

"You will be all right, Julia," he says. "I promise you."

And Rodrigo? she thinks but says nothing.

— 9 —

Julia finds Rodrigo in his single bed, sleeping, his head covered by a pillow. His mother, whom she saw in the street, said he was home and she should knock, but when she did, no one answered. The front door was open, however, and she let herself in, calling Rodrigo's name.

She is about to leave when he casts off the pillow and sits upright against the wall. His hair is uncombed, a weed-like tangle. His right eye is red, and she wonders if it, too, is injured. "Your mother..." she begins, but, too troubled by how he looks, she cannot continue.

He springs from the bed, stumbles and catches himself against the nearby chest of drawers. "I didn't hear you come in," he says. He pulls a comb from the top drawer and strikes it across his head. "I was hoping you'd come."

She glances at his cast. It covers his entire foot, save the ends of his toes, and rises to a few centimeters below his kneecap.

"It isn't bad," he says. "It's supposed to come off in six weeks. I'll be playing a week later." He walks toward her, dragging his foot. He is next to her now, and looking at his face, even if it wears the haziness of recent sleep, she can imagine nothing happened. She feels the tightness in her body dissipate. She feels herself easing into his arms. His embrace is exactly the same.

"I was listening to the radio. I heard what happened." She pauses, stopping herself from crying. "I was afraid."

"It's all right, Julia," he says. "It's a twisted ankle. Don't worry, all right?"

"Only a twisted ankle?" she asks, at once hopeful and skeptical.

She looks at him, and he is smiling his large, confident smile. She smiles back.

"My father wondered how serious the injury is," she says. "He wonders if we should postpone our wedding so you can concentrate on healing."

"Why?" Rodrigo says. "I'll be better than ever in six weeks. When we're married, we'll have forgotten I ever had a cast." He kisses her, and she allows him this intimacy, even if it isn't proper. She shouldn't be in his room alone.

"I'll come back when your mother is here," she says. "I'll come back to sign your cast." She walks toward the door, but returns for one more kiss.

— 10 —

"I spoke with the Imperials' doctor, Doctor Escobar," her father says three days later. "He is well-trained. He spent several years studying in the United States." Her father is sitting at her desk; Julia is sitting on her bed. Her hand runs to her left to touch her pillow. It is too soft and pliable; searching for something more solid, she finds the bedpost. She holds on.

"For athletes," her father continues, "the injury isn't uncommon. It involves the anterior cruciate ligament, if I remember the term correctly. So it isn't only Rodrigo's ankle—it's his entire leg. He will need a year to heal. If it isn't better after a year, he will need an operation. For the operation, he would need to find a specialist in the capital."

"He says he'll play again in a few weeks."

Her father shakes his head. "He'll want to play in a few weeks, but he won't be able to move the way he used to."

"He won't be able to walk?" she asks.

"To walk, yes. But to run the way he is accustomed to running? To fly down the field? No."

"But next year, he'll be better. He will have healed."

"Perhaps." Her father purses his lips. "Doctor Escobar said Rodrigo will need to be careful with how he treats himself. He must dedicate himself to healing and rehabilitation. This will be difficult, I think, because he will not have the luxury of living on his player's salary. The players are paid from week to week. The Imperials will not pay him when he isn't playing. They may give him a little money as compensation for his injury, but this won't be enough to support himself, much less a wife."

She hears his words, but she refuses to acknowledge their implication. She says, "If we have to, we'll live with his mother for a year—until he can play again. And if I have to, I'll work. I know of a cardamom exporting business in Cobán that is looking for a business manager."

She can see the blood rise from her father's neck. His eyes grow darker and his face hardens and narrows. "You must postpone your wedding until next October," he says.

"But Papá, I promised Rodrigo. I made a promise to him as he made to me."

"He made a promise based on what he could offer you. What he offers now is much less secure. He will understand."

"I don't think he will."

"Then explain it to him this way. If you were to lose a leg or an arm and couldn't perform the duties of a wife, would he be obliged to keep his promise? If you were to be struck by a bolt of lightning and burned beyond recognition, would he be obligated to keep his promise?"

"But if we were married already and this happened, I would be obliged to..."

"But you aren't married, Julia. This is the difference." He stands up. His face has turned a deep shade of red, like a tomato. Beads of sweat line his upper lip. "An engagement is a provisional promise, a marriage a lifetime promise. You no longer have my permission to marry Rodrigo."

He takes a step toward her, and Julia flinches, fearing he is about to raise his hand. His hands remain clasped together in front of him, however, gripped tighter than when he prays. His voice is softer now: "Understand, Julia, I want what is best for you. After you graduate, you will spend the holiday here in Santa Cruz. In January, we will enroll you in college in the capital, as we had planned from when you were a little girl."

She turns away from him. She knows he will see this as an insult, and she is half expecting him to grab her, turn her around, even strike her across the face. She would welcome this. This would make them both guilty of a sin, she of disrespect, he of violence. But he does not strike her. His words are quiet but certain: "What has happened to Rodrigo is unfortunate. But if you married him, you would only be adding to the misfortune. It is God's right to distribute good luck and bad, but it is a fool who seeks out bad luck on his own."

She turns to him, searching for softness in his face. "I love him, Papá." She looks to see if his hard expression will ease. If anything, his face becomes narrower. His eyes are like two black dots, two periods.

"I know you love him. But you do not love him—it wouldn't be possible to love him—as much as I love you."

He turns and marches out of her room. In a minute, she hears him in the living room, praying. She tries to do the same. She kneels at the side of her bed and cups her hands. She mumbles words from sermons she has heard; she mumbles entire psalms and verses from Matthew and John. She wants to understand what to do, whom to believe. Nothing comes to her, no path seems the wiser, the fairer. With her eyes closed, she sees her father and she sees Rodrigo. They plead, they order, they beg and command. Their faces alternate in her mind, alternate and merge.

This, at last, comes to her: She knows she will have to betray one.

— 11 —

Rodrigo has torn down the soccer posters that used to adorn his walls. All that remains is a two-inch plastic statue of a black Christ glued to a board with Rodrigo's hand-painted inscription: Recuerdo de Esquipulas. After his team played Esquipulas in the first game of the season, he brought Julia a basket of the town's famous candy: green, red and gold pieces of sugar. In the palm-leaf basket was the statue of the black

Christ, and Rodrigo blushed when he noticed it. After she removed the plastic from the top of the basket, he took the Christ figure, apologizing because such idolatry was against her religion. Later, he found a discarded scrap of wood near the sawmill and made the plaque.

Rain attacks the tin roof above him. It is mid-morning, but the light outside his window is as dark as evening's. He knows the rain, unable to sustain its fury, will slow soon. It does more than this. As quick as it came, it is gone entirely. He hears a parakeet, in the distance, sing hopeful notes.

A moment later, he hears Julia's voice in the next room, where his mother is. "It's sad," he hears Julia say.

"Yes," his mother says.

"But he will be all right."

"God willing."

There is a pause. Rodrigo imagines his mother crossing herself. "Life is cruelest to the young," his mother says. "When you are old, you expect sadness. But when you are young, you think happiness is your right. You are unprepared when it disappears." She sighs. "He says he will marry you. Is this true now?"

Rodrigo doesn't hear what Julia says in reply—if she says anything at all.

"Is he awake?" Julia asks.

"He's in his bedroom."

Rodrigo scrambles to his feet and hobbles over to his dresser, where he quickly combs his hair. He hears Julia tap on his door. "Come in," he says.

Her curly hair has been flattened by the rain. Her cheeks are pale. Her eyes dart around the room, finally resting where his had earlier, on the statue of the black Christ. "Hello, Rodrigo."

With care he walks to her and holds her, and she puts her head in his chest. He feels rainwater in her hair. "What's wrong?" he asks her.

She looks up at him. She tries to smile, but fails.

"Well?" he asks her, and he feels his heart recoil as if to hide itself deep in his chest.

"My father has withdrawn his permission for us to marry," she says. "He says we must wait."

"Why?" Rodrigo asks, although he knows. When Julia doesn't respond, he begins, as he has before, to tell her that he will heal much faster than the doctor said. "We don't need to wait," Rodrigo says. "This is nothing." He points to his leg. After a pause, and with fervor and anger, he says, "When next October comes, your father will think of another excuse to keep us from marrying."

"He says we won't have money to live on."

"The Imperials say they will pay me something," Rodrigo says. He speaks with hesitation because he knows to be suspicious of promises of money. "And until I play again, I'll find a job." He holds Julia by the shoulders and says. "We'll have money, Julia. All right? I promise."

She nods and keeps nodding. He wonders if she believes him.

"I'll have to tell my father we have postponed our wedding," Julia says. "If I told him we planned to marry without his permission, I don't know what he would do."

"Of course," Rodrigo says. He looks at her and wonders if it is he to whom she is now lying.

— 12 —

Julia's father permits Rodrigo to visit her once a week, but he limits the visits to half an hour. Tonight, in whispers, Rodrigo and Julia talk about their impending marriage. Rodrigo has arranged it with a lawyer in Cobán. In two months, on the eighth of October, they'll take a bus to Cobán and return as husband and wife to live with his mother.

"And after we are married," Julia tells him, as she has before, in a slow, even whisper, "I'll find a job in a bank or cardamom business. I'll work until you can play soccer again."

"It won't be long." Even as he says this, he is conscious of his ankle and leg. They are nowhere near healing, he fears. But he says, "I'm going to take my cast off soon. I don't need it anymore."

"Are you sure?" she asks him, her forehead wrinkled in concern. "You'll consult the doctor first, won't you?"

"He'll see how well I'm doing and will wonder why he put the cast on at all. And a few days after the cast is off, I'll be running again. You'll see."

He gives her a broad smile, and she smiles in return. She kisses him, noiseless but warm.

Toward the end of their half hour, he recites a fairy tale he invents and acts with the shadows his fingers cast on the orchid-pattern curtain in front of the near window. There is Julia the princess and Rodrigo the prince and an unnamed five-fingered monster who is on the verge of being slain when Julia's father steps into the room.

"Goodnight, Rodrigo," he says.

— 13 —

Julia and Rodrigo meet at the entrance to the Hotel Mundo one afternoon after she finishes classes at Colegio Verapaz. As he promised he would, Rodrigo has removed his cast. Standing against a bamboo post holding up the hotel office's roof, he looks as he is supposed to: tall and robust and ready to dazzle the world with his footwork and speed. She is so pleased to find him restored to health that she rushes to him and embraces him, laughing with delight. Hidalia leans against the office's counter, one hand on her chin, the other playing with her hair.

"Your cast is off!" Julia says to Rodrigo.

"I cut it off with a knife," he says. "It was easy."

"But it was supposed to be on for another three weeks."

"I'll heal better without the cast."

"And you walk all right?" she asks. "It doesn't hurt?"

A grimace briefly contorts his face. Behind him, Julia notices the hotel's parrot hop across its perch below the orange tree. It looks at her with its black marble eyes.

"It's a little sore," Rodrigo says. He waves his hand. "It's nothing."

They are planning to go to the soccer field in Chixajau, where he will show her how well he is recovering, how well he can run. Afterwards she will tell her father about his rehabilitation. And her father will agree to allow them to marry.

"Let's go," Rodrigo says, and he turns to Hidalia and opens his arms. From beneath the counter, she removes Rodrigo's soccer ball and tosses it to him. He cradles the ball against his waist, and Julia waits for him to take a step. He takes a deep breath and another and a third. She looks up at him and he licks his lips and smiles. "All right," he says, and he takes a step with his good foot, and Julia watches his face flush and his body lean to his left, his weight falling heavily on his healthy foot. He puts his right foot down on the gravel tentatively, like a boy might test cold water with his toes, and she knows how far he is from being healed.

"We don't need to go to the field," she says quickly. "We can have a refresco in the hotel's restaurant." She points behind her at the covered porch in the front part of the hotel. The long driveway to the hotel is covered in gravel, and she knows that for him to walk even this distance, over this rough ground, would be difficult. Rodrigo continues to walk toward the Cobán highway, however, leaning to his left, half hopping.

"Please, Rodrigo," she says. "We don't have to go now. You'll feel better in a few days. You need to rest."

She follows him. He walks up the steep dirt road like a man climbing a mountain with a tree on his back. "You don't need to do this," she says. "I know you'll feel better. I know you'll heal." He doesn't seem to be listening. "Rodrigo!"

Slowly, he turns around. She sees how he is sweating, how red his face is. "No matter what happens," she says, "we'll be married. All right?" This isn't the first time she has said this to him. She has, in fact, said it often, usually in whispers. But the more she says it, the more he seems to doubt it and the more he wants to impress her with his health and vigor.

His face holds a fierce, concentrated look. "Yes," he says. "Good. But I will play again. It's only right. I will play again."

"I know," she says. "I know. Please, Rodrigo, I know."

A white van pulls off the Cobán highway and heads toward them. Julia thinks it's going to hit Rodrigo, and Rodrigo must think this also because he drops the soccer ball. It bounds back to Julia, who instinctively traps it between her feet. The van stops suddenly, its tires grinding against the loose dirt. Pedro Mendez is in the driver's seat, and he steps out of the van.

"What are you doing, vos?" Pedro asks Rodrigo. "What happened to your cast?"

Rodrigo shrugs and Pedro grabs him by each shoulder. "Are you crazy, vos? You'll hurt yourself worse."

Julia is surprised by the genuineness of Pedro's concern. "Get in here," Pedro says, indicating the van. "I'll take you home."

"No," Rodrigo says. But he doesn't say it with any force, and Pedro easily leads him toward the van.

"Julia too," Rodrigo says, looking back at her. Pedro waves for her to come. Julia shakes her head. "I'm going to visit with Hidalia," she says, indicating the hotel office.

"Do whatever you want," Pedro says. Rodrigo frowns and says, "I'm sorry, Julia. Tomorrow. Let's try again tomorrow."

"All right," she says, and she fakes a smile.

She steps aside as the van passes. Rodrigo turns around to watch her, and she waves. She waits until the van is gone before beginning to walk home. She hears a voice behind her: "I thought you were going to visit me."

It's Hidalia, standing outside the office, her hands on her hips. Her black hair flaps in the light breeze like a ripped flag. Julia sees how lonely she is, and she knows how easy it would be to add to her loneliness by saying, "I lied," and continuing her walk. In her mind, she is already walking home, passing the thin pine trees behind barbed wire on the right side of the road and Hugo Tul's carpintería on the left.

But she moves toward Hidalia with steady steps, smiling, her promise kept.

— 14 —

Two nights later, Rodrigo wakes up to find Pedro sitting on the end of his bed. A candle burns on top of the chest of drawers at the far side of the room. In the shadows, Rodrigo has trouble making out Pedro's face. Even in the dark, however, Pedro's white teeth shine. "How long have you been here?" Rodrigo asks.

"I don't know, vos. A long time. But you were very entertaining the way you twisted in your sleep."

"Bad dreams."

"About what?"

"I don't remember."

"It's better not to remember. If you remember your dreams, they come true." Pedro isn't smiling anymore. "You haven't come to see me," he says.

Rodrigo doesn't reply.

"How many times have we seen each other since I came back from the capital? Maybe four—and by accident."

"I was busy with soccer."

"The professional no longer has time for his amateur friends." Rodrigo hears the bite in Pedro's voice.

"We have four practices a week," Rodrigo says.

"You *had* four practices a week, vos. You won't be playing again this year."

"I will," Rodrigo says, although without conviction. He is groggy from his nap. His body is tired, and yet he feels restless. If he could only go outside and feel the wind on his face, he would be fine.

"Whatever you say, vos," Pedro says. "But I think now you will have more than enough time for your old but unwelcome friend."

"Come on, vos, you know you'll always be my friend."

"In your good fortune, I think you forgot me."

"No, I didn't."

"You thought you had been blessed with a new life."

"No…"

"Don't worry. I forgive you. I'll be here even after your cold-hearted novia forgets all about you."

Rodrigo sits up in bed. He wants to grab Pedro and hurl him across the room, but he sees Pedro smiling. "Calm down, vos. I was joking."

Rodrigo remains upright for a minute before lowering himself back onto the bed. "What time is it?" he asks.

"It's late."

"How late?"

"Your mother and brothers are asleep."

"How did you get in here?"

"I walked."

"The dogs didn't bark?"

"Come on, vos. You know dogs are afraid of me." Pedro laughs. Rodrigo remembers Pedro telling him how he used to visit Clara at midnight when Clara was living with her grandmother; he'd scale the courtyard wall and sneak into her bedroom. The dogs always fled from him as if he wore the scent of a wolf. "I was the one who lit the candle, vos," he says, nodding behind him. "I didn't want to turn on the light and startle you."

"My mother put the candle there," Rodrigo explains. "She said it would provide the right light, if I wanted to pray."

"I brought you something," Pedro says.

Rodrigo perks up. "What?"

"Close your eyes."

"Come on, vos."

"Close your eyes!"

"All right." Rodrigo closes his eyes.

"Hold out your hand."

Rodrigo sticks out his left hand. A moment later, he feels a cold, wet bottle in it. He opens his eyes. He is holding a bottle of Gallo.

He hasn't had a beer since his injury. Some days after practice, he would follow Mateo and Frederico into Cantina Imperial, half a block from the stadium, and behind its red curtain spend an hour drinking beer with them. But after his injury, he hasn't thought of drinking. Now, however, he thinks a beer is exactly what he needs. He puts the bottle to his lips and drinks down two quick gulps.

He asks Pedro what work he is doing now.

"I've been doing favors for Señor Prado, the man who owns the white mansion on the Cobán highway."

"The millionaire? What favors?"

"I make sure his mistress never leaves the house."

"Does she?"

"Never."

"And if she did?"

To this, Pedro smiles. "I have orders," he says. A moment later, he says, "Drink your beer."

"I want to save it," Rodrigo says.

"Why? I brought as much as you'll need. We'll have a fiesta."

— 15 —

Rodrigo and his friend Galindo work in the valley, picking coffee beans next to the river, which runs crooked and slow across the center of the plantation. Rodrigo's cast has been off for two weeks, but his ankle and leg ache and he cannot run. He is working at Finca Mundial to earn money until he is ready to play soccer. He doesn't mind the work. Picking coffee is tedious, but it's bearable because he doesn't have to think about what he's doing. Instead, he can picture himself on the soccer field, can see himself sliding a pass to Mateo Rey, can imagine the roar of the delighted crowd.

It's hot, and there's no escape from the sun. The coffee plants are no taller than his chest and they offer shade only to his feet, which he likes to keep bare. His injured ankle feels better when he doesn't wear shoes. He likes the warm feel of dirt on the bottoms of his feet. He imagines the ground as something healing, a balm which will enable him to run and kick again.

— 16 —

When Julia is with Rodrigo, she makes plans to marry him, whispering about their future. Since his injury, though, he has changed. His work under the sun leaves his skin with a glazed, pinkish-red tone. His all-day labors seem to drain the words from him. Sometimes she finds their conversations trailing into silence, rescued only by his recitation of what will happen soon: the day they will marry, the lawyer in Cobán who will marry them, the way they will live as husband and wife with his mother until, recovered, he becomes an Imperial again.

When she is with her father, she discusses her college plans. She fills out San Mateo University's registration form and lists her intended field of concentration as business administration. She signs up for student housing. One Sunday, she even goes to Cobán with her mother and father to buy new clothes for college. She buys two dresses—one red, one black, the Imperials' colors.

When she is with Rodrigo, she sees her life as he sees it and when she is with her father, she sees it as he sees it. She knows she will have to decide between the two lives she has been offered, but every day she postpones her decision. To help herself sleep, she says, "What will happen will happen."

At cultos, sitting in the hard pews, she loses herself in Hermano Hector's words and in the electric piano sounds. She holds up her arms, palms up, and imagines herself floating on clouds, lifted by a wind out of her life and carried like a baby to God's feet. Here, all is peaceful, all is certain. But soon enough, Hermano Hector stops talking. The music stops. And when she follows her father and mother and Angelica into the night, she looks up at the sky and sees how distant the stars seem, and how lonely, sending down their pale, pleading light.

In the calvario, where she often stops after returning from classes at Colegio Verapaz, she finds herself repeating certain words: God, heaven, love, calm, silence. And she asks questions: Who am I? What should I do?

On the last day of September, her book bag filled with the textbooks she'll study tonight in preparation for her four final exams, she stops again at the calvario, escaping a chipi-chipi. The calvario is, as usual, empty. There are no signs of recent visitors: no fresh flowers, no smell of burning candles. She kneels in front of the altar, but she doesn't stare at the icons. Rather, she opens her palms and looks at the lines in them and wonders where they all are leading. She wonders if the lines in her left hand are pointing her toward one destiny, with Rodrigo, and the lines in her right hand are showing her another road, the one her father has mapped for her.

She presses her palms together and closes her fingers around her hands. She squeezes as hard as she can and feels her fingers pulse with her blood. The sensation is thrilling. *This is me. This is my blood. This is my life in me.*

She thinks: *I know another way.* And it's this: She won't marry Rodrigo on October 8th, but she won't leave him to go to the capital to study. She'll stay a year in Santa Cruz and work at El Puerto de Cardimomo. She meets all the requirements for the job the company advertised. She'll wait until Rodrigo is healed and can play soccer again, and they'll marry sometime during the next season.

She asks herself if this is what she wants or whether it's only a way to walk the path between her father and Rodrigo, an attempt to keep them both happy.

No, it is what I want. She takes a deep breath and wonders if she'll have the courage to tell Rodrigo and her father what she wants.

— 17 —

When they started work on the finca a month before, Rodrigo and Galindo talked as they picked coffee, speculating about the lives of their fellow workers and especially the plantation owner. Don Roger's wife died in childbirth but he soon became her twin sister's novio. Although they have stopped talking about the lives of their fellow workers, which like theirs are dominated by heat and rain, Don Roger continues to interest them. His wife's sister is pregnant—it's his baby—but she refuses to marry him. "She feels ashamed because he's her sister's husband," Rodrigo says. "He'll always be her sister's husband, even if her sister's dead."

"Crazy girl," Galindo says. "She should marry him."

They fall silent and pluck the beans. Rodrigo thinks about soccer and Julia and how while he might have lost soccer, at least temporarily, he won't lose Julia. He thinks about their wedding date a week away and he thinks about how he will surprise her when he brings her not to his house but to the house in Cobán he showed her long ago. He has saved enough money to rent it for three months.

He concentrates on his right foot and feels it in the dirt. He feels the warmth of the dirt touch the center of his foot, then spread, soothing his ankle. He imagines the ground as God's balm and the wind through the coffee plants as His incantation: "Heal, heal, heal."

Even as the day turns cooler and clouds gather in the west, Rodrigo feels the heat on his foot. Another few weeks, at most another month—then he'll try running, running like he would on a soccer field, with the fury of wind.

The rain comes, but soft, chipi-chipi. Rodrigo and Galindo work another twenty minutes until they see their fellow workers, men, women, and children, descend from the curving hills. The men are dressed like Rodrigo and Galindo, in T-shirts and faded slacks ragged on the ends and spotted with holes. The women wear faded dresses and cortes stained the color of coffee. The children seem to be barely dressed at all. Rodrigo and Galindo carry their baskets to the barn and dump the contents onto the concrete floor. In the morning, they will move the beans to a patio outside to dry.

The workers, about forty in all, walk toward the gate. The children are especially tired, their steps slow and labored. Rodrigo and Galindo walk near the back of the group. Rodrigo is in no hurry. He knows Julia will be studying tonight. After dinner he will meet Pedro and have a beer with him. Or perhaps he'll go into his courtyard with his soccer ball and sit on a chair and bounce the ball on his left foot, his good foot, seeing how long he can keep it from hitting the ground.

Before they make the final turn around the hill to the gate, they hear shouts, and men and women rush by them, suddenly animated. "What's wrong?" Rodrigo asks Galindo, but even as he does, Galindo begins to run. Rodrigo feels his ankle sting, as if bitten by a dog, and he feels his leg ache. He compensates by shifting his weight to his good foot. "Now!" he tells himself, his command in soccer when he wanted to race past an opposing player. But as he's about to fly, he feels something dull and heavy slam against his right shoulder, and he sees the ground bend. He hits the earth and rolls.

He's on his back, and he isn't able to stand before two soldiers converge over him, their rifles pointed at his gut. He closes his eyes and wishes himself into Julia's living room. He loves the feeling of sitting close to her, smelling her hair, listening to the ripple of her laughter. But he sees her father's shadow on the orchid-pattern curtain covering the window. He never knows when her father will step into the room to interrupt a kiss.

—

In the back of the canvas-covered truck, Rodrigo sits on a bench across from six soldiers. They wear camouflage and hold rifles between their legs. "You didn't run fast enough," one tells him. "A strong boy like you and you didn't run fast enough."

Another solider says, "He ran fast, but I'm faster."

"Liar."

"Your mother, vos."

The two soldiers stand, as if to confront each other, then sit down, laughing. "Angry?" the first soldier asks Rodrigo. Rodrigo doesn't reply. The soldier laughs.

The truck jiggles. Rodrigo wonders how he can escape. He would rather be shot in the back than become a soldier. "Sad?" the first soldier asks. Rodrigo stares at him.

"He's sad," the first soldier announces, and the other soldiers laugh.

— 18 —

When Julia's father comes into her bedroom and announces she has a visitor, she leaves her desk without hurrying. She knows her life has been decided, even before she could decide it, and she knows her father knows it as well. She detects his knowledge beneath his stone face, sensing, even in his show of calm and indifference, a certain pleasure. There is nothing she can do now, and she moves deliberately, but with growing fear, toward the living room.

Galindo, Rodrigo's friend from El Instituto Básico and the coffee finca, is sitting on the couch, looking as sunburned as Rodrigo usually does. His long nose is especially red. He is sitting deep in the couch, and because he is unusually tall, his legs rest in front of him like the legs of a praying mantis. When she sits on the chair across from him, his eyes refuse to look at her. Julia feels her heart rise in her chest and flood her body with trembling.

"Soldiers came," Galindo says, staring at his knees. "They chased us on the finca. I think everyone escaped. Everyone except..." He shakes his head. "I looked back, and I saw Rodrigo. They had him on the ground. I couldn't do anything."

"None of this can be true," Julia says, and Galindo explains in greater detail. Even as she asks more questions, she pictures Rodrigo's wounded foot. She thinks of the speed he no longer owns. As Galindo talks, she tries to find her place in the clouds, at God's feet. Her life is decided; God has decided it. This is, of course, what she should have expected. To have thought she could guide her life to the place she wanted was folly, arrogance and sin.

She notices a wetness reach her lips. Furiously, she licks her tears, but she can't keep them from running.

— 19 —

Julia sits with Rodrigo's mother in the dark kitchen. His mother has made her coffee and she sips it without tasting it. Although they are sitting across from each other at a small, wooden table, his mother seems far away, as if on the other side of the room. Her black hair blends in with the darkness around her. They have already exchanged words of condolence and sorrow.

Time passes, and Julia finishes her coffee. She wonders if the rest of her visit will pass in silence. Rodrigo's brothers, shorter, skinnier and paler than Rodrigo, come into the kitchen to see who is sitting at the table. They say hello, their heads bowed, and leave. More time passes before Rodrigo's mother asks, "Will you have another cup of coffee?"

Julia wonders if she should leave, if this is what Rodrigo's mother expects. They have fulfilled their obligation. But Julia finds herself saying, "Yes, please," and Rodrigo's mother fills her cup. Julia adds sugar and sips the coffee. She doesn't taste anything; she only feels the sting of hot water on her tongue.

"The Imperials were supposed to pay him," Rodrigo's mother says. "He signed a contract, and they were supposed to pay him his full salary, even if he was injured. But they paid him only a little of what he was supposed to receive, and the last time he went to receive his salary, the gerente said he could come for his full salary at the beginning of next season, when he was well. He said the team had to pay a player to take Rodrigo's place."

As Rodrigo's mother speaks, her body is still. Her dark eyes are fixed on Julia. "He said he needed to find work because when he married you, he wanted you to have a home. He knew of a house in Cobán, and he knew your father would approve of it. He wanted to prove he could take care of you. So he found work at the coffee finca. He made nothing, but he said even a little money would help until he could play again." She turns away, as if realizing the futility of talking about what didn't happen, what God didn't will.

Another silence settles over the kitchen. Julia finishes her coffee. She is about to stand and say goodbye when Rodrigo's mother says, "Even when all the children are in the house on the quietest night, it is difficult for a mother to sleep. There is always worry. And now I will wonder every moment where Rodrigo is and what might be happening to him."

"Trust in God," Julia says.

"Yes," she says, nodding. "This is what we must do." In a whisper, she adds, "But in this war, I don't see God."

She asks if Julia would like more coffee and Julia says no thank you and walks out of the dark kitchen and into an afternoon burning with sunlight. The rainy season is over.

THREE

— 1 —

Rodrigo is sweating from every part of his body, leaking from his toes and knees, from his fingernails and eyelashes. He marches, ragged and exhausted under the jungle trees. There is no sun; it's hidden above the giant hands of leaves. He never sweated like this playing soccer. The sweat came from his chest and back and legs, but it disappeared quickly, as if licked by the wind. His sweat doesn't disappear now but collects in his uniform. He imagines he stinks, raw and pungent like rotting fruit, but he can't smell himself. The jungle invades his nostrils, smelling like everything green.

He remembers how, when in long, deep embraces with Julia, he used to sweat, his sweat tentative and clean like drops of a chipi-chipi. He never sweated more than this, no matter how long they remained in each other's arms. Besides, she would soon say goodbye and disappear. And his sweat would withdraw into him and her smell would dissipate and the feel of her hair in his fingers would vanish and he would have no reminders, no proof that she had ever been with him. He might as well have been kissing a ghost.

He wants her here now. He wants to embrace her in all his sweat and stench. And if she wants to run, he won't let her. He'll crush her, kill her, before he lets her go.

No, no, he doesn't want that. He doesn't know himself in this uniform, in this jungle, in this heat. He only wants to run down a sideline, dribbling toward a goal, the crowd cheering, the wind streaming past him. And when the game is over, when the crowd is gone, he wants to meet her at the edge of the field and kiss her lightly, softly, their chests separated and a breeze floating through the space between them.

— 2 —

Every Friday night, Julia and her college friends go to Cine Capital to watch whatever movie is playing. There are usually eight in their group, although sometimes Marisol, Julia's roommate, is too worried about her studies to join them. Tonight they are all here: Oscar, Gerardo, Felipe, Octavio, María, Sandra, Marisol and Julia. They have eaten at a Burger King restaurant at Oscar's insistence because Oscar's father owns a Burger King in Quetzaltenango.

The movie, from Mexico, is about a smiling, capricious dictator. Only one man seems capable of overthrowing the dictator, but he is too preoccupied with his girlfriend, a temperamental blonde, to do much besides brood. The movie juxtaposes scenes of the hero and his girlfriend with shots of the dictator, in full military dress, presiding over state dinners and firing squads. The film's hero is only beginning to awaken to the dangers the world faces with such a leader when the movie sputters and dissolves.

In the theater, there is a collective groan. Words are shouted at the empty screen. At last, people stand, turning toward the projectionist's booth behind them. The booth is dark and empty. Julia and her friends file into the theater's lobby, where Oscar tells them to wait. Meanwhile, he climbs a flight of stairs to the right of the concession stand. The other people in the audience linger in the lobby before, with curses and dark jokes, they leave the theater. Oscar returns a few minutes later with a short, fat man wearing a red suit and white shoes. Julia and her friends form a semicircle around him. When the man speaks, he looks at his shoes. "I'm sorry," he says. "This happens sometimes. What can we do?"

"You could offer us free tickets to another movie," Oscar suggests.

"I couldn't," the man says, throwing up his arms. "I am only the manager of the theater, I am not the owner." He looks around, his small head bobbing on his large body. "I know what we'll do. You can go into whatever theater you want." He points to his right, toward the entrances to the five other theaters in the movie complex.

"But the other movies have already started," Oscar says.

"They haven't finished," the man says with enthusiasm. "You can see half of another movie."

Julia finds the idea comical and preposterous, and she is about to articulate her opinion, but the boys in her group murmur their agreement. They talk quickly about what movie they should see. Presently, Julia follows the group into another theater at the end of the hallway. They enter just as, on the screen, a man dressed in black and lying on the roof of a tall building loses his grip on a woman's hand and she plummets onto the sidewalk below. Afterwards, the man keeps seeing the woman on street corners, in bars and in shadowy corners of his house. He tries to talk to her, but she doesn't respond. He tries to touch her, but whenever he comes close to her, she disappears.

Years pass, and the man marries another woman and they have children and he becomes an old man, retired with his wife to an apartment in a sun-filled city by the beach. One night, the woman from the roof returns. He finds her on his balcony, sitting in one of its plastic chairs, gazing at the ocean. Unlike before, he doesn't attempt to come near her. Rather, he sits in an adjacent chair. They gaze at the moon together, speaking about the first time they saw each other.

The next morning, the man's wife finds him dead in his chair, the breeze blowing his gray hair back, a smile on his face.

The movie isn't scary enough to be a horror film and it's too creepy to be a romance. The boys in her group register their disapproval with one-word critiques: boring, stupid, sentimental. But Julia feels touched by it. She wishes she had seen the beginning so she would know what happened between the man and woman before the woman fell off the building.

They leave the theater. It is midnight, and the streets, crowded when they came, are deserted save for the homeless men who linger in the doorways of closed businesses. Even in Cobán, she never saw such poverty. The men smell of urine and garbage. She finds herself moving closer to Oscar, who seems unconcerned with the danger of the deserted streets. He whistles one of the songs from the first movie they saw.

As they walk past the police station, a fortress in the center of zona una, and pass the Chalet Suizo hotel, she bumps into Oscar. He takes her hand as if to steady her. Because he is tall and thin, she expects his hand to be insubstantial, something bony and hard. It's a firm, full hand, however. He glances at her, smiling. He whistles louder.

They reach the bus stop on 7 avenida. A woman's voice, coming from a high floor of a hotel across the street, says, "This will be extra, understand?" Julia can see her, five flights above, leaning out of the window. She wears no shirt or bra, and her breasts dangle in the air. Oscar shouts, "Jump! Jump!" and everyone in the group laughs. A moment later, the woman is back inside the room. The window slams shut.

The bus comes, grinding up the avenue, spitting black exhaust into the gray night. Julia and her friends step on; they are the only people on board. Oscar uses the occasion to stand in the middle of the aisle in imitation of the salespeople who haunt the same venue and offer cures to the common cold, to tooth decay, to every illness within the body and every deformity without.

"Tonight, ladies and gentlemen," Oscar says, "I offer you a product you've never seen before, never imagined existed. I offer you, in the tiny bottles I hold in my hands, a magic water to call back the dead. Sprinkle it on their crypts and step back because here they come." He walks down the aisle like a zombie, his hands drooping past his knees. Julia and her friends shout with mock fear.

Abruptly, he stands upright and does another imitation, this time of the shoeless boys and girls who find their way onto busses to sing, hoping to be given a few centavos. Oscar's singing voice is deeper than his speaking voice, and it's surprisingly resonant on the rackety bus.

If you shun me because I'm poor,
I understand.
I offer you no riches.
I offer you my heart.

Julia feels a coldness creep into her. She wraps her arms around her chest and looks out the window. She sees a man walking quickly down the street, as if fleeing an assailant. She thinks about Rodrigo, something she hasn't allowed herself to do in weeks. She received one letter from him before she left for college.

In his letter, Rodrigo wrote as if continuing a conversation, mentioning several of his fellow soldiers as if she was familiar with them. She wondered what had happened to his other letters and suspected her father had intercepted them. He was gone on a weeklong trip to Lanquín when she received this letter; it was her mother who picked up the mail at the correos office. At the end of his letter, Rodrigo wrote, "Don't worry, Julia. There is danger here, of course, but I run faster than bullets. One day, I will run back to you." He concluded his letter by writing her name five times, each time in larger letters.

When her father returned from Lanquín, she asked him what he'd done with Rodrigo's other letters. His eyes narrowed in anger. "I did nothing with them," he said. "If he wrote you other letters, they never came." A minute later, he sighed with what to Julia seemed a mixture of disappointment and sadness. "Julia, hija mia, I know that what happened to Rodrigo is unfortunate. It's deeply unfortunate for him and his mother. But you must not let their misfortune prevent you from concentrating on fulfilling your life's goals."

She felt tears fill her eyes, and, quickly, her father came to her, wrapping her in his arms. They were standing in the living room, and she saw their shadows projected onto the orchid-colored curtain over the window. She was angry with her father, but at the same time, she welcomed his embrace and the security of his words. "We are all subject to God's will," he said. "God has given Rodrigo a different destiny than what he expected and hoped for, but this is right because it is what God decided. We mustn't question God's plan. And you have your own destiny to fulfill. I promise it will be bright."

The same night, they had gone to pray with Hermano Hector, who had gathered a group of especially devout members of the Church of God in his house. Sitting in a circle and listening to the Bible verses Hermano Hector recited—"Everyone who hears these words of mine and follows them will be like a wise man who built his house upon the rock"—she began to feel at peace. If Rodrigo welcomes God into his heart, he will be safe. And God, it was clear, had chosen a specific path for her, a path without Rodrigo, To fulfill her destiny, she knew she mustn't think about Rodrigo and the past but of college and her new life of opportunity.

She hadn't written Rodrigo back. The return address on the envelope had been smudged. Besides, in his letter he'd said mail delivery was sporadic; whether it was delivered at all depended on the lieutenant's mood.

On the bus, she feels a body move next to her and turns to find Oscar. He takes her hand again, holding it in both of his. She sees the trace of a mustache above his lip, so thin it seems drawn by pencil. His eyes are a bright gray, a cat's eyes. The others look at the two of them and nod. Something has transpired without Julia knowing exactly what or how.

— 3 —

Palush, an indígena boy from Cobán, is playing a guitar he found in an abandoned guerrilla camp. It's night, and some of the soldiers have gone to bed, slipping into their tents under trees. Palush plays well even though the guitar is rain-beaten and missing its first string. Rodrigo and about ten other soldiers sit in the darkness listening to him.

Palush is seventeen, and his voice has only recently matured; there is still something fragile about it. But it is a clear voice, and, although soft, it seems to silence the other sounds in the jungle. Rodrigo permits himself to relax in the softness of Palush's voice.

Rodrigo wonders what Julia is doing. It has been almost six months since he has seen her, and he has heard nothing from her. In the single letter he received from his mother, she didn't mention Julia. But his mother may have written him a hundred letters and Julia may have written him two hundred. The mail comes infrequently, and Rodrigo knows most of the letters are lost along the way, ruined by rain or intercepted by guerrillas or destroyed by cruel lieutenants who don't want their soldiers distracted from the war. The one letter from his mother is more than most of his fellow soldiers have ever received. Of course it wouldn't matter if they did receive mail. Only a couple of them can read.

Palush sings, and Rodrigo thinks of Julia and wonders if she would love him in his sweat-smelling uniform. He hates the days with their sinister flashes of sunlight through thick leaves. But tonight Palush sings, and the song reminds Rodrigo of Julia, convinces him she loves him and will love him despite his long absence. When he finishes with the war, he will again offer her his heart. And his heart will be enough.

Palush concludes the song by plucking each of the strings, beginning with the sixth, then rising toward the first. Rodrigo waits for him to pluck the last string, but even as he remembers it's missing, he hears another noise, a brief, hollow snap. Rodrigo sees Palush fall backward, clutching his guitar. A second later, the jungle fills with shots.

Rodrigo races to a nearby ceiba tree, its trunk thick and solid. Holding his M16 rifle in front of him, he crouches. Pointing his rifle at the dark spread of trees in the distance, he fires six rounds. A tree branch crashes beside him. He pulls the branch over him, covering himself with its thick leaves. He waits, wondering when he'll feel the sting of a bullet in his back or heart.

In a minute the jungle is quiet again. From somewhere nearby, the lieutenant tells his soldiers to remain where they are.

Silence again. But a moment later, Rodrigo swears he hears music, the guitar resurrected, strummed. And he hears Palush's voice, softer than before, more child-like. The lieutenant hisses for Palush to shut up. What Palush sings next is incomprehensible, the words sung as if underwater. Rodrigo shoves off the branch and races to Palush. He finds him lying on his back with the guitar on his chest. A sliver of moonlight slips through the cover of leaves overhead and falls onto Palush's face. Rodrigo bends to blow air into his mouth, but when he does, he notices that Palush's mouth is full of blood. He turns Palush's head to the side, allowing the blood to drain from it, and urges, "Sing!" But Palush's hands have fallen away from the guitar; it slides off his chest. "Sing!" he shouts again, but he knows he is speaking to a dead man.

The lieutenant orders him to move, but Rodrigo grabs the neck of the guitar as if it were a man he was trying to strangle. He lifts the guitar, ready to slam it against the jungle floor, but he notices the clean hole the bullet made at the bottom of the sound hole. Through the hole, he can see the moon.

He places the guitar beside Palush and rushes again into the cover of trees.

— 4 —

On the top floor of the university's library, Julia and Oscar sit at a desk in front of a window with a view of Volcán Pacaya. It is early evening, and there is a dullness to the gray sky, although the grayness is pierced repeatedly by the flash of the volcano's lava. Oscar is reading an article in *Business Week* magazine about chain hotels in the United States, and every so often he reads her a sentence or two. Her English is only half as good as his, and she doesn't understand a good portion of what he reads. But if he notices her ignorance, he doesn't mention it. She is glad to be included in what intrigues and excites him. The Business Week article, she knows, isn't for any class he is taking. Whenever he is at the library, he reads as many magazines from the

United States as he can. She is impressed, even awed sometimes, by his curiosity and intelligence, and when they are at the library, she often finds herself gazing at him, marking his concentration, the way his gray eyes fly hungrily across pages.

When he looks up again from his magazine, he catches her staring at him. Smiling, he wiggles his finger at her. "You're not studying," he says.

"I am."

"My face isn't a worthy subject."

She smiles playfully at him. "I think it is."

They have been novios for two weeks, although without her father's permission, it isn't official.

She returns to her *Business English* textbook, mumbling the vocabulary words to herself, hoping to hold them in her memory. She soon finds her attention drifting again, this time to the view in front of her.

Before long, Oscar notices where she is looking. Every so often, lava shoots from the volcano, streaking the evening sky with its fiery orange light. "I've heard all sorts of predictions about when it will erupt again," Oscar says. "I've heard some people claim that the next time it erupts, the capital will turn into a smoldering ruin."

"Is that possible?" Julia asks with concern.

"It's possible." Oscar shrugs. "But it's also possible we could sit here for a hundred years and see nothing more than what we see now." Gently, he cups her face between his hands and stares into her eyes. "This wouldn't be tragic."

— 5 —

Julia's father comes to the capital one Saturday to meet Oscar and give him permission to become Julia's novio. They eat lunch at El Pavo Grande on 13 calle, sharing plates of tacos and enchiladas. Both Oscar and her father are dressed in ironed blue pants and clean white shirts.

Oscar is Evangelical, and this pleases her father, who pauses from his eating to deliver a mini-sermon. "The Catholic Church is misguided," he says, emphasizing his point by thumping the red tablecloth. "It makes saints of indígenas who never knew or accepted Christ. It takes pity on communists who want to give away what people have earned by hard work and the grace of God."

His eyes are fixed on Oscar, who sits across from him. Julia, sitting next to Oscar, stares alternately at her father and at the yellow and green sign on the wall behind him advertising Corona beer. "The priests," her father continues, "give false hope to campesinos, supporting their claims of land ownership. The priests say they are men of peace and compassion, but by feeding people's minds with fantasies and illusions, they only encourage a hopeless fight."

"I agree," Oscar says, and he devours the last of his taco. He tells Julia's father what he has told Julia on several occasions: The war is bad for the country not only because people continue to be killed, but because it has hindered the country's economic progress, stifling development and discouraging foreign investment. "Meanwhile, other Latin American countries, countries such as Costa Rica, continue to progress," Oscar says. "They attract businesses because the businesses do not have to worry about guerrillas sabotaging electrical plants or assassinating political leaders.

"We need peace," Oscar says, "and whether we achieve it with a greater, more determined campaign against the guerrillas or at the negotiating table is less important than how quickly we achieve it. The faster, obviously, the better."

Julia's father leans back and gives Julia a quick glance. She sees the small smile beneath his serious, absorbed look. She suspected her father would like Oscar, but having it confirmed leaves her feeling no emotion. Her new life seems written already: She will marry Oscar and they will live in Quetzaltenagno; he will manage his father's apple orchards and oversee the buying of more Burger King restaurants and she will become a mother. She knows this is a good life, a life any woman should want, and if it doesn't excite her in the ways she knows it should, she cannot conjure a better alternative.

She feels herself drift from the conversation. How quickly it all happened, she thinks. How quickly her life was decided again.

She remembers a time she stayed after her last class at El Instituto Básico to finish painting, on the back wall of the school's hallway, a dancing horse, part of a scene depicting the night of El Señor de Esquipulas. She was walking down the concrete steps of the school when Rodrigo called to her from the pine trees on her right. After they'd kissed and kissed again, she noticed, in the pasture below them, vultures encircling the carcass of a calf. The vultures seemed to dance around it as in a ritual. Whenever she wasn't kissing Rodrigo, deep in his embrace, her eyes found the vultures. It was this way for an hour, kisses and vultures, until the rain fell and they raced home.

She knows she has been thinking about Rodrigo too often lately. Sometimes she contemplates what he'll be like when he returns from the war—if he returns. Her father told her about the training boys who have been forcefully recruited into the army undergo, and when she imagines Rodrigo, she pictures his face raked with scars and his teeth gritted in pleasure at some violence he has seen or committed. If a part of her is hopeful he will be spared such a transformation so she can love him again, the greater part of her thinks: *If God had meant us to be together, we would be together now.*

Sometimes she thinks she should write Rodrigo or leave a letter with his mother in order to break their engagement officially and to explain her new life and the destiny God has chosen for her. But such a letter seems both unnecessary, because surely Rodrigo's mother or someone else in Santa Cruz will have told him where she is now, and unnecessarily cruel.

Her father and Oscar are looking at her as if they've asked her a question. She thinks about asking them to repeat what they've said, but she knows what answer they want. So she gives it: "Yes."

— 6 —

The soldiers are lounging under trees, sulking in their sweat. The lieutenant announces he has letters, but this interests only a few of the men. Rodrigo doesn't stir. Exhausted, he is trying to nap, trying to ignore the mosquitoes buzzing in his ears. He is surprised when the lieutenant comes up to him and hands him an envelope.

Rodrigo sits up. The envelope, larger than regular size, has no return address. With fingers shaking in anticipation, he tears the side of it and pulls out its contents. He finds a single sheet of paper, ripped out of a notebook, and two photographs cut from a magazine and glued onto thicker paper. The photographs are both of the same naked woman, one a shot of her on her back, the other on her stomach.

Rodrigo scans down to the signature on the note. Pedro. He swats the mosquitoes from his ears. Rodrigo reads: "When you come home, we'll have fun. The women are waiting—all but your traitorous novia. I'm sorry, vos."

He reads the last lines again and a third time. He drops the letter and kicks it with his boot. He slams his palms together, crushing mosquitoes between them. Unfolding his hands, he finds them dotted with mosquito parts and small pinpricks of blood.

— 7 —

Reflecting on her first year of college, Julia notes this paradox: although the year seems to have gone by quickly, its routines—including late-night studying (usually with Oscar) and weekend movie-watching (always with Oscar)—seem part of an old ritual. How quickly her new life overshadowed her old life; how quickly her old life became history, something whose memories she might collect in a box marked "Girlhood."

To celebrate the end of the school year, Oscar invites Julia to eat lunch with him at the Hotel Dorado in zona diez. They sit in the outdoor café overlooking a pair of tennis courts. On the court nearest them, four gringos bat the ball back and forth across the net as if they're playing volleyball. Julia has only played tennis once, in Cobán. The owner of the Imperials also owned the two tennis courts behind Cobán's outdoor market, and Rodrigo borrowed a pair of rackets. But when they played, Rodrigo could never find the right stroke. His shots either fell listlessly into the net or sailed over her head and into the fence behind her. She, on the other hand, managed to acquire a quick proficiency. He soon grew frustrated and, in a rage, crushed a ball so hard it flew over the fence and onto the roof of a bus filling with passengers to Lanquín.

Oscar orders them both iced coffee, one of the café's specialties, and they listen to the waiter, who wears a long-sleeved white shirt, recite the day's specials. When they have ordered, Oscar begins to speak, but he quickly stops and bows his head.

"What is it?" Julia asks.

Oscar is wearing black slacks and an azure shirt with a black crown above the left breast. His dark hair is slicked back and his face, which sometimes seems too thin, looks full and strong. His lips are dark red, and she once heard one of their friends, in a joke, call them a whore's lips. There is, it's true, something feminine about them. Today they seem soft and desirable and a perfect complement to his square, masculine face.

Her mood is light because classes are done and she did well in all of them. Oscar, however, seems both nervous and preoccupied, and she touches his shoulder. "What's wrong?" she asks.

"I have a question to ask you," he says. He gives her a hesitant, hopeful smile. Even as her heart pounds in anticipation, she feels a tenderness overcome her, a desire to kiss him, to hold him.

"Yes?" she asks. "What is it?" She knows what he's going to ask and she knows what she will say. It is what she is supposed to say, but it's also, she is sure, or nearly sure, what she wants to say.

He removes from his pocket a black box and, with trembling fingers, opens it. Inside is a diamond ring. "It's for you," he says. "If you want it." He shakes his head quickly. "What I mean to say is, will you marry me, Julia?"

She stares at the ring and its illuminated diamond. In her life, she hasn't seen anything as bright.

She is aware of time passing. Before long, Oscar looks up at her, his gray eyes, for once, clouded, doubtful. His bottom lip trembles, and again she feels tenderness toward him. She opens her mouth to accept his offer, but before she can speak, a tennis ball plops onto the brick patio in front of them, bounces against the ceiling of their orange umbrella and falls onto her lap.

With alarm, Oscar turns toward the tennis court. Already, she hears an apology, first in English, then, weakly, in Spanish. She looks at the ball. It has been a long time since she has seen a tennis ball, and this isn't like the one she and Rodrigo played with, which was worn to near baldness. This ball is electric green and smells like a chemical she can't identify. Oscar takes the ball from her lap and hurls it back onto the court. Julia breaks into laughter.

"Is it funny?" Oscar asks her. He doesn't seem sure.

"Yes, it's funny," she says. She finds relief in her laughter. "It's funny."

Hesitantly, Oscar, too, laughs. "I didn't hear what your answer was," he says. "Did you give me an answer?"

"Yes," she says.

"You did?"

"Yes."

"What was it?"

"Yes."

"Yes? Oh. Good."

He reaches to pull her toward him, but the waiter comes with their iced coffee and Julia cannot keep herself from laughing.

Later, when she is eating her chicken stir-fry and he is eating his Chilean sea bass, she says, "When will you speak with my father?"

The four gringos have quit their tennis game and are eating lunch at the table next to theirs. All of them seem to have acquired strong sunburns. "I already have," Oscar says. He no longer seems nervous. He sits upright in his chair, and every so often he reaches to touch Julia, as if to confirm he can.

"When?" Julia asks.

"Last weekend."

"On the phone?"

"No." Oscar licks his lips. "I met him in Zacapa, at his suggestion. For such an important question, I knew I had to speak to him in person."

Her father's admiration for Oscar, she knows, could only have grown after Oscar traveled three hours to meet him.

"You had lunch at the Hotel Wong," Julia says.

"Yes, we did. He told you?"

"No. But I know my father. When I was younger, I went to Zacapa with him and my mother. And I know he has been back since, for meetings."

Oscar looks at her as if expecting her to say more. "And, after lunch, you visited the Museo de Paleontología in Estanzuela," she says.

"Yes!" Oscar says. Touching her shoulder, he speaks about what he saw in the museum, about the mastodon tusk and the giant armadillo shell. Julia remembers them from her visit to the museum. But what she remembers better than the fossils was what she and her mother did afterwards. Her father remained to talk with the museum's director, and she and her mother returned to Zacapa to sit on the shore of the Montagua River. It was a brown, slow river, nothing like the quick, blue river in Santa Cruz, and watching it in the thick heat of the afternoon made Julia sleepy. Her mother told her about what her own mother had said about rivers, how they are always moving but appear unchanging. "Perhaps the same is true of people," her mother said. "Or at least some people. From one day to the next, we look mostly the same, but our souls are always journeying, always coming closer to God and God's grace."

This conversation occurred the year before Julia's family converted to Evangelism. At the time, her mother had a close relationship with the town's priest, an

American named Padre Michael. Her mother was part of a group of fifteen people in the church who used to meet with the priest once a month to talk about God and the Bible and how what they read in the Bible applied to themselves and their town. On the banks of the Montagua River, her mother told her about the day the group met at the river in Santa Cruz and, at meeting's end, as if by silent agreement, waded in.

"Let's do the same here," Julia said to her mother. So they removed their shoes and socks and they bunched their skirts between their knees and stepped into the river. The water was warm, even warmer than Julia expected, and it was swifter than it seemed from the bank. "Are we supposed to say something?" she asked her mother.

Her mother said, "Let's listen to the river."

They could hear the sounds of trucks and busses from the highway and the snorts of cattle from a nearby field. But they could also hear the river whistling around their legs.

Oscar says, "Your father introduced me to the museum director. I don't remember his name, but he studied in the States. He described what this country was like before humans were around. I thought your father would argue with him about evolution; I was prepared to hear your father quote the Bible."

"My father is an engineer," Julia says. "He respects science. He says the Bible speaks truths and science speaks truths and between them and beyond them there is much we don't know and may never know."

"He's right," Oscar says, nodding.

As if thinking of something else, Oscar smiles.

"What is it?" Julia asks.

"I didn't know if you were going to say yes to my question," he says. "This is one mystery of the universe solved."

— 8 —

In the November-to-January break between her first and second years of college, Julia works at La Casa Indígena, a store in Antigua that sells purses, dresses, shorts, table cloths and other items made of tipica fabric. Despite the store's name, the two owners, a pair of elderly cousins, have no Maya blood. They are light-skinned and speak Spanish the way Julia has heard it spoken by tourists from Spain.

Although Julia was hired as an assistant manager, she does little more than ring up sales and stare out the broad window next to the cash register, watching tourists stroll up and down the cobblestone street. She lives in a room at the back of the store with one of her classmates, Raquel, who spends every evening at bars in town. Her goal, she told Julia, is to meet a rich gringo. As far as Julia can tell, Raquel eats nothing but mangoes and tortillas. Even so, her waist is ample above the black mini-skirts she prefers. Every night, she lavishes her lips with dark red lipstick and her cheeks with heavy blush.

Oscar visits her every weekend, coming in from Quetzaltenago, where he is spending the summer managing his father's apple orchards. What work he does on the orchards isn't clear. When Julia asks him, his answers are vague—"I make sure the workers work" is one of his favorite replies—and he soon changes the subject to topics he likes better, such as politics and travel. For their honeymoon, a year hence, he plans to take Julia to Costa Rica, where they'll spend three days in the capital, three in the mountains at Monte Verde and three by the sea at Manuel Antonio Park.

During his visits, he stays in the Hotel Ramada on the edge of town, and when she finishes work on Saturday afternoons, she sits with him beside the pool, sipping fruit drinks, sweet mixtures of strawberry, mango and watermelon. He wears sunglasses with gold rims and comments on the tourists who use the pool to swim laps, stroking in monotonous rhythm. "This is why the United States is such a success," he says with admiration. "Gringos never rest."

On Sunday evening, when he boards the bus to Chimaltengago, his first stop on his way home to the Western Highlands, he insists she kiss him as he stands on the bus' bottom step. She is far shorter than he, and he therefore must bend to reach her lips.

Always as she watches his bus leave the station, spitting black fumes at her, she feels a quiet relief, as if an unmelodic music that had been playing ever since his arrival had been turned off. But this feeling of pleasure in her freedom never lasts longer than a day before she feels uneasy and incomplete and begins to miss him.

At night, sitting alone in the room she shares with Raquel, she does her best to read the Bible, but she finds her thoughts falling into idleness, wistfulness, even sin. Her favorite daydream is to imagine herself alone at night in her bed, the lights off. She hears a man enter the room. She is too afraid to speak or move, and soon the man discovers her and falls with violence and passion on top of her. She is too frightened to resist, and by now she doesn't want to because she realizes the man is Rodrigo, smelling like he used to after a soccer game and speaking words of love to her in his sure, deep voice.

One Wednesday night, feeling restless, she surprises Raquel by agreeing to accompany her to Macondo, a bar on the north side of town, although she tells Raquel she will not drink liquor or dance. She refuses Raquel's offer of lipstick and perfume, but agrees to wear one of her dresses, a red cotton dress that exposes a half moon of her back. The dress is too small for Raquel.

Julia knows Oscar would not approve of what she is doing, but she knows Oscar has friends in Quetzaltenango with whom he goes to restaurants and movies and even bars, although he, too, refuses to drink or dance.

Rock music from the United States blares from speakers on Macondo's ceiling. Raquel hands her an agua mineral, and they find seats on the second floor above the bar counter. At the table next to theirs, a brown-haired gringo with glasses is reading a book. Raquel tries to catch his eye, but he is intent on his reading.

Julia and Raquel sit in silence for a few minutes. "What do we do now?" Julia whispers.

"We wait until more people come."

They finish their drinks and Raquel goes to get them more. The gringo looks up and gives Julia a smile. She wonders if she should say something to him, but decides it wouldn't be appropriate.

Raquel doesn't return, and Julia sees her below at the bar counter, talking to a tall man who, although dark-skinned, doesn't look Guatemalan. She looks around her at the red walls, the concrete cracked in places. She looks again at the gringo, who is staring at her. "Hello," he says.

"Hello."

He continues to gaze at her, so she asks, "Isn't it difficult to read here with so much noise and so little light?"

For a moment, she doesn't think he understands her because he says nothing. After putting his book down, however, he answers in clear, accented Spanish: "I can barely read the book anyway." He holds it up so she can see the title: *El Labrinto de Soledad.* "I'm hoping to improve my Spanish, but this is more complicated than I thought."

He asks her if she lives in Antigua, and she tells him about her job. He tells her he is in Antigua to study Spanish. He is, he says, an archeologist—or, rather, he is studying to be—and he wants to work one day in Central America. She tells him about the ruins of Najquitob, a village near Santa Cruz. The ruins are buried deep in the ground, she says, but occasionally people in the village find pieces of slate and stone. "They are great ruins of the Pokomchí people and of King Mamamun," she says. "They are ruins of palaces and fortresses. But they sit underground because no one has come to uncover them."

The gringo asks her where the village is. As she is explaining, Raquel returns with the tall man she was talking to below, and she introduces him to Julia. His name is Mario, he is from Italy, and she is going with him to Latinos, another bar. "Would you like to come?" she asks her, and when Julia says no thank you, she seems relieved. Raquel glances at the gringo before descending the stairs with Mario.

The gringo asks who Raquel is, and when Julia explains, he says, "I've seen her here the last three nights."

He asks if he can sit at her table, and when, after hesitating, she agrees, he introduces himself as Richard Saberstein, from Chicago. He might be twenty-five-years-old, he might be thirty-five. It is difficult to tell with gringos. His glasses make him look older than he probably is.

She asks him if he has ever been to Tikal, and he nods. "It's beautiful," he says, although he doesn't speak with particular animation. Usually, gringos are effusive in their praises of Tikal's Mayan temples and the wildlife-filled jungles around them. "You could do your work in Tikal," she says.

Richard shakes his head. "Too much is already known about Tikal," he says. "Too many archeologists have already had their chance with it." He leans forward in his chair. "I want a new place, an undiscovered place." His voice is louder now. His glasses keep sliding to the end of his nose, and he keeps jamming them toward his eyes. "I want a place like what you were describing. I want to be the first, understand? I want to amaze people with what I discover."

He stops, sighs and leans back in his chair. Something about his enthusiasm reminds her of Rodrigo and his confident soccer talk. "But I have two more years of coursework before I can even begin thinking about doing an excavation of my own. And it's bad luck to plan or even think too far ahead, isn't it?"

Julia nods.

"I was reading about what people in Guatemala believe," he says. "They believe it's impossible to plan with any certainty even the simplest event—a meeting the next day, for example—because a person never knows what's going to happen from one minute to the next. Disaster could strike anytime."

Julia says, "Some people believe this."

"Do you?"

"We plan our lives with God's blessing. And sometimes God doesn't bless our lives. Or He doesn't bless them in the ways we think He should."

"God has a plan for us?"

"Yes, he must." She looks at him closely. His eyes skip around the room. "Don't you believe He does?"

Richard smiles. "I'm an atheist," he says. "You've probably never met an atheist."

Julia has heard sermons condemning atheists as ignorant sinners. "You don't believe we live under the grace of God?"

Richard shakes his head. "I wish I could. But I've seen too much go wrong to think we live with grace."

"Perhaps you haven't been able to see God's grace in what you've witnessed." She is repeating words she's heard before—from her father, from Hermano Hector. They've seen God's hand in the worst disasters—floods in Thailand, famine in Africa, their own country's endless, brutal war.

"Perhaps," Richard says. "But the grace I'd like to see is in other people."

"God gives us the freedom to be good, but He doesn't guarantee we will be," Julia says. "This is our responsibility as Christians."

"I think it's our responsibility as human beings, never mind our religions or lack thereof," Richard says. He smiles. "But, it appears, we essentially agree." He gazes at her. "I was talking with my Spanish teacher today about religion. She's part of a group in her church called the Carismaticos. It's a Catholic group, although it sounds more Evangelical to me." He turns away, tapping his fingers on the table in time to the music from the ceiling. "I was born Jewish," he says, turning back to her. "I don't suppose there are many Jews in Guatemala."

"There are some in the capital," she says. "A small group."

"Muslims?" he asks.

"There is a mosque on the road between the capital and Antigua." She had long wondered what the building with the spires was when Oscar told her. He said the owner of Noches de Arabia, a restaurant near the university, is a Muslim. "They're like us," Oscar said. "They don't drink."

Below them, on the dance floor to the right of the bar, two couples gyrate to the music. "Listen," Richard says, "do you want to dance?"

Quickly, Julia shakes her head. "My fiancé..." she begins.

"Oh," Richard says, frowning.

"He's in the army," Julia says. She didn't mean to say this. Something about the music's martial beat led her to thinking again of Rodrigo. She wants to backtrack, correct herself, but she knows she'll sound foolish. She feels compelled to say something else, so she adds, "I'm Evangelical. I shouldn't be here."

"Oh." A moment later, Richard asks, "What's wrong?"

Her eyes, she realizes, are damp, and she dabs at them with the red cloth napkin in front of her. He asks her if she'd like another mineral water, and she says she had better go. When she stands, so does he. He looks smaller and thinner than he did when seated. They say goodbye, and she walks out of the bar and down the block, turns left and finds herself standing in front of La Merced, a Catholic church and museum, its yellow archway aglow from the spotlights below it. She notices that the ticket-taker, a man wearing a blue baseball cap and sitting on a fold-up chair, is asleep, filling the archway with his steady snores. She sneaks past him and climbs the stone steps to the roof.

The sky is cloudless and star-filled. The three volcanoes—Agua to the south, Acatenango and Fuego to the southwest—surround the town like sleeping guard dogs. She thinks about the right way to know God. She wonders if God finds it easier to see her here, under the open sky. She thinks about where Oscar is and imagines him at a movie with friends, eating popcorn in the eighth row—Oscar always sits in the eighth row—and whispering jokes at the screen. She thinks about where Rodrigo is and imagines him safe, camped out under the same luminous sky. She feels, for the moment, at peace, grateful for the abundant brightness of the sky.

She hears a scuffling noise and turns to find the guard standing at the top of the staircase. She cannot see his face; even with the bright sky, it's covered in shadow. "What a beautiful night, mi amor," he says. A second later, he mumbles under his breath, another creepy endearment—or a threat—and approaches her with slow but determined strides.

Julia looks over the edge of the roof and sees below her the lighted courtyard of what must be the priest's residence. The priest himself—or one of his visitors—is standing in the middle of his yard, transfixed, it seems, as she was, by the sky. "Father!" Julia calls to him, and he looks up. She can see his face perfectly, as round and open as the full moon.

"Yes, mi hija?" he asks.

The guard is at her side now.

"What's wrong, mi hija?" But the priest sees the guard now and says, "Who are you, son? Are you Juanito?"

The guard hesitates. "No, Father, my name is Armando."

"Do I know you, my son?"

"I'm new, Father."

Julia slips past the guard and rushes down the stone steps and out of the church. The streets are empty, and she finds herself running, imagining what might be lurking in doorways and behind trees. She stops when she reaches the Parque Central, which is lighted and crowded with gringos and indígena women and girls selling purses and table runners out of baskets they carry on their heads. Julia wishes Oscar were here to put his arm around her, protect her from whatever might approach her out of the night. At the same time, she wants to return to La Merced to speak with the priest. She wants to thank him. She wants to tell him she is in love with two muchachos—or neither of them. She wants to tell him she is an Evangelical who misses being Catholic. She wants to confess this: She sometimes believes in nothing at all.

Julia looks up at the stars. *All this must mean something.* If she reached up, she is sure she could feel their fire on her fingertips.

— 9 —

The moon is invisible from under the great black covering of trees. Rodrigo's fellow soldiers are sleeping in tents, crooked pyramids on the forest floor. Rodrigo is leaning against a tree, thinking: *I might as well be in a jail cell.*

From high branches of the trees, monkeys howl. Rodrigo imagines them forming a wide circle around the tree he's under.

Rodrigo has a pen and notebook. That afternoon he saw the notebook on a village road during a march and he picked it up and tucked it inside his uniform. He borrowed the pen from a lieutenant the week before and never returned it. He tears a piece of paper from the notebook. He can't remember the date, so he leaves a spot on top of the paper blank. On the first line, he writes Julia's name. After a long greeting in which he asks about her and her parents and wishes them health and happiness, he tries to explain about the monkeys. "They yell the whole night," he writes. "A man cannot sleep because of the noise the monkeys make."

This isn't true. Only Rodrigo seems to be having trouble sleeping because of the monkeys. He and his fellow soldiers have walked eighteen kilometers today, and he feels sore in his thighs and knees, but especially in his right ankle, his soccer injury. He knows he should be tired, but he also knows that if he tried to sleep he wouldn't succeed. He would lie on his back, listening to the monkeys. And it's more pleasant to sit under a tree than lie in a tent.

He writes Julia's name again, writes her name in large letters, the way a monkey would howl it. Below it, he writes: "Your name is what they are shouting. Your name is what doesn't permit me to sleep."

This isn't true either. It is not Julia who keeps him awake, although if he thought about her long enough, she would, troubling him with how she looks; he can't remember exactly. He remembers her curls, her forest of curls, but he can't remember how long her hair is, how far down her back it falls. He remembers her nose better: small, with a tip that always shined as if it had oil on it. About her eyes, he remembers little. Dark, but how dark?

He tries to see her but cannot, not completely.

It is not Julia who keeps him awake, although this is what he writes her in the letter. He writes how the monkeys howl her name—how the forest reverberates with Julia, Julia, Julia—how her name chases away his sleep.

It is not Julia who keeps him awake, because he stops thinking about Julia and remembers when he was a boy, perhaps eight years old, and the circus came to town. After much pleading, he convinced his mother to take him, and they sat in the top row of bleachers. There was a monkey in the circus, a lanky creature with a gray chest and violet eyes, and although chained to a pole, he pranced around like a prince.

During a break between acts, the monkey was set free to roam in the tent. An announcer's voice said, "Now Don Geronimo, our dear old monkey, will select one child from the audience to take a stroll with him around the ring. Get ready, children—if he points at you, you're the lucky one."

The old monkey stood in front of the bleachers where Rodrigo was sitting and scratched his head. The audience went silent, as if someone were saying a prayer. The monkey scanned the faces in the bleachers, scanned the children. Then Don Geronimo pointed at Rodrigo. "It's me!" Rodrigo said, but a man in the front row pushed his little girl toward the monkey, and Don Geronimo took the girl's hand and walked her around the ring.

Rodrigo puts down the pen. He has lied to Julia. He closes his eyes and discovers he's very tired. But he knows he won't be able to sleep. The monkeys aren't calling Julia's name but his own. They're telling him about the place they've saved him on top of the trees—above the tents, the soldiers, the war. They're telling him to come join them under the moon.

— 10 —

A week before Christmas, Oscar, Gerardo and Marisol come to visit Julia in Antigua. Gerardo stays with Oscar at the Hotel Ramada and Marisol rooms with Julia, sleeping in Raquel's bed. Raquel no longer works at La Casa Indígena; the cousins dismissed her after she failed to come home two nights in a row. Occasionally, Julia sees her around town, usually from a distance. She looks heavier and is more careless about how she combs her hair.

They eat lunch at Burger King, despite protests from Marisol, who has come with a guidebook intended for tourists from Spain and reads off the names of restaurants they might have selected. In her gold sequined dress, which emphasizes her ample breasts, and with her shining brown hair combed smooth over her pale forehead, Marisol looks like a French model. Everyone eats chicken sandwiches save Oscar, who devours three Whoppers. Julia wonders where he finds space in his stomach. He is, if anything, thinner than when she last saw him.

Afterwards, they find a seat in the Parque Central and listen to an Andean band play guitars and flutes in front of the fountain. Gerardo, who is short and plump, tells jokes above the music, including one about a series of deaf men who go to the pharmacy to buy condoms. Julia is surprised by how lewd the jokes are, but she can't help laughing.

As Gerardo begins another joke, they hear a whirling sound. Above them, a helicopter, painted olive, buzzes past. A moment later, from the east, soldiers come marching as if on parade. The Andean band stops playing. The girls who sell change purses and table runners stop their progression from park bench to park bench and keep as still as startled deer. Cars stop in the middle of the cobblestone street on the north side of the park, and the soldiers march around them. Julia looks at each soldier's face as he passes, but she cannot distinguish them. They might all be Rodrigo.

They continue marching west, toward the bus terminal and market. Even when they are out of sight, the park remains quiet.

Julia listens for the last of the soldiers' boots pounding against the cobblestone. And even when she knows she should no longer hear the echo of their steps, she does.

I've betrayed him. She wants to be alone, praying at the altar of the calvario above Santa Cruz, smelling dried roses and birds of paradise and whatever else is left in old milk cans by hopeful penitents. She wants to pray for Rodrigo and ask his forgiveness for ignoring him, for committing her life to someone else.

She feels Oscar's arm around her. He looks at her, his gray eyes bright, intense, concerned. "What's wrong?" he asks.

"Nothing."

When this doesn't seem to satisfy him, she says, "The soldiers."

"I know," Oscar says. "But the war is almost over, thank God."

"It is?" Julia asks, and she allows herself to feel more hopeful. "But it seems the negotiations are always failing."

"Both sides are still at the table," he says. "And, from what I've read, they're moving closer to an agreement. When the war is over, this country will be great again. And we'll be part of it." He pulls her close to him, and she feels settled by his confidence. "Imagine what we'll do when we don't have to worry about guerrillas or soldiers. People from all over the world—regular people, people who aren't hippies or backpackers or international aid workers—will start coming here again."

She looks up at him and he smiles. "Trust me," he says.

— 11 —

It is Oscar's idea to camp on Volcán de Agua, and Julia and Marisol agree only after he assures them that the tents he brought from Quetzaltenango will keep out rain, insects and snakes. After lunch—this time, at Marisol's insistence, at Vino y Queso, an Italian restaurant—they take a taxi the ten kilometers to Santa María de Jesús. To Julia, the town looks like Purulhá, its houses tucked between overgrown vegetation. Its primitiveness and its smells are like Purulhá, and she remembers Rodrigo before his soccer game, kissing her in the bougainvillea.

Julia and Marisol want to hire a guide, but Oscar and Gerardo dismiss the idea. They set off in tennis shoes, following a wide street that, if it continued, would rise straight to the volcano's peak. The street ends, however, replaced by a grassy field. They climb a zigzagging trail up the volcano, pausing every ten minutes to catch their breath. The sun, which dominated the sky as they set off, is hidden between a patch of white clouds. Julia finds herself sweating, although the day has turned cool.

Two hours into their climb, they see, coming down the mountain, a man and a woman. The man is a gringo, tall and blond and sunburned. The woman is black, and Julia thinks she looks like Alejandra. But it has been too long since Julia has seen her to be certain. The groups exchange greetings, and as the man and woman continue their descent, Julia looks back and finds the woman gazing at her. She feels they are both about to say something, but neither of them does, and the woman again turns and disappears around a bend. "Alejandra," Julia calls in a whisper.

"What did you say?" Oscar asks. Julia has spoken with Oscar about Alejandra, but she isn't sure he would remember her and does not want to explain. "The wind," she says as the wind rises and throws Oscar's hair over his eyes.

When, an hour later, they see another pair of gringos, Oscar asks them how far they are from the crater. The man, breathing heavily, says, "Forty-five minutes, if you are quick."

"And if we are slow?" Marisol asks.

The man smiles. "All night."

By dusk, they have failed to reach the peak, and Oscar suggests they look for a campsite around the next bend. When they turn the corner, however, they find soldiers sitting in front of a campfire, their canvas tents staked along the side of the trail. Two soldiers and a lieutenant approach them. After checking their cedulas and chatting with Oscar about the possibility of rain, the lieutenant says, "There are reports of guerrillas in the area. Camp near us. You'll be safer."

The lieutenant looks at Julia, and something about his stare—appraising, cold—makes her afraid. But it isn't only fear for herself or Oscar, Marisol, and Gerardo. She thinks of the men Rodrigo must be with, what they might be turning him into.

"Thank you," Oscar says. "We'd like to reach the top tonight."

"It's late," the lieutenant says, his eyes again on Julia. "It's better to stay."

After the lieutenant and his soldiers walk back toward their fire, Oscar urges his group on. As they continue their climb, Julia sees the soldiers' faces in the flickering firelight. They are all boys, and they have the smooth skin of boys, but their eyes are weary and ancient.

When they have turned the bend, Oscar scoffs. "He says it would be safer near them." He chuckles and shakes his head. "I say it would be safer sleeping in the middle of their fire. Let's go as high as we can. I'd rather take my chances with guerrillas."

They turn three more corners before Marisol says, "My feet hurt. I'm sure I have blisters."

"All right," Oscar says. "We'll be fine here."

He steps off the side of the trial and into the forest before returning a minute later. "There's some flat land in here—enough to put two tents on."

As he and Gerardo set up the tents, Julia and Marisol unpack the food they brought. They were going to light a fire and cook hotdogs, but with soldiers nearby and perhaps guerrillas also, they can't risk this. Instead, they make sandwiches with tomatoes and sliced ham. The air is even cooler now, and Julia finds herself shivering as they sit on a fallen tree at the edge of a trail, watching the sky expire. They hear birds sing their last songs. They eat and talk and Oscar and Gerardo eat more.

"I wish we could have a fire," Marisol says when they have finished eating. "I'm very cold."

Gerardo puts his arm around her and slips his hand inside her jacket. He pulls her flush against him, and soon they are kissing. Oscar takes Julia's hand and walks with her a few steps down a trail. They look up at the sky, but there must be clouds above them because they can see no stars. "You're cold," Oscar says.

"Yes, I am."

"Here," he says, and he pulls her to him. He kisses her, his bottom teeth clipping her bottom lip. "I'm sorry," he says. "I can't see well." Again he kisses her, softer this time.

"Come here," he says after they have been kissing for a long time. He takes her hand again, and they stumble in the darkness back to their campsite. "Here," Oscar says, indicating one of the tents. The other tent is set off at some distance, behind a pine tree, and Julia hears Gerardo and Marisol whispering. "But Marisol and I are sleeping here," Julia says, touching the tent's front pole. The tent wobbles.

Oscar glances at the other tent before turning back to Julia. "I think they have other ideas," he says. "Nothing will happen, I promise. We will be like brother and sister tonight."

She takes a deep breath. She thinks she hears a cackle, one of the soldiers—or a guerrilla—laughing at a joke. She unzips the tent flap and crawls in. She hears Oscar relieving himself, a long rush of water.

Oscar comes into the tent and crawls beside her. They have one sleeping bag and one blanket. The opened sleeping bag serves as the mattress, and although it is thick, Julia can feel a tree's root beneath her.

"Tired?" he asks her.

"Yes," she says.

"Well, we'll sleep."

He leans over and kisses her, a brief, chaste kiss on the cheek. "Good night," he says. A few minutes pass. Despite the tiredness she feels in her feet and legs, she is restless. She wants to leave the tent and breathe the cool night air, but she is scared of what is outside. She closes her eyes and sees the soldiers and their flat, sad faces. *It wasn't my fault*, she thinks, although she doesn't know what she means. The words, however, give her relief. *It wasn't my fault. It was what God willed.*

She thinks about the enormous, white Catholic Church in Santa Cruz and the quiet calvario. She thinks about the Church of God with its rows of benches and its unadorned altar. She thinks of mosques and synagogues. She thinks of all the prayers offered to God around the world and wonders which prayers He hears. If He hears anything at all.

She thinks of Oscar's words: *The war will be over before long.* She hopes it will be. But in her mind she again sees the soldiers and she feels the tension of their presence. She hears Oscar's breathing deepen, and although she is pleased he didn't press her for deeper intimacies, she knows it won't matter. Marisol and Gerardo will think the worst, and when classes resume, everyone will know they have been lovers.

She finds herself, at last, falling asleep when she hears Oscar stir. "Did you hear that?" he asks.

"What?"

"That noise?"

Her heartbeat quickens. "No."

"Listen."

They listen for a moment.

"I don't hear anything," she says.

"Maybe it was nothing."

They listen again. Nothing. He rolls toward her and kisses her neck. He whispers, "What do you think Marisol and Gerardo are doing?"

"Sleeping."

"Ha. I don't think so."

He moves his mouth across her neck to her lips. She feels his hands move up her chest. For a moment, she says nothing. She says nothing as he unclips her bra. His hands feel good, very good, but this, she knows, is wrong. Good, but wrong. Wrong, but good. "What are you doing?" she asks.

"I love you," he says. "Every night I fall asleep thinking about you."

He touches her breasts with his large hands, and she is half excited and half afraid. "Don't you love me?" he asks. "Don't you?"

"Yes," she says. "I do. Of course."

"Good."

"But Oscar..." Before she can continue, he kisses her again, covering her lips. She feels his body press on top of hers, and this isn't unwelcome. He struggles with her pants, and soon they are around her knees.

"You love me," he says. "You make me happy because you love me."

She feels herself shiver—in fear, pleasure, pain. She is worried she is going to humiliate herself by throwing up. This is all she can think about as he presses himself inside her.

"You love me," he says. "You're going to be my wife."

He shudders, and at the same time she feels a pulse between her legs. She closes her eyes, hoping she won't cry.

"I love you," he says, kissing her hair. "You love me and I love you. All right? All right, Julia?"

She doesn't say anything. He withdraws and falls beside her. He presses his mouth to her ear.

"Please?" he whispers. "Please, Julia?"

She feels his wetness begin to leak from her.

"Please?" he asks again. He isn't touching her anymore.

"Yes," she says, because she doesn't know what else to say. "Yes."

"Good," he says. He kisses her ear. He kisses it again. He seems about to say something, but he doesn't. Julia feels his warm breath in her ear.

Later, as he's sleeping, she hears deep in the night, as if from the top of the volcano, a guitar, five, six, seven notes, then silence.

In the morning, Oscar tries to wake her with a kiss on the cheek. Although her eyes are closed, she has been awake most of the night, imagining the tent as a tomb. She doesn't respond to Oscar's caresses, and soon she hears him unzip the tent and greet Marisol and Gerardo.

She feels the ground beneath the sleeping bag with its roots and pine needles and she feels small aches in her back and waist and legs. She feels a dampness around her—on the floor of the tent and on its sides and even in the air, which seems thick with mist. She knows it would be more pleasant to leave the tent and shake the soreness from her limbs and the moisture from her clothes and hair, but she is concerned about seeing Oscar, concerned about what looks Gerardo and Marisol will give her.

She knows women her age who have done what she and Oscar did, some who do it with ease and regularity. They speak of the pills they take and the instruments they insert between their legs as they would of aspirin and hair clips, and she listens with interest, but she never thought she would know, first-hand, what they were discussing until she was married. And when she was married, it would be different; it would be something more beautiful than the base mechanics of preventing conception. Now she has knowledge, and she feels ashamed of it. She wonders if Oscar, disgusted by how little she resisted him, will leave her now. She wonders if she is pregnant. She wonders if she should hope she's pregnant so Oscar will be certain to marry her.

She hears Marisol call her, and in a moment, she hears a rustling sound above her. Marisol's face hangs over hers, her hair falling on Julia's forehead. "Wake up," she says. "It's time to climb to the top of the world."

Reassured by Marisol's everyday tone, Julia puts on clean clothes and shoes and leaves the tent. Gerardo says good morning to her and Oscar smiles, a smile he might give her on any morning. "They made breakfast," Oscar says.

"Sandwiches!" Marisol announces. "Bread with strawberry jelly."

"And water to drink!" Gerardo adds. "A feast!"

Marisol hands Julia a sandwich, and they eat, sitting on a log as mist tumbles down the volcano, leaving the peak in light.

— 12 —

Sunlight slips through the mahogany, chicozapote, cedar and palm trees and spreads across the thatched roofs of the dozen houses in the village. Rodrigo hears a rooster's familiar welcome to the morning. He hears a pig's grunt. From one of the houses, he sees smoke rise and curl toward the sky.

Guerrillas are here, the lieutenant told them. Or they were here. Or they are planning to be here. Rodrigo doesn't remember.

Rodrigo and the other soldiers are crouched at the tree line on the village's western edge. Rodrigo has never been to this village, but it looks as familiar as the villages around Santa Cruz. He looks to see where the soccer field is and spots it to his right, on a plateau perhaps fifty meters distant. The crossbar on the near goal droops in the center. The high corners are obviously the place to aim, he thinks.

"Now!" the lieutenant hisses, and the soldiers spring from their crouches and race to the houses they've been assigned. Rodrigo follows Miguel, another soldier, to a one-room, adobe house on the northern edge of the village. Miguel pushes open the wooden door. An old man is sitting on a bench in the center of the room. An old woman in a thin yellow güipil and a gray corte is standing in front of a cooking fire. In the back of the room, in a bed, a girl is breastfeeding a baby. The two women scream and begin to cry, and the man stands, holding up his hands and speaking in a language Rodrigo doesn't understand.

"Out!" Rodrigo says, waving his rifle at the old man. "Outside! Now!"

The old man's hands tremble. Miguel steps up to the old woman, grabs her by the shoulder and pushes her toward the door. Rodrigo does the same with the old man. "I'll get the girl," Miguel says, striding toward the bed where the girl shivers over her baby. Seeing Miguel approach, she cries out and holds up her hand. Miguel slaps her hand with the end of his rifle, and the girl shrieks.

If Miguel was a friend of his, Rodrigo would say, "Come on, vos, leave her alone." But Rodrigo cannot remember the last time he spoke more than a few words to anyone. All the same, he opens his mouth to speak, but nothing comes. The girl's screams are loud, louder, and then, suddenly, strangely, there is quiet.

Rodrigo isn't looking at her anymore. He has turned to march the old couple out the door. The sunlight is fierce now, and Rodrigo shields his eyes as he pushes the old couple toward the village's center square, which is nothing more than a broad patch of dirt. On the north edge of the square is a church. Atop its metal roof is a large black cross. It glimmers in the sunlight, and Rodrigo wonders if it is made of jade.

He pushes the old couple into the center of the square. There are perhaps twenty people here, all old people and women with babies, and soon more come, staggering in front of soldiers' rifles. Samuel, another soldier, drags an old woman into the square, his arms around her chest. She collapses onto the dirt. No one moves to help her. Rodrigo hears two quick gunshots followed by a rooster's crow. He looks around for Miguel. He sees a pair of chickens on a nearby rooftop.

Rodrigo feels sweat flood his scalp, fill his shirt, collect in his boots. He wants to remove his helmet and run his hands through his hair. He wants to remove the jacket he is wearing; he wants to peel off his boots.

The lieutenant asks the people in the center of the square where the young men are. No one replies. "Where are the muchachos?" he demands again. "Have they joined la guerrilla?"

"They're dead." The speaker is the old woman Samuel dragged to the square. She is on her knees. Her pink güipil is ripped and her right breast, wrinkled, brown, is visible. "The guerrillas came and killed them and now you are coming to kill them. But you cannot kill the dead."

"So guerrillas came?" the lieutenant shouts. "You harbored guerrillas?" The lieutenant spits. "You are all traitors?"

He looks behind him, eyeing his soldiers, before turning back to the crowd. "Your muchachos have all joined la guerrilla, but if they are expecting to come home when they are done with the war, they will be disappointed."

The lieutenant turns around and points to Rodrigo, Samuel and Ofelio, another soldier, and waves them forward. "I want this man," he says, pointing to one of the old men. "And this man. And this woman." The woman he points to is the woman on the ground.

It is Ofelio who takes the lead, pushing the two men forward to the west side of the church. Samuel drags the old woman by her right hand. They stand them up against the side of the church. One of the men, who is wearing a white T-shirt and dark green pants and no shoes, falls onto his knees and cries and pleads. The other old man is wearing a straw hat and looks straight ahead. Because of his hat, the ferocious sunlight doesn't strike his eyes.

Following the lead of the other two soldiers, Rodrigo lifts his rifle. He feels his arms shake and his finger quiver. He glances up at the black cross and thinks it looks like a great black bird. He thinks of the black cross he glued to a piece of wood and nailed to his bedroom wall after his injury, how it was supposed to guide him to recovery.

Slowly, the old woman spreads her arms. Both of her breasts are now exposed; they are small and wrinkled and as brown as the dirt below her. Rodrigo thinks about how close she is to dying already. She might die tomorrow, and if they left her to die they could spare themselves the bullets. Behind him, Rodrigo hears the lieutenant spit. He smells smoke and, glancing to his left, sees a rooftop in full blaze.

"Why are you waiting?" the old woman asks. "If you will be murderers, begin your killing."

The lieutenant gives the word.

When the woman falls, when the two men are crumpled on the dirt, Rodrigo doesn't stop shooting. His fingers will not let him stop. He blazes bullets into the side of the church, opening a fist-sized hole in the mud wall. He wants to keep shooting, to knock down the wall, the whole church, until he is able to see what's on the other side.

But he feels a hand clasp his shoulder, and he hears the lieutenant's hard voice. "Stop," it says. "Stop."

— 13 —

One day in the middle of her second year of college, Julia finds herself riding the bus beyond Antigua and San Mateo University's satellite campus, where her computer class meets, and into Jocotenango. This will be the first class she will have missed. It doesn't matter. When the school year ends in October, she'll never be a student again; she'll marry Oscar, who will have completed his degree, and they'll move to Quetzaltenango. Oscar's father is building them a two-story house overlooking one of his apple orchards.

She steps off the bus. The town's feria is in progress, filling the streets in front of the Catholic Church. She advances with the crowd, passing cantinas and the Lotería booth, its tables crowded with large women, and El Pistolero, where boys line up to shoot corks at musical targets. Bursts of clanging guitar sounds mix with people's loud conversations and children's shouts.

She walks to the end of a street where a small crowd is gathered around a wooden booth. A light bulb hangs from the center beam. Although it is only five in the afternoon and the sky is clear and blue, the light is on. A tall, lean woman with black hair cut straight across her forehead stands behind the counter. She has the smooth, unblemished skin of a young girl, but her eyes are lightless and solemn.

Julia watches the boys around the booth flip ten centavo pieces at the rings. One of them succeeds in landing his piece in a ring's center, and he shouts in triumph. The black-haired woman hands him a quetzal and his coin, saying, "Play again. You have luck on your side."

The boys evidently are part of a group because when after a few minutes and no more success, one announces he is tired of playing, the rest follow him toward other games. This leaves Julia alone with the black-haired woman. The woman says, "I've seen you before, haven't I?"

"I don't think so."

"I have. I'm certain of it."

"I haven't been to a feria in more than ten years."

"It wasn't at a feria. You were at a window. I thought you must have wanted to come outside."

"It wasn't me."

"No?"

Julia shakes her head.

"I must be mistaken," the woman says. "But you are Evangelical, aren't you?"

"Yes."

If the woman finds pleasure in Julia's transgression of her religion now, she doesn't show it.

Julia says, "Here, give me ten coins." She hands the woman a quetzal and the woman hands her ten ten-centavo pieces. In the exchange, the woman's hand touches hers, and Julia feels how cool and soft it is.

Julia tosses the coin and it lands in the red felt surrounding the rings. Her second and third tries also fail. On her fourth try, she hits a ring, but the coin bounces off of it. The rest of her tries are no more successful.

"I have no luck," Julia says.

"You could try again."

"Ten tries is enough to prove I have no luck."

She turns to leave, but bending down to the grass below her feet, she discovers that her purse is missing. She runs her hand across the grass, as if she couldn't trust her eyes to spot it. She stands up. "My…purse…" she stutters.

"Yes?" says the woman.

"It's gone. It was here."

She stoops again. She pushes her fist against the canvas flap of the coin-toss booth. She is able to push the flap up until she sees the woman's feet. Julia stands again.

"Did you find it?" the woman asks.

Julia looks at her with suspicion, but she hesitates to accuse her. "I don't have any money," Julia says. She feels her voice rise. "I won't be able to get back to the capital tonight. I won't have a place to stay."

"I'm sorry," the woman says.

"Please," Julia says, hoping to stare her into a confession.

The woman leans over the counter. "You could work here tonight," she says. "I would let you take my place. I've never been to a feria, I only work at them. I would pay you what the dueño pays me. Tonight you could sleep in this booth with me and tomorrow you would have enough money for the bus to the capital."

"I want my purse," Julia says.

The woman holds Julia's gaze. "Don't you want to work here tonight? Okay, I'll even work with you. It will be nice, the two of us. We'll talk like sisters, and when the feria closes, we'll plan our escape."

Julia thinks the woman is crazy. Again, she says, "I want my purse."

"But you could have more," the woman says. When Julia doesn't respond, the woman looks down, and Julia sees disappointment in her face. She feels a moment of pity, but it is quickly replaced by what she knows: The woman is a thief.

"Your purse is at your feet," the woman says. "It's been there all along."

She is tempted to call the woman a liar, but when she bends down again, she finds her purse where she left it.

Shaking, Julia marches toward a set of pay phones near the town's municipalidad. She calls Oscar, who answers on the second ring, and asks him if he'll pick her up. "I am leaving now," he says, and the purposefulness in his voice reassures her.

And yet ten minutes after her call, she loses interest in his arrival. Sitting on a bench in front of a statue of a jocote, the fruit painted in rainbow stripes, she thinks about the black-haired woman and what she offered. *But the woman is crazy. She's a thief and she's crazy.*

She hears a jingling of guitars from El Pistolero and the heated cry of the Lotería barker announcing the figures on the balls he draws—the apple, the devil, the dreaming man.

— 14 —

The slant of sunlight through leaves makes Rodrigo's eyes water. He has never cried in the war, only leaked water from his eyes, irritated from the sunlight's sting. He and his fellow soldiers are marching single-file through dense trees. Vines as thick as corn stalks climb, snake-like, around trees, strangling them even as they feed off them. He once heard the lieutenant refer to these vines as women, and even though Rodrigo laughed, he doesn't agree. They are more like war, feeding off the country, village by village, until the country is dead.

Rodrigo has only this last march back to the base in Poptún, and then he'll be allowed to go home. He has spent twenty-two months and six days in the army, and this morning the lieutenant told him that when they arrived in Poptún, he would be discharged.

They move at a languid pace, as if they were children on a morning walk to school. Rodrigo wants to hear the steady pounding of boots, a quick march. He hears only dull, lethargic thuds.

There is a crackle of bullets, and the man in front of him, a tall soldier whose helmet is too small, falls. Swiftly, Rodrigo moves behind a mahogany tree. Secure in his position, he sees men on a far slope. He counts nine of them, their dark green camouflage unable to hide them in the jungle's light browns. He points his rifle at one and pulls the trigger. The guerrilla clutches his stomach, then falls. Rodrigo trains his rifle on another, a bearded man with long hair, but before he can fire a shot, the bearded man falls from the bullet of another soldier.

The guerrillas retreat, their ambush a failure, and Rodrigo shoots one in the back as the rest race over the crest of the hill and into a thick maze of trees. Rodrigo hears the lieutenant's voice, and he sees his fellow soldiers emerge from behind trees. Soldiers move quickly toward the fleeing guerrillas; Rodrigo, however, is casual in his pursuit, cursing the distraction. He hears more shots, soldiers firing blindly into trees, and he steps up to where two soldiers stand above a dying guerrilla, the one he shot in the back. They have turned him over, and he is holding his hand over the place in his stomach where the bullet departed. He is a young boy, no older than fifteen, Rodrigo guesses, his face as fat as a baby's. Rodrigo turns away, disgusted with how easy it was to shoot him.

One of the soldiers announces, "He's dead." The other soldiers return from their aimless pursuit of the fleeing guerrillas. They have lost one man—the soldier who was walking in front of Rodrigo—and two others are injured.

The march to Poptún, Rodrigo knows, will be slower because of the dead and injured men, and it is this misfortune alone he curses.

— 15 —

One morning after Julia's Latin American history class, Julia's new friend Lilian invites her to hear a presentation by Sabina Ramirez, a journalist from *La Libertad*, a feminist magazine based in Antigua. Sabina Ramirez is coming to speak to a student group Lilian founded called the Women's Solidarity Union.

Julia met Lilian the previous week, when Lilian stopped her after class to tell her she admired the presentation Julia did on the fall of the Somoza regime in Nicaragua. Julia agrees to meet Lilian at the meeting, but before she leaves her dormitory room, Lilian calls her to tell her the meeting has been cancelled; Sabina Ramirez, she explains, thinks someone might be following her and doesn't want to put Lilian and others in danger.

So instead of attending the meeting, Julia rides with Lilian on a bus into zona una and sits with her on the second floor of El Chino Lindo. They eat noodles with broccoli, carrots and peas, and Lilian tells her about what Sabina Ramirez planned to speak about: the martyrdom of María Elena Moyano, a woman from Peru who'd founded an organization called Vaso de Leche but had, last year, been assassinated. "Her organization gives milk to poor women and teaches them about their rights," says Lilian, whose dark skin and brilliant eyes remind Julia of Alejandra's. "But to some people, this is a threat. They think if women have strength and health and the will to organize and speak, they will steal someone's power."

Lilian talks to Julia about how she dreams of expanding the Women's Solidarity Union from its base at San Mateo University into towns and villages across the country. She wants the Union to teach women about family planning and nutrition; she wants it to teach women how to organize in order to speak as a larger, more powerful entity to government officials. "Sometimes I picture myself doing what María Elena did," Lilian says. "She wasn't a guerrilla and she wasn't with the government, she was only a woman acting peacefully to do what she believed needed to be done to make her community stronger. But, look, María Elena is dead, and Sabina Ramirez cannot even come to speak to us because of who might be following her. I don't know if I have the courage to act as they have acted."

As she decides on the future of the Women's Solidarity Union, she says, she will work to change her own life. "I have three brothers, and my father and mother listen to them, but when I speak they tell me it isn't right for a girl to have such bold ideas," she says. "And although Lorenzo, my novio, has heard me say many times that I want more than his mother and my mother have, I think secretly he hopes I will be a traditional wife."

"But how will you win their respect?" Julia asks. "No matter what you say to them, they may continue to ignore you."

"The first step is to gain economic independence," Lilian says. "Lorenzo knows I will not marry him until I have a career. I intend to be a lawyer. And when we marry and have children, I will continue to work. I must. This is the only way to assure my independence. If I am independent, I will have the same power as Lorenzo and whatever he says to me I can accept or refuse."

Lilian asks Julia if she plans to work after she is married, and Julia says she does. In the moment, it is what she wants. But after the bus brings her and Lilian back to the university and they have said goodbye, Julia doesn't know if Oscar would agree to allow her to work. She doesn't know what work she might be able to find in Quetzaltenango.

When, three weeks later, Julia doesn't see Lilian in her history class on three consecutive days, she calls her. Ana, Lilian's roommate, whom she knows from another class, answers and tells her Lilian has had a problem.

"What kind of problem?"

There is a long pause. "She was pregnant and had the operation, un aborto. But the operation made her bleed too much, and she had to go to the hospital." Another pause. "Her father discovered what happened."

"Will she be coming back?"

"Because I know Lilian, I think the answer is yes. But I do not know her father."

In Santa Cruz, Julia heard of a woman in the village of Río Frío who was said to perform abortions with a branch from a eucalyptus tree and tea made from flor de muerto. She'd even heard of girls who used the woman's services, but she thought it was all rumor. There was no greater sin, Hermano Hector often preached, than killing a child. Even as Julia feels horrified by what Lilian did, she imagines her friend with blood rushing from between her legs and her father's words of condemnation raging in her ears, and pity replaces her revulsion, concern overcomes her displeasure.

Later, when Julia again considers what Lilian did, she feels no less abhorrence at the act, but at the same time she recognizes the courage it must have taken Lilian to undergo the illegal operation. When she prays for Lilian, she prays for God to forgive her sin but also for her friend to remain resolute and strong.

— 16 —

The pick-up truck leaves Rodrigo at the intersection of the Cobán highway and Calle Tres de Mayo, and he walks up the hill toward Santa Cruz. It is past midnight, and everything is silent. The few working streetlights give a weak yellow glow. He passes Doña María's house on the hill to his left, its front steps carved by an azadón into the grass, and Blanca Oralia's house set behind a wood fence. Chickens crowd the courtyard, as they always have. He turns to his right and sees, high on the far hill, the calvario. It seems to glow, as if candles are burning inside. He wonders what day it is, what religious celebration might be taking place.

He reaches the street's first building, Don Alberto's tienda, a Coca-Cola sign between its two windows. He walks past Don Marcos's farmacia and El Dragón, the cantina with its orange lights and jukebox glowing between the red curtains in the door. He walks to Avenida La Parroquia and turns right toward his house. He tries the front door, but it's locked. There is no light inside. He walks around to the back, to the courtyard. The dogs wake up and bark, but he whispers to them and they smell him and settle down and return to their places under the tin roof. As always, the back door is open. He steps into his house for the first time in almost two years.

In the hallway, he listens for the sounds of his mother and brothers sleeping. After a moment, he does hear them, faint but familiar. His brother Augusto is sleeping in Rodrigo's old bed, a sheet wrapped around all but his face. Rodrigo doesn't want to frighten him. He walks down the hallway again and into the courtyard. In the middle of the courtyard, his mother stands wrapped in moonlight like a ghost.

She speaks his name and comes to him as swift as light. "Thank God," she says. She's in his arms as hot and trembling as a lover, and he smells her hair, smells smoke and flowers, and he feels her tears dampen his chest. She lifts her head and pulls back to look at him again. "Are you all right?" she asks, and she touches his arms and neck, his cheeks and nose. She runs her hand across his forehead. "Are you all right?" she repeats.

Rodrigo nods. His mother falls again into his chest and hugs him in her thin arms. Her tears come again, fast and warm. He wants to tell her he would have been home months earlier, but he'd been forced to stay in order to complete a campaign to rid the villages around Poptún of guerrillas. But this doesn't matter now. For him, the war is over. "And you, mother?" he asks. "Are you all right?"

"Now I am," she says, nodding, rubbing her face against his chest. He runs his hand through her hair, still long and black.

He asks about his brothers. They are fine, his mother says.

He knows he should refrain from his next question. He fears the answer because he thinks he knows it. But he wants it confirmed. "And Julia?" His mother stops crying. She steps back from him. Again she's in moonlight, beautiful and pale.

"She's in the capital. At college."

His mother turns her head, and he sees her profile. "You haven't forgotten her." It isn't a question, so he doesn't answer. Slowly, his mother turns to face him. "You must forget her. She has another novio. The wedding is in October."

Rodrigo doesn't say anything and doesn't move. Sighing, his mother comes to him, and he's grateful to have her in his arms again. No one has touched him like this in two years, and her tenderness makes him feel like weeping. But he's thinking of Julia and her wedding. He must leave soon for the capital, the next morning even, although he wants to leave now, to run all the way, all night. He'll hold his mother a little longer, though. She lingers, as if she knows his plan.

After his mother leaves, Rodrigo doesn't bother to sleep, but sits in the courtyard, staring at the stars. He sits a long time. When the sky changes, giving way at last to a gray, predawn glow, and the air comes alive with cock crows and bird songs, he stands and walks from the courtyard onto Avenida La Parroquia. He will catch the seven o'clock corriente to the capital, but before he leaves he wants to see Julia's house again.

He walks across the park. Ricardo, Doña Luvia's disturbed son, sleeps on a bench against a wall painted with a dancing devil. The dog at Ricardo's feet growls as

Rodrigo passes. Julia's house is set off behind an arch of roses. A light bulb sticks like a glowing fist from above the front door. Rodrigo thinks if he wishes hard enough, Julia will come from the house. He wishes she would—he wishes his mother's words were lies—he wishes nothing had changed since the day she told him she would marry him.

Julia lost faith in him. To have found another novio, to have planned a wedding—she must have thought he would die in the jungle. Several times, he thought he would die. But always he vowed: *If I survive this war, I will have Julia again. And this will make everything I've seen and done all right.*

He closes his eyes and wishes away her engagement, wishes away the jungle smells that cling to him, wishes away the last two years. He wishes she would open the door and fly toward him before the sun rises.

When he opens his eyes, she is standing under the light bulb. Her hair has grown wild and long, as if she were unwilling to cut it before he returned. But she is thin, too thin, as if during her vigil she hasn't eaten. She is beautiful, of course, always beautiful, even if she is thin. He starts to call her name, but she speaks first. "Buenos días, Rodrigo." Her voice is too low to be Julia's, and now he realizes his mistake. He greets Julia's mother, his heart still rattling against his chest in anticipation of a miracle.

"Julia is gone."

"I know."

"She's engaged."

"I know this also."

Her mother walks toward him and stands with him under the arch of roses. She is not like Julia, Rodrigo thinks. But she is beautiful still. Her hair is thick and black like Julia's, although it lacks Julia's curls.

"You still love her."

"Yes. Always."

Julia's mother looks him over, then stares without shame into his eyes. "You must have thought of her all the time, wherever you were," she says. "Maybe it helped you live. If so, I'm glad. And you're okay? It's a miracle. It is."

Rodrigo says nothing. The air is ripe with sound. A hundred cocks crow. A hundred birds sing. She is close enough so Rodrigo feels her breath on his face. "I had a first love. His name was Ramiro. He died a long time ago. But I haven't forgotten. So how could you forget?"

She glances back at her house. "My husband just woke up, do you hear him?" She turns again to Rodrigo, who shakes his head. "He's wondering where I am. He's coming. You see, I only have a moment."

She draws close to him again. "I'm sorry, Rodrigo. I am. I always liked you. And you must have suffered. We all do in the war, but you—well, you know more than we ever will."

She puts a hand on his cheek, then turns toward the door. But she turns back quickly. "Stay home, Rodrigo. Please. Forget her. Your need will pass—or at least it will ease. It will. I promise. Please."

Behind her, the door opens. Rodrigo sees her husband standing in the doorway like a lieutenant.

—

Rodrigo is tired. No, more than tired—he's agotado. On the corriente to the capital, he is wedged between an indígena woman feeding her baby through an open zipper in her güipil and an unshaven man wearing a red baseball cap. Rodrigo holds the metal bar on the seat in front of him, and he knows the bar should be cold, it's always cold, but he doesn't feel it.

He can't help thinking about how Julia has given up on him—gone to the capital, found another novio—and how he could get off the corriente, go home and forget. Sleep. Forget. Sleep. But he imagines her standing behind a fence. All he has to do to reach her is leap it; it's only as tall as his chest. But his legs are like stiff boards. And his ankle is tender. It will never heal completely. After marching on it for two years, he understands this. So in front of the fence, he hesitates, worried about the pain he'll feel if he jumps. She notices his hesitation and frowns. He smiles, trying to reassure her. But Julia turns around and begins to walk away. "Wait!" he calls, but she doesn't hear him.

The corriente screeches and stops. Rodrigo sits up, jarred awake. A man sitting in front of him removes a costal from the overhead rack, throws it over his shoulder and steps off. The woman is asleep next to him, her baby cradled in her arms. Rodrigo has been sleeping on the woman's shoulder, as if she'd offered it, tenderly, in place of a pillow.

———

The building where Julia lives shoots up from the ground thicker and taller than any tree in the Petén jungle. Julia lives on the fifth floor; he found her address in a directory at the university library after entering the library from a service door in the basement. Now he stands to the side of the building, leaning against a red brick wall, waiting until he can follow someone in the door.

The people who enter are boys in red ties and white shirts and gray slacks and girls in white, beige and yellow dresses. They look cool and unruffled, even in the capital's heat. Rodrigo fears he cannot follow one of these well-dressed boys and girls into the building without provoking their suspicion. Rodrigo wears black slacks and a blue short-sleeve button-down shirt, but neither is new. He feels as large and menacing as he did in his soldier's uniform.

More people pass. He waits. The sky turns a deep blue. The stars emerge, tentative, like deer's eyes in brush. He gazes alternately at the pale stars and at the door, the light above it covered by a soccer-ball-sized globe. An old man, short and with spotted skin, steps up to the door and inserts a key. The man is wearing the dusty clothes of a casero. He clicks one lock open, then the second. Seeing his moment, Rodrigo creeps up behind him. When the man pushes open the door, Rodrigo trails him, his chest centimeters from the man's back. The man steps into the hallway, and Rodrigo sidesteps to his right and presses himself against the near wall. The man walks toward the stairs at the back of the hallway. He reaches them, puts his right foot on the first stair, then turns around and stares at Rodrigo.

"Why are you here?" the man asks loudly, as if he's lost his hearing. His front teeth fall over his lower lip in a grin that seems animal-like.

"I'm here to see my novia," Rodrigo says.

The man looks him over. "But if she is your novia, she would let you in the door herself."

"I'm surprising her. We haven't seen each other in two years."

Rodrigo feels like telling the man more—about how beautiful Julia is, about the two years in which he hasn't seen her, two years of sweat in the jungle, long marches, daydreams, nightmares. He feels like telling him about how sometimes her name alone, whispered again and again, was enough to keep him moving and hoping.

The man smiles. It's a warm smile. "Where have you been these two years?"

"The war."

He looks Rodrigo over.

"Which side?"

"The good side."

"There is no good side. You were a soldier."

"Yes."

"Against your will?"

Rodrigo hesitates. "Yes."

The man nods. "When I was taken, I was tending my father's cattle. We used to have a herd of twenty-six, the largest in our village. When I returned home after three years, we had no more cattle. My father was dead, and no one knew where my mother was. I found my sister living in an avocado tree in the mountains. Yes, in the tree itself, in a house she'd made from branches. She had a gun. She shot deer and squirrels to feed herself. She was fatter than I was." The man laughs. He looks Rodrigo over again. "I believe you," he says. "But if asked, I will say I have never seen you in my life."

He waves, a sort of salute, and marches up the stairs. Rodrigo hears the tread of his feet grow distant and disappear. Rodrigo's heartbeat quickens. He hasn't slept since his morning ride on the corriente. He spent three hours finding the campus. Twice, he took wrong city busses. One left him outside the city's basurero. He smelled the stench and saw the vultures at the same time. He'd never seen so many vultures; they formed five separate circles, each circle with a dozen birds, hovering over heaps of garbage.

He mounts the stairs and begins his climb to Julia's room. His heart knocks against his chest like it did in the jungle when, crouched behind a bush or a log, he had to distinguish a guerrilla's face from a square of sunlight; had to distinguish a guerrilla's footsteps from the scampering of monkeys across the jungle floor, the ruffling of wild turkeys' wings, the low, persistent grunts of tapirs. He opens the door onto the hallway of the fifth floor. He walks four steps and he's at her door, room 504. He lingers, afraid of what awaits him.

He inhales, exhales, inhales. He knocks on the door twice, standing stiff and straight as if he were a soldier again. The door opens. A woman stands in front of him, and he thinks it's Julia, changed completely in the two years since he's seen her: taller, plumper, lighter skinned. This shakes his resolve, but in the next second he knows it's not her. "Con permiso, señorita," he says. "I'm looking for Julia García."

The woman gives him a questioning glance before telling him to wait. She tries to close the door, but he sticks his foot into the doorway to stop her. He takes a step inside. He knows it's rude to enter without permission; he knows the woman might fear he's someone menacing—a thief, a rapist. But he can't help himself. After two years in the jungle, two years of whispering Julia's name, writing her name, dreaming of seeing her again, he is tired of waiting.

He walks toward the second woman in the room, the woman sitting at a desk against the far wall.

———

Looking up from her half-finished Mario Vargas Llosa novel, Julia sees him standing in the doorway. He looks the same as he did the day he first kissed her. But when he steps closer, moving under the ceiling light in the center of the room, he looks nothing like the boy she remembers. His face is badly shaven—tufts of hair spot his neck—his jaw is longer and his eyes are darker and more intense. Yet it is Rodrigo, and even as her heart surges in fear and anticipation, she feels a sense of calm. This, too, is God's will. She finds herself neither happy nor sad to see him because to be either would be to delight in or to rue the sun rising or the night falling. This was supposed to happen.

She sees Marisol dash out of the room.

She asks Rodrigo to sit down.

———

Rodrigo hesitates, having imagined their reunion differently. He expected her to rush toward him, the sight of him alone enough to call her back to the good life they dreamed of, their happiness instant and overwhelming. He takes a half step toward her, hoping she will see him, truly see him, and her cool, even gaze will soften with joy. But if he had been hoping for her delight, he also prepared for her caution and reserve. Another moment passes, and he does sit, in the hard chair next to her desk.

She is the same, he thinks; she has the same hair and eyes. Only her face is different, less round, less rosy.

"How are you, Rodrigo?" she asks.

Rodrigo has so much to tell her, but when he does speak, his words come with too much bluntness, as if he's speaking to a doctor after a battlefield injury: "I'm finished with the army. I can play soccer again. We can get married."

She doesn't respond to what he has said. Instead, she asks about his mother and brothers. He answers her quickly, waiting for her to tell him what he wants to hear, what he knows she still feels. She tells him about her father and his back problem. "He finds he can't work as hard or as long," she says. "He's seen the best doctors. They don't seem to help. It's funny. He thinks he got the injury from playing soccer."

She continues to talk, a rapid-fire catalogue of everyone they both know. She doesn't look at him, and he sees her shyness as proof of her love. This restores his confidence. When she says, "I'm engaged," her words seem coaxed, as if someone behind her had prompted her by whispering in her ear.

——

Rodrigo doesn't seem to hear her when she mentions her engagement or if he does, he ignores it, because he tells her he never stopped loving her. He loves her now. And she loves him—doesn't she?

Julia doesn't deny it. She thinks if she ever loved anyone it was Rodrigo, at least as he was the times he called her name from whatever place he'd found to hide. His words were as crisp and right as an order, and she drew toward him as if he was pulling her with a rope.

She doesn't say anything; she lets her eyes speak, hoping they say, *Yes, I'll go with you back to the time we had. I'll be the girl I was if you will be the boy.*

There is a silence before Rodrigo asks, "Did you get my letters?"

"One," she says.

"I must have written you a hundred. Some I sent. Some I wrote with sticks on the ground. Some I wrote to you in my head when I was marching." He pauses. "Do you love me?" he asks.

"I love…" she begins, starting the light, sweet routine she used to tease him with when they'd sit together on her couch. But she catches herself. For a long time, she doesn't say anything. It's as if she's deciding what to do. But she knows the decision isn't hers. It's all in God's hands. *We are boats and He is the river. We have no paddles. We have no sails. We follow his current.*

Rodrigo leans toward her and reaches for her hand.

Good, his eyes seem to say. Good, it's settled. And, a moment later, she finds herself held aloft in his arms, and she readies herself to be carried like this all the way home.

—

"I'm all right now," he says. "I'm cured. I'm as fast as ever. I'm as strong as ever."

He holds her aloft with ease. "You know how much I love you, how much I've always loved you. I've never stopped. And you, too—I can see it. I know you love me too."

As she is suspended above him, he imagines the years ahead, seized again, pulled from the chaos of jungle and bullets and sweat and blood. Everything will be as it once was, as it should be.

Behind him, he hears a stampede of heavy feet.

—

She hears the boys' breathing before she sees them. They are like bulls in a corral. She wants to close the door, but it is open wide, and she sees them charge toward the two of them. They are bulls. They are wild; they are angry.

—

Rodrigo feels arms reach around his waist. Someone cuffs his ear. Julia is out of his arms now, standing at a distance. He wonders how she could have gone so quickly from him. He feels himself being dragged to the door. He jams an elbow into a boy's stomach and the boy stumbles into a lamp. Another boy wrenches Rodrigo's right arm behind his back. He tries to break the boy's hold, but another boy grabs him around the neck. There are at least four boys against him.

Rodrigo remembers how at Finca Mundial the soldiers led him into the truck, how they pressed his hands to his sides until the truck was moving.

—

Julia wants to speak, to tell the boys to let Rodrigo go, but when she opens her mouth, nothing comes. It is perfect silence. When, at last, she finds words—"Stop! Por favor, stop! Animals!"—the boys have dragged Rodrigo out the door.

Rodrigo marches, his eyes staring straight ahead, his shoes scuffing the hallway's thin, gray carpet. He knows he can't outfight them. More boys join them in the hallway. A tall, light-skinned boy with gray eyes and a hint of a mustache appears, and the boys guarding Rodrigo stop, their fingers biting into his arms. The tall boy stares into Rodrigo's eyes.

"I don't know who you are," he says, his teeth clenched. "But you better not come here any more. Do you understand me, vos?"

Rodrigo isn't afraid of the tall boy, who cannot weigh two-thirds of what he does. His voice is too high to intimidate or frighten. Showing his disdain, Rodrigo smiles at him.

"Joto!" the boy shouts at Rodrigo. "Hueco!" The insults seem silly, child-like. In the army Rodrigo has been called worse than a fag.

—

Marisol looks at Julia, no doubt expecting gratitude, as if she'd pulled Julia from a rushing river. Julia's lips are pursed and her head bobs in a slow, continuous nod. Marisol is waiting to hear Julia's words of thanks. What she hears is: "He was the best soccer player in our town."

Marisol, expecting more, says nothing. For a long time, silence. Marisol releases a breath. A moment later, she asks, "Was he the boy you were going to marry?"

Julia doesn't need to answer. She drops her head into her hands and cries.

—

Rodrigo is moving again, down the steps. Outside the building, they shove him, face first, onto the cement. He struggles, but they have his arms locked behind his back. He hears the boys shout, and he knows what's coming. He feels it wet and warm on his hair. "What a good latrine we have," one boy says, and they all laugh.

Rodrigo breaks the hold on his right arm and spins onto someone's shoes. He grabs a boy's leg and pulls him onto the ground. He feels other hands claw his back, and he throws back his elbow, finding something solid and feeling it give. He stands, and the boys, all of them on their feet, run to the door. He stalks after them, too tired to reach them. Someone must have been holding the door open, because they are inside the building quickly, protected by the twin locks. The boys peer at Rodrigo through the heavy glass door, and although they continue to shout insults at him, he can see fear in their eyes. He knows that if given a fair chance, he would beat them all.

Rodrigo turns and walks away, his nostrils assaulted by the smell of urine in his hair.

——

Julia covers her face with her hands, pressing them hard against her eyes. But even in the blackness in front of her, she sees Rodrigo, a soccer ball tucked beneath his arm, asking her to come play with him.

She isn't finished crying when Oscar comes into her room. He puts his arm around her and she allows herself to cry into his chest.

"It's all right, Julia, he's gone."

A moment later, with her tears slowing, he asks, "Who is he?"

Julia doesn't answer.

"Who is he?" Oscar asks again.

It is Marisol who replies: "He's a soldier. He's in love with Julia."

— 17 —

Rodrigo stays at the Hotel Ajau, a four-story brick building next to the Monja Blanca bus terminal in zona una. He has a room on the rooftop. There are two beds in his room above the slate-colored floor, and he tries to sleep first in one, then the other. He hears a pair of foreign lovers—Americans, he guesses—talking in the room next to his, their speech interrupted by the wet, deep sound of kisses.

He'd seen them on his return from Julia's dormitory. The man is tall and brown-haired with a large, thick nose. The woman is blond and blue-eyed. He wonders why they're here, in a cheap hotel with mold on the walls. They should be staying at El Camino or El Dorado in zona diez, where most tourists stay. He knows they're not poor. Perhaps they are the kind of Americans who think it is romantic to pretend to be poor.

He is too tired to listen long to their lovemaking, but as he falls into dreams, he hears what sounds like a cat's cry or the slice of chalk against a blackboard—no, the cocking of a rifle—and he is awake, thinking he is in the jungle again. He hears the sound again. It is only their bed, scarping against the floor, screeching their love.

— 18 —

Julia cannot sleep. Oscar left her room late, satisfied, at last, after hearing her disclaim any lingering interest in Rodrigo, after hearing her proclaim that she loves only him.

She knows she told him less than the truth. "I love Rodrigo." She tries this on her lips, a whisper. Louder: "I love Rodrigo."

Or is it this: "I loved Rodrigo"?

Who is Rodrigo now?

Who am I now?

In the dark, her room is unfamiliar, the proportions of its furniture—her bed-side table, her chair, her dresser—larger, the walking space smaller. But even if she were to turn on the light, she fears she would find the scene disorienting, the room narrow and confining and strange. She wonders how quickly she got here, to this turbulent life, when a few years ago, in Santa Cruz, her life seemed as languid and easy and unvarying as the afternoon chipi-chipi.

When she thinks of Rodrigo now it is as he was in that life, a vibrant, happy part of what seemed unalterable, forever secure. And to have him come to her today and, before her eyes, be broken and hauled out of her room like a criminal was to see her own past, with its promise forever ahead of it, be, in a violent instant, annulled.

When she cries now, softly, so as not to alarm Marisol, it is for Rodrigo and for what he must have suffered in the war and suffered tonight. But the greater part is for herself and for what of her life cannot be reclaimed, for what of her life is already gone.

— 19 —

The next morning, Rodrigo takes his urine-smelling shirt to the pila on the first floor and washes it, scrubbing it with hand soap. After rinsing it, he rings it out as best he can and returns to the roof. He hangs the shirt on the clothesline where the maids have hung bath towels. He has brought only one shirt, one pair of pants, one pair of underwear and one pair of socks. He didn't think he would need more. He hadn't been thinking beyond seeing Julia. This seemed its own end, sufficient, final. He was sure he could convince her to return with him to Santa Cruz. If all had gone as he'd hoped, they would have left on the late afternoon corriente.

But now he needs a new shirt; he doesn't want to wait until his old one dries. He walks down the three flights of stairs bare-chested and passes the woman with the long jaw who sits behind the counter beside the front door. She frowns. He steps onto the street, into the bright day. He doesn't have to go far to find a shirt. A Ropa Americana store is on the corner of the next block, and from the piles of clothing on the floor, he picks out two shirts he likes, one yellow with black stripes and the other purple with buttons down the collar and an eagle emblem on the breast. The two shirts cost him five quetzals.

The army gave him two hundred and fifty quetzals when he finished. He has already spent thirty-eight—seven on food during his trip back to Santa Cruz, ten on the corriente to the capital, ten on the room, four on lunch, two on city busses and now five on two shirts. Still, he feels rich, and he decides he wants breakfast, although it's almost noon.

There's a comedor across the street from Ropa Americana, and he orders eggs and beans and coffee. The woman brings them to him quickly, as if guessing his hunger. After he eats, he feels he could eat five more platefuls without being anything less than starved.

He decides he'll have a beer. Beer always satisfies him. Even jungle villages that could be accessed only on narrow, winding paths had cantinas or tiendas that sold Gallo and Venado. The officers frequently sent their soldiers down such curious paths to find liquor. On one occasion, the pair of soldiers they sent never returned, and the officers didn't know whether they'd run off or been killed.

Rodrigo remembers when he and Ubaldo, a fellow soldier, went on one of these missions, setting out before sunset into thick jungle. They walked until their uniforms were soaked with rain and sweat. After what Rodrigo guessed was more than five kilometers, the path broke into a clearing where there was a cluster of houses. The first house they came to had a door made of bamboo. Ubaldo wanted to bash it down, but Rodrigo pushed it gently open. Ubaldo shone a flashlight into the darkness; three women—two young with smooth skin, the other old with gray hair—were sleeping in a single bed. They did not wake. Rodrigo pointed his rifle at the three women as Ubaldo shouted, "Get up." When they woke up and saw the two soldiers, they screamed.

"No, no, no," Rodrigo said. "We need liquor. The lieutenant sent us. We'll pay."

It was several minutes before the women calmed down. Finally, the old woman asked them to please step outside the house; she needed to dress. Ubaldo insisted that he and Rodrigo remain—"They might be guerrillas," he told Rodrigo, "they'll kill us"—but Rodrigo convinced him that the women were harmless. A minute later, the old woman led them to another house and woke up another old woman. The second woman led them to a wooden shack. It had plenty of liquor, and Rodrigo and Ubaldo spent all the money the lieutenant had given them.

Before they returned through the jungle, Rodrigo and Ubaldo drank a frasco of whiskey each, then shared another during their walk. Between sips, they mimicked the monkey howls. When they arrived back at camp, the lieutenant saw they were drunk, and he slammed the butt of his rifle against Ubaldo's knees. He was about to do the same to Rodrigo, but he stopped, saying, "Your legs are weak enough already, vos. I don't want anyone having to carry you." Rodrigo and Ubaldo watched the officers drink themselves into quietness.

In the comedor in the capital, Rodrigo's beer lasts only a few minutes. Unsatisfied, he orders another and then a third. Even after a fourth beer, he fails to achieve the feeling he likes. He considers ordering a fifth beer, but decides to leave. The bill is twenty quetzals.

He takes a bus to the university and sits in its central plaza under a statue of Simon Bolivar, watching students come and go. Two girls with long legs and short, shining hair look at him, stop and smile. He stands and approaches them. "Excuse me. Do you know Julia García?"

They frown, disappointed at the mention of another woman, and shake their heads. Yet they wait, as if expecting him to say more. He doesn't oblige them.

The afternoon passes. He asks two more women, walking together with books pressed to their chests, and a boy on a bicycle who stops to rest in the shade beneath the statue, but they don't know Julia either. The boy tells him at length about his own novia, a woman named Lesbia, who two weeks before lost her virginity to him. "And now I don't want to marry her," the boy says, shaking his head. "And I promised. What an ugly situation, no?"

Rodrigo thinks about telling his own story to the boy, but the boy shrugs, hops on his bicycle and pedals off.

He decides to wait again by the door of Julia's dormitory, to risk another encounter with the pack of boys. He walks away from the statue and onto a narrow street, past the men selling blank cassettes and batteries out of dirty cardboard boxes, past the women selling plastic bags full of peanuts and mangoes. He turns down another street and finds himself heading toward the happy, swirling lights of Cantina Real.

It's dark inside. Round tables are covered with plastic red and white tablecloths advertising Rubio cigarettes. It's five in the afternoon, and he's the only one in the cantina. A short woman with bleached streaks in her long hair steps out of a back room. He hears a baby crying behind her.

He asks for a bottle of Gallo and a frasco of Venado. She brings them to him and asks him to pay now, explaining that she has to look after her baby. After he pays the woman five quetzals, she goes again to the back room, and the baby stops crying. Rodrigo hears cars rattle outside the front door. He taps his fingers on the tablecloth. Drinks. Taps. He looks at his watch. Quarter after five. Drinks. Drinks. Drinks.

"María," he calls toward the back room. "María!"

The woman doesn't come. He again shouts, "María!"

She comes, and he hears the baby cry. He hates the lonely sound of a baby's cry. He asks for another Gallo and another Venado.

"Go to your baby," he tells the woman after she serves him, although what he thought he would say to her was: Stay here and talk with me. This time, she doesn't ask him to pay in advance.

Two men in shirts opened to their bellybuttons come in, greet Rodrigo and sit at the table across from his. "María!" the heavier of the men yells, and the woman appears again. Again, the baby cries, and Rodrigo covers his ears.

After the men have ordered, Rodrigo requests another beer. When the woman brings the beer to him, he pays his bill. He drinks quickly, knowing how late it is. One of the men says, "She had eyes like in the song." The man sings, off key and fumbling over the words: "How enchanting your eyes, woman, beneath your night-black eyebrows." He smiles. "And she was rich, hombre. She had the best clothes—Italian clothes. She didn't need me to buy her anything. Besides, she didn't want clothes from me. She didn't want jewelry."

"What did she want?"

"You know."

The other man laughs in mockery. "Liar."

"True, hombre. All true. We took a little holiday to Puerto Barrios, rented a room overlooking the sea. We had a king-sized bed, nice and soft. But we didn't sleep, hombre. You know we didn't sleep."

The other man laughs again and shakes his head. "You're lying, vos."

"It's true, hombre. All true." He laughs as if he is, in fact, lying.

Rodrigo stands, says goodbye to the men, steps outside. The sky has turned a deep blue; the stars are faint but warming. Remembering Julia, he turns up the street and runs. At the intersection, he forgets to watch for cars. One screams to a stop. The driver, a white-eyed man with a mustache, leans out of his window and yells profanity at him.

Rodrigo waves an apology and keeps running. After a minute or two, he stops, wondering where he is. He looks around. The streetlights above him come on suddenly, as if he'd woken them up. He races down another street, turns left, walks through a park, jogs down another street and then stops in front of Julia's building. It's almost seven o'clock. He sits on a bench in a patch of grass to the side of the entrance. No one walks by for a long time.

Finally, the old casero comes, wearing the same dusty uniform. Rodrigo stands, grateful to have a friend again. He smiles at him. The man doesn't smile back.

"Let's go in," he tells the man.

The man shakes his head and frowns. "They told me about you."

"Who?" Rodrigo asks, although he knows.

The man shakes his head again. Rodrigo says, "I've loved her my whole life. She's my fiancée." He feels something catch in his throat. "Her father never liked me."

The man is shaking his head as if he's heard the story before, but Rodrigo presses on: "I played soccer. I was good. I was magnifico. Here." He jukes left, dances right, swings his leg to kick. "See? But I twisted my ankle, ripped the muscles in my leg." He bends down to touch his right ankle, as if telling the man weren't enough. "I had to stop playing. I needed work. I worked on a coffee finca."

The man is still shaking his head. His head is slightly bowed, and Rodrigo sees the brown shine of the man's bald spot. "One day, the army came. They took me." He can't stop himself. He sobs—once, twice. "I was a soldier."

The man lifts his head to look at him. His look is hard and straight. "I know," the man says. "Believe me, I know. But this is my job, mi hijo." He walks toward the door and inserts the key.

"You know?" Rodrigo asks, speaking to the man's back. "You know what?"

The man doesn't answer, but clicks open the second lock and pushes in the door. Rodrigo rushes toward the man and jumps on his back, knocking him to the floor. He punches the man twice on the shoulder, then grabs the man by the ears and lifts his head. "What the hell do you know, stupid old man?" Rodrigo says. He crushes the man's face against the floor.

At the back of the hallway, a girl is standing at the bottom of the staircase. He thinks it's Julia, so he approaches her. She screams, turns and races up the stairs. "Wait!" he calls, but when he reaches the foot of the stairs, she's gone. He thinks about climbing the steps to Julia's room. At the same time, he imagines what awaits him—the gang of boys, intent on hurting him even more than they did the day before. It doesn't matter. He'll beat them. He begins to climb the stairs.

But above him he hears a flurry of footsteps and angry, excited shouts. Rodrigo turns around. The casero is kneeling on the floor of the hallway, as if in prayer. There is a streak of blood in front of him.

Rodrigo runs past the casero and out the door. He turns right down the street, races into a park, cuts down another street and stands before another cantina, its red lights soft and beating like a heart. He catches his breath. He is exhausted and dizzy. He feels his stomach cramp, and he wants to vomit, but he can't and his inability makes him frustrated and angry. His stomach twists, and he curls over, his balance thrown off. He catches himself against the hood of a car. He feels his stomach rise and fall, and then quickly he feels what he's eaten and drunk race to his throat and onto the car hood. He falls to his knees. Clutching his stomach, he puts his head against the tire. He closes his eyes and vomits again and falls asleep.

A car horn wakes him. He wipes his mouth with the bottom of his shirt and stands. Looking around, he sees a man and woman walking toward him. He walks swiftly away from the car. In the park, he sits on a bench, feeling relieved but exhausted. He remembers what he failed to do. He glances around the park. It's empty. Cars pass on all four sides, their yellow lights slicing the gray night.

He decides he'll stand across the street from Julia's window. He'll wait for her and hope she notices him, hope she calls down to him. All he needs is one word from her, his name or some simple affirmation, to keep fighting. He saw a movie in which a boy waited under a girl's window to prove his love and win hers. The boy waited in the rain and in the heat and under the ferocious glare of the moon. Rodrigo had seen the movie in Santa Cruz, projected onto a cracked wall inside Don Armando's pharmacy, and as the boy in the film endured his vigil, the audience shouted their mocking advice: "Find another muchacha, fool!" "She's ugly, vos!" "Go pay a puta!" The cracks on the wall made the boy's face appear lined with age.

But, in the end, the girl did come to him, didn't she?

Rodrigo walks to the side of Julia's building, stands in a bath of streetlight and stares up at her dark window. No light comes on. No voice calls down to him. He stands until his legs wobble from fatigue. He whispers her name, then shouts it.

—

Julia sees him from her window, standing under a streetlight, looking up at her room like a dog from under the table. She feels like a princess in a fairy tale, locked in a high tower. But if a part of her would like to push open her window and climb a rope of hair down to the street and run off with Rodrigo into the night, another part of her keeps her in place, keeps her silent. She knows if she left with Rodrigo her father or Oscar would find her and return her to where she is now.

Today her father called to ask her if Rodrigo had been to see her, and she'd lied to him. But he'd called Oscar and Oscar hadn't lied. When her father called her again, she had to confess, and her father said if Rodrigo came to see her again, he would come to the capital and do to Rodrigo more harm than Oscar and his friends had done. At this, Julia cried, alarmed at his threat of violence. With such little provocation and often with glee, men turn to their fists and machetes and guns to stop what they want stopped or to achieve what they want done. Their willingness to fight, their very joy in the prospect, seems endless, which is why, she knows, the war has gone on for more than three decades and continues, ruining families and villages and sending thousands of boys to early deaths and turning other thousands into monsters.

She didn't want her father's martial bluster. She wanted him to ask her how she was feeling about Rodrigo's return and what she thought of marrying Oscar now. She wanted him to heed his religion and find pity and kindness for Rodrigo. But all she could say to him, her voice a mix of protest and tears, was, "You don't understand me."

He said, "Believe me, Julia, Rodrigo is ruined. He came to our house and your mother talked to him and I saw him leave. He was limping. His injury isn't healed. And I know what happens to soldiers. They have done the vilest deeds and, because they've been rewarded for what they've done, they think their behavior is normal and good. What he did in the war he'll do to whomever he sees."

His voice turned more tender: "You are safe, Julia. Oscar will protect you, and if you need me, I will come. I'll leave my work, my work doesn't matter, it will keep. You matter more to me than anyone in the world."

She cried at this, too, because this was the father she had always adored and believed in, the man who offered her safety and love. How could she resent a man who loved her like this? It was like resenting God for making the world the way He had.

She cried at her confusion.

Sitting in front of her window, she cannot bear to look at Rodrigo anymore. She falls onto her bed and thinks how she might leave her window on wings made of her talent and desire and faith and fly into the night and toward what she wants, toward herself, toward freedom. Wherever they are. Whatever they are.

— 20 —

At the hotel, Rodrigo has a hard time climbing the three flights of stairs to the roof. On the second floor, he pauses to sit on the stairwell. The two gringos step out of the public shower. The man wears a hotel towel around his waist, barely large enough to cover him. The woman is wrapped in her own towel, pink with small gray elephants on it. Wet, her hair is not blond but reddish. It clings tightly to her skull and neck. Rodrigo is too tired to move, and the two lovers separate in order to walk past him. Busy whispering in their language, they say nothing to him.

When he reaches his bed, he's too tired to listen for their lovemaking. He wakes at noon to the screeching of their bed.

— 21 —

On the third night after Rodrigo's visit, Oscar sits with Julia in her living room. He talks about who will be coming to their wedding and what bands will play— a marimba band and a popular music band and even a punta band, Los Hijos del Futuro, from the Caribbean—although the two of them, honoring their faith, won't dance. Three times, she interrupts their conversation, feigning to have to use the bathroom but actually going to her room to look down at the street. The third time, Rodrigo is gone, and she is startled to see the empty pool of yellow light where he was standing.

"What's wrong?" Oscar asks her when she returns to the living room.

She says she isn't feeling well. This doesn't stop Oscar from kneeling at her feet and wrapping his arms around her. With Marisol gone to visit Gerardo, he knows they have privacy. But, as usual, she rebuffs his advances. Ever since what happened on the volcano, she has given him no more than kisses. She half expected him to lose interest in her after their volcano climb. But her coolness toward him has had the opposite effect. He is more ardent than ever, and on several occasions, he has begged her to marry him sooner than their wedding date.

She no longer asks herself if she loves him. The answer to this question used to vary depending on her mood and the time of day and what memories intruded on her thinking. Now it's unimportant. They will be married on October 7th.

To enhance his frustration, she allows him only a kiss on the cheek before he leaves. He exits her room with the heavy tread of a beggar sent off without a centavo or a piece of bread.

Immediately, she returns to the window. She finds the same empty spot of light. She watches the spot until the night grows even blacker around it and she hears

Marisol come home. At some point, she falls asleep, but it doesn't impede her view. In front of her closed eyes is the empty spot of light, burning, burning.

— 22 —

Every day, Rodrigo sits under the statue of Simon Bolivar, hoping to see Julia pass, but each day it's for less time. On his fifth day in the capital, he sits for only half an hour before he walks to Cantina Real. The woman brings her baby out as she serves him his drinks. At a corner table, she breastfeeds her son. She smiles when she sees Rodrigo looking at her. "Do you work near here?" she asks him.

"No," he says. "I'm a soccer player. I play in Cobán, for the Imperials."

She looks him over, as if deciding whether to believe him.

"We're playing tomorrow against Los Rojos in El Estadio Nacional."

She says, "I went to the stadium once, three years ago, to see a game. The stadium was filled. I had to stand up the entire game."

"I always play in front of big crowds," Rodrigo says.

He doesn't know whether the woman believes him; he thinks she doesn't. Nevertheless, she moves with her baby to the table across from his. The place is dark and empty and smells of spilt beer and mold.

The woman's cheeks are bright pink, sun-tinged, which Rodrigo finds strange because he pictures her confined to the dark cantina all day. "Is this your first child?" he asks her.

"No," she says, looking down at the baby. She looks at Rodrigo. "I mean, this isn't my baby. He is my sister's. My sister cannot feed him, so I am feeding him."

Rodrigo finishes his beer.

"I had a baby," she says, looking away, "but he died. He was my first."

"I'm sorry," he says. "But this baby will love you like a mother."

"Yes, but when he returns to my sister, he will forget what I gave him."

"He won't," Rodrigo says. "He will have two mothers." Rodrigo pauses. "What does your husband think of your sacrifice?" he asks her.

She doesn't reply. Instead, she moves closer to him. With one arm, she cradles the now sleeping baby against her chest. With her free hand, she reaches to take the bottle from in front of him. On its way, her hand touches his; it lingers a moment. He is startled by how good her fingers feel. As if by instinct, his left hand begins to reach for her. He is about to cover her hand with his own when he remembers why he is in the capital.

Her hand leaves his hand. She goes to sit across from him again. She asks him about soccer and he tells her all he can remember and invent about his time with the Imperials.

— 23 —

Tonight he waits under the streetlight outside Julia's window until he feels his legs quiver from fatigue. This will be his last night in the capital, and he prays to God that she will see him, that she will come down from her room, that she will rush into his arms. But it is a mechanical praying, tired prayers without hope. And even as he waits, he thinks about the woman in Cantina Real. He thinks about how nice her hand felt. He thinks about how nice her body would feel pressed against his.

Because he is thinking of the woman in Cantina Real and not thinking of Julia, he knows God will not reward him. God will keep Julia locked in her room. He will suffer on the street all night because he is thinking of a woman besides Julia.

But if you would come to me, Julia, I would think only of you now and forever.

At Rodrigo's feet are three bottles of whiskey. He paid for two; the woman in Cantina Real gave him the other as a gift. He is glad to have the extra bottle. He needs to fortify himself against the silence of Julia's window.

Another memory returns to him: the woman from the feria. With heaviness and regret, as if recalling a crime for which he escaped punishment, he remembers the words of love he spoke to her, remembers what they did on the floor in the back room of Don Federico's cantina. Yet even as he wishes he had never stepped into the room, had never lain with her on the cold floor, he remembers the way she held him when he was done, keeping him inside her and running a finger softly up and down his neck. It was he, at last, who broke their bond, who pulled away.

— 24 —

Julia cannot sleep. *I am not a princess trapped in a tower.* She thinks of Lilian and Alejandra, and she knows they would never be so cowardly as to leave someone they used to love—or love still—in the dark, in the silence of the street. They would offer him kindness. They would ask him what he saw and suffered in the war. They would listen to his stories.

And if after he tells me everything he has done, everything horrible and boring and frightening and sad—and if after I tell him about everything I've done, about Oscar and the night on the volcano—if after all this, he wants to kiss me, and I want him to kiss me…

Julia peaks past her blinds and sees Rodrigo standing in the streetlight, bringing a bottle to his lips. She remembers him on the sidelines in El Estadio Imperial draining a water bottle into his mouth. She remembers him looking up at her, waving at her as if she were the only person in the stadium. "Wait," she whispers to him, and she rushes toward her door. Softly, so as not to wake Marisol, she opens it. As softly, she closes it.

She runs down the steps, swinging her body around the landings so quickly, she is dizzy by the time she reaches the ground floor. Here, she stops. There is an old man, the building's casero, pushing a mop across the floor. Under the weak light bulbs, the tile floor looks like burned gold.

The casero stops his mopping to look at her. She sees the bruises on his face, the dried blood at the corner of his lips. "It is late, señorita," he says.

"I know."

"You have someone to see?"

She nods. She doesn't need his permission to pass; nevertheless, she remains where she is, but whether out of politeness or because she is concerned he would stop her, she isn't sure. He isn't her father or Oscar, but she doesn't move.

"I think I know who you want to see," the casero says. "The soldier." The casero points to his bruised face. "I have him to thank for this."

"You must be thinking of someone else."

"He wanted to see you. It was my job to stop him."

"Rodrigo wouldn't hurt anyone…anyone who…" Julia pauses, knowing she cannot speak with certainty about Rodrigo anymore.

"The war makes strangers of people we know well," the casero says. "Better to return upstairs, to the room and bed you know."

An anger Julia has felt before in the presence of her father and Oscar rises in her again. It is anger at their presumption, their certainty that they know what is best for her. Now even this stranger—this stranger with a mop—would presume to direct her life.

Without answering, Julia bursts past him, pushes open the door, and rushes outside. She sprints left, to the south side of the building. She sees the streetlight and, beneath it, nothing.

No, something—three empty Venado bottles. She lifts one of the bottles. The smell assaults her. She returns the bottle to the sidewalk. She remembers Rodrigo's father from long ago, sleeping in a doorway of the closed market in Santa Cruz, flies crowded around his mouth and eyes.

There is a distant car horn. Nearer, there is a woman's voice singing in a foreign language.

Julia looks into the night, but the night is all she sees.

— 25 —

It is Saturday, and Rodrigo has only enough money left for a bus ticket. The last corriente leaves the capital at four p.m. He decides to visit the statue of Simon Bolivar a last time.

Stunningly, Julia is here, in the long stretch of grass across from the statue. She is with her friends, and they are sitting on chairs set up for a marimba concert. Rodrigo walks to the edge of the grass and stares at her from under an orange tree. The boys in her group have noticed him, however, and the tallest of them, the gray-eyed boy with the hint of a mustache, stands and gestures toward his pocket. He pulls up his fingers in the shape of a gun.

Julia isn't looking at Rodrigo but at the marimba band, its members dressed in tuxedoes and red bow ties. The band begins to play, its sound amplified by microphones. The music is quick, furious even. Rodrigo remembers the sound of bullets in the jungle, the stinging sound of bullets in the air. He wanted to be so small, he wanted to be invisible. Now he wants to be huge, to be as big as this orange tree. He wants to be unmistakable, unavoidable. *Look at me, Julia,* he begs softly. *Look at me and see how much I love you.*

He waits a long time, but she stares straight ahead at the marimba band. *It's all right, Julia,* he thinks, turning from her. *It's all right. I'll play soccer again. And I'll come back here with the Imperials, and on the night before our game I'll wait for you under the streetlight. And this time, you'll come to me.*

He sees a fallen orange. He traps it between his feet, dribbles it from his right foot to his left. *See, I can play again.* He dribbles it from his left foot to his right. He stops, pulls his foot back and shoots the orange high into the sky. It catches against the deep blue of the sky and hangs in the air like a miniature sun, glowing.

See, he says. *See.* Before the sun falls. *See?*

FOUR

— 1 —

In their house on the outskirts of Quetzaltenango, Julia is drawn to the large sunroom on the second floor with its view of apple orchards. Oscar's father had seen such a room in a mansion he visited in Italy and decided he wanted a similar room in the house he was building his son and future daughter-in-law. During their first week home after their honeymoon in Costa Rica, a trip marred by Oscar's being scratched by a monkey in Manuel Antonio Park, Julia insisted they eat all their meals in the sunroom. Octavia, their muchacha, serves the meals on blue plates from France.

Sitting in her sunlit perch, Julia thinks about the unlikeliness of her presence here. If she'd had foresight and had confided to her girlhood friends about what was to come, they would have called her loca and, laughing, told her to keep dreaming. But the same girls, Lorena and Erica and María del Luz, came to her wedding, riding on the bus Oscar's father had rented to take them from Santa Cruz to Quetzaltenango. They had sat in subdued silence during the service, and only when the marimba band had finished its first set and given way to Los Hijos del Futuro (the dreadlocked lead singer urging everyone, especially the Evangelicals present, to dance) did she see them smile, relax, laugh. She and Oscar didn't dance, but she wished she could have joined her three friends and formed the fourth part of their circle as they swirled around the dance floor.

Her happy mood carried into her honeymoon, and she thought having the sunroom, with its elevated view, would help her sustain it. But now, with Oscar gone to Puerto Barrios to investigate opening a Burger King, she feels a heaviness sink inside her. She knows this mood; it's persistent and enervating.

Today she stands for an hour at the window, gazing at the distant hills. They have been stripped of trees, and their deforested peaks remind her of the heads of vultures. They are not the dense green hills of Alta Verapaz, the rainforests and cloud forests around Santa Cruz. Quetzaltenango is more populated than Alta Verapaz, and the people here have been more successful in dominating nature. Their dominance leaves her feeling stripped of mystery and music. Where, she wonders, do the birds go to sing?

— 2 —

Forty-eight hours into his trip to Puerto Barrios, Oscar calls to tell Julia he will be gone another few days. He hasn't found a suitable location for a Burger King, but there is a hotel he thinks might be a good investment. In the background, she hears what sounds like the beating of waves against sand and a high voice shouting playful endearments. Attempting a joke, she asks," Are you cavorting with the mermaids?" But there is static on the line, and when it clears, he has hung up.

Oscar's mother, Doña Felipa, a short, slim woman with strings of gray in her long brown hair, visits her the next day, and they drink coffee and eat sweet bread in the sunroom. After a few minutes of talk about Julia's honeymoon, she says, "You must be careful about the cleanliness of people here. I don't know what people are like where you come from, but here they are dirty."

Julia sits up in her chair. "How are they dirty?"

"They never wash their hands. Everything they touch is dirty." She sighs. "When I go to the panadería in the morning, I am always the first to arrive. I can assume the girl behind the counter bathes before she starts work—her face always looks scrubbed—and I don't want her touching anything before she picks up my bread. And I always bring exact change because money is the dirtiest object of all, and I don't want her giving me any soiled bills."

Julia says, "But your own money must be dirty, too, if it has been touched by hands other than yours."

"I have the maids wash it," Doña Felipa says. "My husband thinks I'm loca, but he gets sick more often than I do—coughs and flu and who knows what else—and it's because he touches dirty money. Every afternoon the maids wash every bill I have, and when they're dry—I have a special screen to dry them on—I put them in my purse." She sips her coffee and eats a piece of sweet bread.

"I'll have a screen built for you," Doña Felipa says. "You'll be healthier, and that's especially important when you have children." She glances speculatively at

Julia's stomach. "There are some tasks I can trust the maids to perform," Doña Felipa says. "I allow them to go to the market and buy our food because the food will be cooked and the heat will burn away the germs. But I cannot trust them to buy clean bread. This I must do myself, even if I am getting older and it is an effort to go to the panadería."

She gives Julia a solemn look. "Perhaps you and I could alternate buying the bread. I could trust you to be first in line at the panadería in the morning, couldn't I?"

Julia must have nodded because Oscar's mother beams. "Very good. Thank you, mi hija."

— 3 —

Rodrigo is surprised by the number of men who greet him fondly, pat him on the back, speak to him reverently of his soccer days. Don Laurindo remembers his goal against Puerto Barrios. "You kicked it from twenty-five meters," he says, sitting with Rodrigo, Don Hector and Don Adolfo in El Dragón. "The goalie tried to stop it. Mula. The ball broke his hand."

Don Hector remembers his assist against Escuintla. "The score was tied," he says. They are drinking Venado as if it were water and they were thirsty on a hot day. "You kicked the ball into the clouds. It disappeared." He laughs, showing yellow teeth above his black beard. "We were wondering if some angel stole it. But then it fell on Mateo Rey's spikes. Remember? It was like God dropped it there."

Don Adolfo remembers nothing in particular, only him dribbling up the field and dancing past defenders as if they were no more mobile than trees. This is the image Rodrigo likes best, his effortless ease with the ball, his grace and his dominance of lesser players. He drinks the clear, tasteless Venado and thinks how magnificent he was. He drinks and smiles. Drinks and laughs. You were magnífico, he hears them tell him and he tells himself.

Women seem less interested in his soccer career, although this isn't true of Clara, a heavyset, light-skinned woman who lives with her infant daughter in a small block house on Calle Tres de Mayo. Clara used to be Pedro's novia, although Pedro assured Rodrigo that Clara's daughter isn't his.

Clara grows tomatoes and corn in her backyard and makes lunches of tamales with beans or chipilín, which she sells in the market to the men who have neither the time nor the money to go to a comedor. Sometimes Rodrigo comes to buy from her, and he always stops to talk with her. When she asks what were his favorite games, he mentions the games the old men remember, and he describes them the way they described them, in the wistful poetry of old age, and she smiles and looks at him with affection.

On most mornings he works scouting forests for a lumber company in Cobán, a job Pedro helped him find. It is hard work to hike beyond the villages of Pambach and El Palmar and villages he doesn't know the names of. When he finds a suitable forest, he asks in the nearest village who the owner is. Usually the owner lives in the capital. He returns to the company's office and submits to his jefe the name of the forest's owner, and sometimes the company cuts down the forest he has found and sometimes it doesn't. When it does, Rodrigo works a gas-powered chainsaw, trimming branches from tree trunks. Sweating and filled with sawdust, he finds he misses Clara.

One day, he visits Clara in the market after lunch. She has finished selling, although she still has a few tamales in her bucket. He offers to carry her bucket to her house, and she accepts shyly, her face turned from him.

On the short walk to her house, the rain falling light and cool, he tells her he still wants to play professional soccer. "But you're hurt," she says.

"I can still play," he insists, and he believes it, or wants to, and he sees she does too, or pretends to.

"Where would you play?"

"Maybe I'll play on a team in town to prepare myself."

"It'll take a little time," she says.

"And when I play in town, the Imperials will hear about it and they'll want me back."

Clara smiles. "They'll see you're as good as before."

They reach her door. Politely, he hands her the bucket. She takes it and lets it dangle between them. A moment passes, and she asks, "Would you like to come inside to eat tamales?"

He nods, his smile wide. "Yes, thank you."

Her invitation into her house is as good as an invitation into her bed, and they both know this. She tells him to wait outside until her grandmother leaves. Her grandmother, who is taking care of Clara's daughter, lives two blocks from Clara's house.

Clara points to the house across the street. "Please stand over there, Rodrigo. Pretend you're waiting for a bus." She goes inside.

The bus comes before Clara's grandmother leaves the house. The bus spits black smoke at Rodrigo. He turns and watches the smoke ascend the wall of the house behind him, curl around the overhanging tin roof and slip into sky.

The door of Clara's house opens, and he sees Clara kiss her grandmother, a gray-haired woman wearing a faded white güipil. Her grandmother turns up the street, and Clara shouts after her, "Gracias, abuela." With slow but eager steps, Rodrigo crosses the street.

Clara's house is dark and dank smelling. The front room has a blue couch, a small table and a bookcase with religious pamphlets and three worn Bibles. There is a small television in the corner of the room. It is unplugged and its face is dusty. Clara tells him to sit. The cushions on the couch are worn and comfortable. He leans back, anticipating Clara's body. She is large-boned with large, round breasts. Her face is moon-shaped with high cheeks dotted with freckles.

She comes with coffee and tamales, and as he eats, she watches him. Clara's tamales are stiff and dry, not soft and moist like his mother's. All the same, they're filling. "The tamales are very good," he says, and she smiles.

She leaves the room when her daughter cries. Rodrigo eats quickly and with some satisfaction, although he misses a bottle of beer. Beer would make the meal perfect. He finishes his coffee, and when Clara returns, she comes with a fresh cup. It's scalding, and he takes small sips until it is cool enough for him to guzzle.

He finishes the last tamale. He leans back in the couch, content. He imagines Julia in Clara's place, imagines Julia bringing him coffee and tamales. He imagines Julia nursing their baby in the next room—a boy with soft, dark skin and night black eyes. He'd be a good boy. He'd sleep often, sleep deeply and without trouble. When he'd sleep, he and Julia would make love. In love, he would taste every part of her, the ends of her hair, her eyelashes, the corners of her lips. Their lovemaking would last all evening, outlast the birds and their songs, outlast the busses and their bellowing engines, outlast the last drunk and the last street dog howling at the moon.

Clara is standing in the doorway. He rises, excited to be moving toward her and the promise of her sex. At the same time, he is defeated because of what he would rather have, what he should have had. This life, he thinks as he moves toward her, belongs to another man.

He puts his hands on Clara's waist and feels the flesh above her hipbones. He kisses her, hard and deep. Her mouth is as dry as her tamales. His hands rise from her waist to her breasts; her nipples stick up against the soft fabric. He takes her hand and leads her to the next room, toward her bed in the corner.

When their clothes are off and he is inside her, he says, "Look at me, Clara. Look at me." She does look at him, but it is himself he sees, in her eyes, his face distorted and unsmiling.

— 4 —

Octavia is a thin indígena girl with a crimson birthmark in the shape of a half moon on her left cheek. As she stands in the doorway of the sunroom, holding Julia's cup of coffee, Julia invites her to sit down. Julia hasn't seen Oscar in two weeks. His mother has been an infrequent guest, and when she does come, it is only to scold her for not buying her the right kind of bread.

Julia repeats her invitation to Octavia, and with a look of great discomfort, as if she'd been asked to sit on broken glass, Octavia settles into a chair across the coffee table from Julia.

"How old are you, Octavia?"

Octavia looks around, as if thinking the question might have been addressed to someone else. Her answer comes in a soft mumble: "Sixteen, señora."

Even after six months of marriage, Julia isn't used to being addressed as señora. The word is too heavy, too tired and too old, to be her title.

"Do you live with your family?" Julia asks.

"Yes."

"How far from here?"

"In a village outside of Momostenango, señora."

"Did you ever go to school?"

"No."

"Did you ever want to?"

Octavia looks around again. "No."

"Did your brothers and sisters go to school?"

"I had one brother. He was going to school when the army took him."

"The army made him a soldier?"

"Yes."

"What happened to him?"

"He was killed. Afterwards, my father received a telegram and some money."

"I'm sorry."

Octavia looks uncomfortably at the coffee in front of Julia.

"Would you like some coffee, Octavia? You could sit here and drink coffee with me."

"No, thank you, señora."

Julia realizes Octavia wants to leave. But looking at her watch, she sees that there are two hours left before lunch; she doesn't know what she'll do in the two hours. Lately after breakfast, she has gone back to her bedroom, hoping to sleep, but she has found herself thinking about dying and how lonely the dead must feel. She imagines the afterlife as a forest at dusk. The lucky ones, the blessed ones, are guided out of the forest by God, but the sinners must wander in the forest forever, seeing other souls around them only as shadows.

"I had a novio who was impressed into the army," Julia says. She expects Octavia to respond to this, to give at least a murmur of recognition and sympathy. Octavia, however, makes no sound. Nor does she look up. "I was going to marry him," Julia continues. "We had the date set, even if my father didn't give his blessing. But a week before our wedding, the army came, and now I am here."

Octavia looks up. "You are with Don Oscar."

"Yes," Julia says. "But Don Oscar isn't here often, is he?"

Octavia doesn't reply.

Julia knows she is speaking too freely, exaggerating even, but she cannot stop talking. She hasn't heard herself speak in a few days, and she is pleased to find conversation coming to her easily, even if her audience is mute. "He said he would be back a week ago," she says, "but I knew not to count on it. I think he is with the mermaids again in Puerto Barrios."

Octavia gives her a brief, curious glance. In a small but eager voice she asks, "Do mermaids exist?"

"Yes," Julia replies. "During the day, they swim in the Caribbean Sea and at night they put on sweet perfume and short dresses and visit the cheap hotels."

When Octavia doesn't respond to her joke, Julia laughs to fill the silence. She thinks of saying something else, but decides against it. She sips her coffee. She opens her mouth to speak, but closes it.

At last, she says, "I wanted you to be the first to know, Octavia. I'm pregnant."

—

When Oscar comes home two days later, he breaks into a large grin at the news. "Oh, mi amor," he says, and kneels at her feet. He pulls her to him and places his head against her stomach. He begins to cry. His crying is soft, as if he is trying to hide it, and she is moved by his emotion. She touches him on the head, patting down the loose strands of his hair.

Oscar's mother comes the next day. After congratulating Julia on her pregnancy, she says, "I have arranged with the owner of the panadería to deliver us bread himself. We will be free of worries."

— 5 —

The rain is falling, although it's light, lighter than most chipi-chipis, more cloud than rain. The soccer field is surrounded on all sides by a high fence, but, as usual, the gate on the east end is open. Boys from El Instituto Básico play in their gray school slacks and white, short-sleeved shirts.

Rodrigo stands just inside the gate, watching. He isn't much older than they are, but they seem to him young and gangly, and when they shout, their voices are like girls' high, laughing voices. They notice him—they know who he is, they have heard the stories about his playing days—and they play harder in order to impress him. Their earnestness makes their dribbling erratic. Their kicks are too high and long.

After a few minutes, the ball trickles out of bounds to Rodrigo, who traps it between his feet. "I'll play," he announces. The boys—there are ten of them, five on each team—shout their agreement, and Rodrigo trots onto the field. He joins the team defending the south goal.

When he gets the ball, he dribbles slowly up the left side. The boys on the opposing team are reluctant to challenge him, but a small boy with curly hair finally does. The boy crouches in front of him, and Rodrigo jukes left with his shoulder, jukes right, then moves left again, dribbling the ball off his right foot.

The boy is quick, however, and he inserts his foot between Rodrigo's legs and pokes the ball loose.

Rodrigo stops and backtracks, but he isn't quick enough, and the boy takes the ball and dribbles toward the opposite end. Rodrigo gives chase, but the boy is well ahead of him now, and Rodrigo's breathing is labored. He stops and watches the curly-haired boy fire a shot on goal. The goalie dives, but too late. The ball rolls into the left-hand corner of the net.

The boy's teammates celebrate, and the boy races past Rodrigo with his index finger extended toward the sky.

On the next possession, the ball is kicked again to Rodrigo, and again he squares off against the curly-haired boy. He decides he can simply outrun him down the sidelines, so he kicks the ball ahead of him and races toward it. He is amazed to see the boy turn and easily match his strides. The curly-haired boy reaches the ball first and kicks it out of bounds. Panting, Rodrigo strolls after it, picks it up and walks to the sideline. He lifts the ball over his head and throws it to a teammate, who kicks it back to Rodrigo. Again the curly-haired boy stands in front of Rodrigo, and Rodrigo is too tired to maneuver past him. He kicks the ball to a teammate and shouts, "Go on!" He puts his hands on his knees and crouches to catch his breath.

His ankle doesn't hurt, and this surprises him. He was prepared to feel the resilient, small pain. Even so, he can't outduel the curly-haired boy. When he tries again, the curly-haired boy remains in front of him, shielding the goal. Rodrigo stops, backtracks with the ball, then sends a high kick over the curly-haired boy's head. The shot surprises the goalie, who moves too late on it; the ball settles into the right corner of the net.

Rodrigo's teammates cheer, and he hears them speak about his past, his other goals on a great team. But he knows his goal isn't worth celebrating. Even the worst goalie in League C would have stopped the shot without much effort. He knows this, too: because of his exhaustion, his goal will be all the glory he'll achieve on the field today. "I'll play goalie," he says, and he jogs slowly to the south end and takes up a spot between the goal. His breathing subsides. He makes two saves, one on a strong kick from the curly-haired boy, before the rain picks up and darkness falls and the boys run home to dinner.

Rodrigo walks slowly toward his house, letting the rain fill his hair. His mother will have dinner ready, and he's eager to eat, but he can't move any faster. He's too tired. His right leg hurts. He wonders if he pulled a muscle.

— 6 —

Three days after returning from his latest trip to Puerto Barrios, Oscar asks Julia whether she has been attending the Church of God in his absence. When she nods, he says, "And have you made friends with the women at church?"

Julia nods again, lying. In Quetzaltenango's Church of God, she sits in the front row and holds up her hands and closes her eyes and prays. She tries to find something in the darkness in front of her eyelids, and sometimes in the pauses between the preacher's impassioned sermons and the electric keyboard music, she does find levity. It's as if she has risen in body above the church and has been able to observe herself from the ceiling. From this vantage point, she sees herself as only one of a hundred sinners, a thousand, a million. She and all her brothers and sisters in sorrow and sin are weak and pitiful but deserving all the same of God's love and kindness and forgiveness. This peaceful sensation always ends abruptly, as something—Oscar's mother bumping into her side or a man behind her praying too loudly or a note missed on the keyboard—sends her back to where she is, sitting on a hard bench among strangers.

"I was thinking," Oscar says, "about how the next time I go to Puerto Barrios I would take you with me. But in your condition, I think it's best you stay here."

She never would have thought to ask Oscar if she could come with him, but as she stares out of the sunroom's window at the bleak, bald mountains and the blistering light, she thinks she cannot stand another day here. She says, her voice rising in a plea, "I want to come with you, Oscar. Please. I want to come with you to Puerto Barrios." She surprises herself by crying, and surprises herself further by how loud and prolonged her crying is.

He seems pained by her emotion. His face grows thinner. He takes her hands and places them between his. "The next time I go, I won't be gone long. I've almost finished negotiations over the land where we'll build the Burger King. And I'm supposed to talk with my father again tonight about the hotel. If he gives his approval, we'll have both the restaurant and the hotel, our own little Caribbean empire. When

I come back from Puerto Barrios, you and I will spend a morning at the market in Chichicastenango. You've never been to the market in Chichi, have you?"

She shakes her head.

"You'll like it. It's a pleasure to look at what is being sold, but it's even more interesting to watch the gringo tourists to see what they buy."

She feels a wave of nausea rush over her. After it passes, she discovers Oscar looking at her carefully. "Did you say something?" she asks.

"No." He gives her a forced smile and she forces a smile in return. He tries to hold his smile, but she sees something intrude on it, something troubled. He releases her hands and says, "I know you'll feel better tomorrow. I'll have my mother visit you."

Julia goes to bed at eight o'clock, heeding her doctor's orders to rest. From her bedroom, she hears a knock on the front door and hears Oscar welcoming a visitor, his father, Don Ricardo. After their greetings, they begin to talk in earnest. "I have thought it over," Don Ricardo says, "and I don't want to buy the hotel. It's not what we know, and Puerto Barrios is too far for us to manage a business at which we are amateurs."

"I'll manage the hotel."

"From here? Impossible. And you can't move with Julia and your child…"

"I wouldn't move. I would go to Puerto Barrios one week out of every month."

"In order to look after a single hotel and a single restaurant? And in the meantime, what about our orchards? Who will manage them?"

"I will—three weeks out of four."

"This is both too little time to spend on a pair of business and too much time away from your home and our businesses here. And so I say no to the hotel idea."

"But Papá…"

"We have to work in our areas of expertise. We know apple orchards and we know Burger Kings. If you are interested in moving into the hotel business, perhaps we could consider opening a hotel here or in San Marcos."

"Papá, the hotel is beautiful. And its clients are strictly gringos and other foreigners. Gringos want to visit the Caribbean. They are less interested in visiting the Western Highlands."

"I see. This is what entices you, your fascination with gringos."

"I'm more fascinated with their money, Papá. If we look beyond the end of the war and think about what businesses are going to prosper, we have to think about tourism. When this country is at last at peace, tourists will come from everywhere, in greater numbers than ever. The hotel business is a natural place to meet this international market. And unlike with our orchards and Burger King, we will be able to acquire dollars and other foreign currency."

"We have the largest, most prosperous orchards in the country, Oscar. We sell in every major city. We stock the shelves of all the supermercados in the capital."

"I know all this, Papá. I am thinking about the future."

"The orchards will be as successful tomorrow as they are today. People won't stop eating apples. And our Burger King gives us enough of a bond with our hermanos in the United States, don't you think?"

"I don't envision only one hotel. In ten years, I could see us owning a hundred hotels, an entire chain. We could start in the Caribbean—in Puerto Barrios and Livingston and all along the Río Dulce—and move west."

"I think it's enough to own a second Burger King in a place so far from our base. We will have to trust some negrito to run it and it may be bankrupt within six months, no matter how often you check up on it. This makes me wonder if we even need this second Burger King."

"But I've been working on these projects a long time," Oscar protests. "All these trips I've taken…" He falls silent. For a long time, he doesn't say anything. When he again speaks, it is about his mother and her health.

When Oscar comes to bed two hours later, Julia is still awake, although she feigns sleep. She listens as he stirs, flipping from his back to his stomach to his side. At last, his breathing slows and steadies. His deep breaths and half snores bother her, and she only falls asleep toward dawn.

At breakfast, Oscar says nothing to her, only stares out the window at the bleached, barren hills. She wonders if he finds this landscape as unsettling as she does, if this, rather than an untapped market for fast food and gringo tourists, is the reason he wants to escape to Puerto Barrios. She has never been to the Caribbean, but she saw Alejandra's pictures of it and she remembers what Alejandra said about its green waters and startling orange sunsets.

"Perhaps you and I could buy the hotel and this would be our business," she tells Oscar. "You could manage it and I could keep the books. We could do it together. And, as you told your father, we could buy other hotels. We could make hotels our business." She pauses before saying, "I'd like to help you, Oscar. I'd like to work."

He looks at her, and she thinks he is considering the idea seriously. Something rises in her, something hopeful.

"Perhaps," he says. "But you'll be busy with the baby. How will you work and look after our baby? And maybe my father is right. Maybe the orchards are enough." He turns away from her. "But, yes, I would like to try," he says. "Here I do what my father tells me to do. I make sure the truck drivers have the right quantity of apples to deliver. I make sure the supermercados pay us what they owe. And with the Burger King, I do less. Our manager is perfectly competent."

"See?" she says. "The hotel would be ideal for you. It would be your place to prove yourself, to use your talent. It would be your own business—our business."

"I don't know," Oscar says.

"Talk to your father again," she says. "Ask him for a loan."

"I don't know," he says again, this time with a hint of anger. "Stop bothering me. I'll think about it." He stands and leaves the room.

— 7 —

Julia delivers her baby, a girl, three weeks early. Her daughter is tiny and pale and wrinkled like something old. Julia had been told she was having a daughter, but she expected a different baby, a more robust and vigorous and beautiful baby. Looking at her daughter, she is reminded of the sad infant mammals she once saw locked in cages at the Biotopo del Quetzal, too weak to live in the wild.

Julia and Oscar name her Georgina after Oscar's grandmother and the lovely hot springs, their waters growing cooler every year, above the town of Zunil to the south of Quetzaltenago.

The doctor says Julia is too fragile to breastfeed, and Veronica, an older woman who cared for the children of two of Oscar's cousins, moves into their house to serve as Georgina's nanny. She tells Oscar what infant formula to buy, and every night after Veronica puts Georgina to sleep, Julia hears her washing Georgina's soiled diapers in the pila in the courtyard.

Veronica brings Georgina to Julia twice each day, before lunch and before dinner, and Julia holds her daughter in her arms as she would a vase from a museum. Veronica instructs her about what she must do to make the baby comfortable, but

Veronica never seems satisfied with how Julia follows her advice and neither does Georgina, who cries often when she is with her mother.

When, at night, Georgina cries from Veronica's bedroom, Julia always wakes up feeling something more painful than longing. She never moves, however. Rather, she listens to her daughter's crying like someone paralyzed and rarely succeeds in falling back to sleep.

In the months after her wedding, she talked to her mother once a week on the telephone. But with Georgina's birth, her mother calls more frequently, although their conversations tend to be short. Both Oscar and Julia's father have complained about the high cost of their telephone calls.

When Georgina turns a month old, Julia's mother calls and says, "You sound tired, mi hija."

"I am," Julia says.

"You'll be less tired in twenty years, when Georgina is grown." It is a joke, and her mother laughs, but Julia is too tired to laugh.

"You are unhappy," her mother says.

"No."

"Yes, you are, but this is natural. In the first months after a child is born, a mother feels more unhappiness than happiness, and when people ask if you are happy, you must say yes and this makes you more unhappy."

"I'm not a good mother," Julia says flatly.

There is a pause before her mother says, "Does Georgina have enough food?"

"Yes."

"Does she keep dry? Is her health good?"

"Yes."

"This means you are a good mother." She pauses. "When you were born, I had the same doubts you do, and my mother said to me what I have said to you."

There is another pause.

"Julia?"

"Yes?"

"I miss you."

"I miss you too." Julia stares across the bald hills. "And I miss Santa Cruz. I miss our mountains."

"They are the same as you remember. Close your eyes. Can you see them?"

Julia does close her eyes. "I see them," she says.

"See—you'll always have them." Her mother pauses. "Your old novio, Rodrigo, is living with Clara Juarez."

"The muchacha whose parents died in the bus accident in Chamelco?"

"Yes, poor girl. And Rodrigo is playing soccer again. People who care about soccer here are very excited."

"How does he look?"

"He's heavier—thicker is more like it. I think I'll always remember him as a boy—very slim and very pretty. Oh, and he's drinking."

"Rumors," Julia says, although she knows it's true.

"I wish they were rumors. But I've seen him twice asleep in the doorway of the calvario."

"What were you doing at the calvario, Mamá?"

There is a pause. Julia can hear her mother's light breathing. "I go sometimes. I go because...because I miss the times when you and I used to go. And there is a new priest in Santa Cruz. He is a norteamericano, a man from New York, and I have talked to him on two occasions."

"About what?"

"About our country, Julia, and where God is in our country. Please don't tell your father. And, anyway, I go to cultos, too. I have always respected Hermano Hector. And now he has an assistant, a woman, who gives sermons two days a week. Her name is Esmeralda and she speaks with great enthusiasm. She is a pretty woman, and I think all the men in the congregation are already in love with her."

"When you saw Rodrigo, did you speak to him?"

"One time I woke him up and invited him inside the calvario to pray with me, but he said he had to go home. I watched him and I saw him go to Clara's house. Poor girl. Her daughter is looking more and more like Pedro Mendez."

When Julia doesn't respond, her mother says, "It's funny to think you were engaged to Rodrigo. He was always going to be a boy of this pueblo, no matter how successful he was at soccer. But look at you—you are the wife of a prosperous hombre de negocios. You should hear your father talk about you. From his conversations, you would think Oscar owned the entire city of Quetzaltenango." Her mother frequently ends conversations like this, with a celebration of Oscar and the life she thinks they lead.

Her mother begins to say goodbye. Julia hasn't seen her since the week Georgina was born, and her mother's coming and going then was quick—four days—and

Julia won't see her again until Christmas. She feels like saying, "Wait." Instead, she asks, "Am I all right, Mamá?"

"Of course, mi hija."

Julia thinks her mother has hung up or been cut off, but above a faint crackling sound, she adds, "I love you, mi hija. You know how much I love you, don't you?"

"Yes, I do."

"Your father always claims you are exactly like him, but I know he's mistaken. You are my daughter, too. And if we are good wives to our husbands, we mustn't neglect ourselves. Their lives touch ours, but they shouldn't eclipse them. We know more than they about what is right for us." She pauses. "Do you understand?"

"Yes," Julia says. She feels reassured; she feels stronger.

"You are my daughter," her mother says again. "Goodbye, mi hija."

After hanging up, Julia marches to Veronica's room and, above Veronica's objection, brings Georgina into her arms, covers her in a shawl and steps outside. Georgina cries, a prolonged protest of Julia's unfamiliar arms and elbows, of her chest and smell. But soon she settles down, and as Julia walks into the orchard, with its fragrance of soil and apple blossoms, Georgina sleeps.

— 8 —

In El Dragón, Rodrigo sits at a table with Don Adolfo, who talks again about Rodrigo's soccer days, although to Rodrigo, it's as if the greatness Don Adolfo speaks of belongs to someone else. Rodrigo accepts the beer Dolores, the barmaid, brings, and he drinks at the same voracious pace as Don Adolfo. He smiles at Don Adolfo's stories, but he isn't listening now; he is listening to the song on the jukebox. It's an old song, one Dolores plays often in the slow afternoon hours.

The singer's voice is soft and pleading, and although Rodrigo nods at something Don Adolfo says, he is really nodding at the song. No woman Rodrigo knows would refuse the comfort of a castle for a lover who offers her only hot kisses and a straw mattress. Rodrigo laughs loudly and bitterly, and Don Adolfo frowns before smiling again and resuming his story.

Julia has a child now, a pale, pug-nosed infant who, even at three months or however old she is, seems to have inherited Julia's abundant black hair. Pedro showed him a picture of the baby and Julia and Julia's husband. Julia's mother had left the photograph on the counter of Doña Renata's tienda, and Pedro, who had followed her into the store, had slipped it into his pocket.

"Look," Pedro said to him, "the husband looks like a gringo, a gringo who hasn't seen the sun in years." Pedro shook his head in disgust.

"His family owns apple orchards," Rodrigo said, explaining Julia's choice. Even now, Rodrigo feels the need to protect her, defend her from people like Pedro who are beneath her, who don't understand her.

Pedro offered him the picture, inviting him to tear it up, but he put it in his pocket. Later, with scissors, he trimmed Julia's husband from the picture. He put the sheared photograph of Julia and her baby in a fold of his Bible. He imagined meeting a stranger on a bus one day and, after pulling out the photograph, saying, "This is my wife and daughter."

After Rodrigo and Don Adolfo have finished six beers each, Don Adolfo asks Dolores for two frascos of Venado, and after they've downed these, he requests two glasses of boh, which Dolores' mother makes from corn stalks and distills behind the cantina. Rodrigo remembers having boh when he was young, but it was sweet boh, hardly more than punch. The boh he drinks with Don Adolfo is thick and sour, and it burns his throat. But he's pleased with its effect. He feels as if his neck has shot up like a flower, and with his new height he's able to peer over Don Adolfo's head.

But, a moment later, he sees he hasn't grown suddenly taller; rather, Don Adolfo has placed his head on the table and is sleeping. Rodrigo laughs, and his laugh is free of bitterness. He is glad to be where he is. He'll never play professional soccer again. He'll never be Julia's husband. But his job is satisfactory; it pays enough, and he no longer minds his long marches into hills to find trees. Often before he begins his climb, he'll drink, and the climb is less cumbersome if he is half drunk. It's work, anyway, and he's capable of doing it. And he has Clara, who gives herself to him whenever he wants. Because of problems she had delivering her first child, she'll never be able to have another baby, but he doesn't want a baby with her.

He drinks a second boh, then a third. The men at other tables are all friends of his, and he stands to salute them. "I am content!" he announces. "I am content because I have work, I have a woman! What more do I need?" His throat catches on the last question and he shivers. He grabs a chair to steady himself. The room wobbles, and he thinks everyone must be laughing at him. There's Rodrigo, they're saying. He used to be the most envied man in Santa Cruz, but now he can't keep up with schoolboys on the soccer field and he's the novio of a woman who's no better than a whore.

"Go to the devil!" he yells at the blurred faces. "To the devil, all of you!"

He stumbles out the door and into the black, barren streets. The street shakes as in an earthquake. He doesn't turn toward Clara's house but his own. The hill to his house is steeper than he remembers. When he turns down Avenida La Parroquia, it's dark. There are no working streetlights, and the Sierras, his neighbors, have turned off their porch light. Rodrigo feels his stomach give. Startled, he vomits on his feet. "Mierda," he whispers, and vomits again. He falls against the dirt embankment below the Sierras' house.

Before he becomes unconscious, he thinks of his father and how he left his mother with nothing. *I'm the better man,* he thinks, although he realizes he hasn't given his mother a single centavo in months. Slipping toward sleep, he decides he'll give her everything on his next payday. He'll buy no more beer, no more boh. And this, too: He'll play professional soccer again. Simple. He'll make a good living again. He'll give her more money than she'll need.

See, mother? Everything will be all right.

— 9 —

Leaving the whorehouse, smelling of a woman whose name he can't remember or never knew, Rodrigo wonders what Julia smells like in love. He has kissed Julia's lips and felt her breasts—which, to his surprise, were large and firm—but she always smelled of nothing more than what was around her, grass or rain or the river. He never drew any deeper smell from her, never smelled her like he's smelled these women whose names he doesn't know.

They smell like flowers near wilting. They try to disguise their smell, throw perfume everywhere on their bodies, even, he is sure, between their legs. And they are surrounded by other smells, the smell of mold on their walls, the smell of must on their mattresses. But Rodrigo knows their real smell. They are dying flowers.

Rodrigo and Pedro are walking back from the whorehouse in San Cristóbal, their thumbs extended to hitch a ride because Pedro's truck wouldn't start. Only a few cars pass them. They don't stop.

"Julia smells just like them," Rodrigo declares.

"Sure, vos." Pedro slaps Rodrigo's shoulder. The impact jars him, makes him stumble.

He has tried to imagine Julia's smell, and sometimes he imagines her smelling like these women, and sometimes he imagines her smelling like roses or mandarinas, and sometimes he imagines her smelling like nothing he's ever smelled before.

"No, vos," he tells Pedro. "I'm lying. I don't know what she smells like when… when…"

"Trust me," Pedro says. "When she fucks, she smells the way any woman does."

"I don't know," Rodrigo says, and his ignorance makes him mourn, and without Pedro seeing, he cries.

— 10 —

In the village bordering the apple orchard, the Catholic Church is lodged within a barn, its wood painted red and a pair of two-story tin doors its only entrance. Inside, broken and dust-covered idols are propped on a table made of pinewood. Empty glass containers, their prayer candles burned to nothing, and milk cans holding dry roses flank the idols. On the back wall, two slabs of wood form a cross. It is cool and dark within the church; what little light there is comes through the open front doors and the cracks in the wood.

Julia comes here often with Georgina, hauling her the two kilometers in a cloth on her back like a campesina would. Today, Georgina sleeps against her back as she sits on the bench in front of the altar. Julia closes her eyes and prays. As usual, her prayer has little content. It is a prayer of words strung together, words such as forgiveness and peace. She says her mother's name and her father's and her sister's, and she says Oscar's name and Oscar's mother's and father's. She says Rodrigo's name, and she follows his name with other words. Soccer. Grass. Wind.

She feels Georgina stir behind her, and soon her daughter begins to cry. With distress, Julia realizes she has forgotten to bring Georgina's bottle. Georgina's cries grow louder.

"The baby is hungry."

The voice comes from the right-hand corner of the barn, near the doors. Julia sees in the shadows a woman sitting on a chair one might find in a classroom. The woman is wearing a simple gray and blue güipil and a blue corte. In the poor light, Julia can't tell whether the woman is young or old.

"I know she's hungry," Julia says, "but I haven't brought her bottle. We'll have to go home."

For a moment, the woman says nothing, and Julia stands to leave. But as she is walking toward the door, the woman says, "You can give the child your breast."

"It has no milk."

"It will be sufficient to soothe her."

Julia doesn't believe the woman. But Georgina's cries continue, so she returns to the bench in front of the altar. She puts Georgina on the dirt floor of the church. She opens her blouse and unsnaps her bra. Her breasts stand revealed to the icons in the dim light. She has seen women breastfeed in markets and on busses all over the country, and seeing them again in her mind, she pulls Georgina to her left breast.

Georgina's mouth hurts her, and she wants to push her daughter away. But she remembers the woman behind her; she doesn't want to appear weak in her presence. The pain is dull and persistent, and she closes her eyes and grits her teeth, hoping she can endure it. Her daughter whimpers and seems about to cry, and Julia despairs. But a moment later, Julia feels something swell in her, something near her heart, and she feels a slow, watery release in her breast. What she gives Georgina can't be more than a trickle, a stubborn few drops. It is enough, however, to keep Georgina from crying, to keep her hopeful at Julia's nipple, her mouth moving over it with vigor.

Julia touches Georgina's head, moving her closer to her, pressing her tiny body into hers.

— 11 —

Rodrigo finds a seat at the top of El Estadio Imperial in Cobán, closer to the sky than the field. He wants to be anonymous. Yet he would not mind if someone from the crowd, some old man or a woman his age, came up to him, scrutinized him and said, "I remember you." There is no one around him, however. The stadium is only three-quarters full. The Imperials do not have a good team this year.

The game is only a few minutes old when Rodrigo stirs, uncomfortable in the concrete seats. He feels his body respond to the motion on the field as if he were playing. He begins to sweat, even though the day is cool and overcast, threatening rain.

The Quetzaltecos, the Imperials' opponents, score a goal, and the crowd groans. Rodrigo hears a few curses. He is tempted to yell one himself.

He does squats, feeling sweat pour from his forehead. *Jesus María*, he thinks, *I should be playing.* But even as he thinks this, he remembers what an effort it was to climb to the top of the stadium and how hard he was panting when he reached his seat. *A dog. I am a dog.*

From his knapsack, he pulls a frasco of Venado. He didn't think he'd need to drink. He thought he would be able to concentrate on the game, even enjoy it. With a few gulps, he has drunk half the bottle.

Last night, his mother came to see him at Clara's house, bringing a pamphlet she had been given or had sought in San Cristóbal. It was for a group called Alcoholicos Anonimos. The group meets in the basement of the Catholic Church in San Cristóbal every evening, and his mother asked him if he would go.

Rodrigo said to his mother, "You are telling me a joke, correct?"

His comment made her frown. "Please, Rodrigo, go to one meeting. Please."

He didn't feel like arguing. He was tired. He said, "Okay, Mother."

But he knew and she knew he did not mean it, and she left him like she was leaving a funeral.

Late in the second half, Mateo Rey intercepts a pass at midfield and races toward the goal. The crowd stands in anticipation and is rewarded when Mateo slices a shot into the lower left-hand corner of the goal, a ball's length out of the goalie's reach. The crowd hoots its approval, and Rodrigo, who is feeling better after finishing a second frasco of Venado, crashes his palms together to join the applause.

But when Rodrigo settles back onto his concrete seat, he feels nausea rise up in him. He looks around, again hoping to catch someone's eye, someone who might remember him. "I could have had three goals by now," he says to no one, and no one listens.

Near the end of the game, Mateo Rey has another chance to score, off a corner kick, but the goalie makes a diving save. The game ends in a tie, and the crowd leaves the stadium half-satisfied. Rodrigo watches the stands empty. The sky seems closer to him than when the game began. If he were a little taller, he might reach up and pull water from the clouds.

He leaves his empty frascos of Venado in the stands and walks toward the field. He stands against a rail above it, trying to smell the grass, trying to remember the feel of the grass against his cleats. He wonders where he would be if he had never been injured. The answer is too easy to linger over, but he does so anyway.

When he is outside the stadium, walking toward the bus stop, he turns a corner and runs into Mateo Rey, his wife and their two young boys. For a moment, Rodrigo doesn't think Mateo will remember him. But: "Rod-riii-go!" Mateo says, smiling broadly. They shake hands. Mateo's hair is shorter than when Rodrigo played with him, cropped close, soldier-like, in the new fashion. He is wearing a tan button-down shirt and blue slacks. He smells of perfumed soap, the soap always stocked in the Imperials' locker room.

"Where have you been?" Mateo asks him, and Rodrigo explains in a few words about the army and about the work he does now. This last part is a lie. Two weeks ago, he was fired from his job. The company could no longer trust him to work. Often he would start to climb into the mountains, but after a few sips from his frasco he frequently found himself too tired to continue, and he'd find a warm, dry spot and drink until he fell asleep. Sometimes he stayed outside all night, waking with dew on his face.

"Oh, vos, bad luck," Mateo says. He looks Rodrigo over. "You look heavy," he says. "You haven't been working out?"

"I can't," Rodrigo says, "because of my injury." It is the first time he has used his injury to excuse anything. He knows it isn't sufficient. He could work out with weights or a bicycle.

"This is my family," Mateo says, and he introduces Rodrigo to his wife and children.

Mateo takes a step closer to Rodrigo, and Rodrigo knows he must be able to smell his hot, alcohol breath. "Do you think you'll go back to school?" Mateo asks, and Rodrigo shrugs and says, "I never liked school."

"I finished colegio last year," Mateo says. "I took classes during the off-season. I have a job lined up at El Sol, the silver exporter in Carchá."

"But you're playing soccer," Rodrigo says. "You don't need to…"

"Today I'm playing soccer," Mateo says. "Tomorrow? I saw how the team treated you, vos. One injury and…Well, besides, there's always some new boy coming up, thinking he's the next Pele." Mateo pauses and smiles. "Or the next Rodrigo Rax."

Rodrigo grins in appreciation of Mateo's compliment.

In contrast to the sternness of his most prominent features—his hard jaw, his crew-cut hair—Mateo's eyes are soft and round. "I used to drink," Mateo says, his voice calm, easy. "Even during the season, I drank. Coach warned me about it. He said I was going to fail him, fail everyone on the team. He told me about a church here in Cobán, the Elim."

"Evangelical," Rodrigo mutters.

"Some of the men in the church used to drink, but they all turned sober. They formed a group to help other men. When they heard about my situation, they would come visit me every night. They would bring me Coke and coffee."

Rodrigo thinks of Julia and the cultos he attended with her and how he'd sit beside her and watch her devotion. He thinks, too, of his father.

"Will you come with me one night?" Mateo asks. "It's the Elim, two blocks from the park. There are services every night beginning at seven. Our group meets afterwards."

Rodrigo looks behind Mateo at Mateo's family and thinks how, except for an unmown patch of grass, he could be in Mateo's place. He bites his lip and says to Mateo, "I was good, vos, wasn't I?" It isn't a question, and Mateo doesn't respond. "I was good, but when my ankle turned, I lost something. And once you lose something, it's easy to lose something else. Everything falls away from you, and you can't hold on. It's like being in a hurricane."

Rodrigo feels more words rise in him. He feels an entire speech about to come, a speech of loss and complaint, but Mateo says, "There's a way to regain what you've lost, at least the most important things you've lost. There's a way to find your soul again and give your soul to God. And in giving your soul to God, you've reclaimed it from the devil."

Mateo touches Rodrigo on the shoulder and presses his fingers gently into Rodrigo's flesh. "Listen, vos, I never thought I'd become an Evangelical. My family is Catholic; ever since I was sixteen I carried the Christ floats in the Semana Santa parades. Fifty pounds on my shoulders, and I loved it. But in my heart, in my soul, I was lost and sick. I'd always mocked the Evangelicals. I hated their singing, vos, and their loud preaching over microphones. I thought it was rude, vos. But they were helping turn people toward a better life, and I needed a better life."

Mateo removes his hand from Rodrigo's shoulder and gazes at him with sympathy. "You were my teammate, vos. But now you're something more important to me. You're my brother and I want to help you. I'll come to your house on Monday at six and we'll ride the bus together to Cobán."

He asks Rodrigo if he is still living with his mother, and Rodrigo tells him where he is living, although not with whom. Mateo doesn't ask. "I'll come on Monday, vos."

"Okay," Rodrigo says.

"Good," Mateo says, and they shake hands.

Mateo begins walking again with his family, but he turns around, and Rodrigo thinks he wants to ask a question. He fears it's about Julia. He used to tell the world about Julia. But Mateo only gives him a wave before resuming his walk.

—

Trying to sleep in Clara's soft bed, Clara breathing uneasily beside him, Rodrigo remembers hunting deer long ago in the mountains with his father, who carried a rifle taller than Rodrigo. They never saw a deer, but this didn't matter. His father found a stream, sat down and opened—he is sure of it now—a frasco of Venado or another brand of whiskey. Thirsty, Rodrigo asked if he could have a sip, but his father shook his head and told him to drink from the stream. They talked in soft voices about soccer and deer and trees. Soon, his father fell asleep on his back beside the stream. Rodrigo joined him, sleeping with his head against his father's forearm.

But as he tries to linger in the memory of gently humming mountain water, tries to picture his father sleeping warm and large beside the stream, he sees the rifle at his father's feet. His father, he fears, hasn't fallen asleep but has shot himself. Rodrigo panics, wondering if this is what really happened to his father.

No, he assures himself, his father is alive. Safe somewhere.

But again he sees the rifle, and this time it isn't his father's rifle, it's his own. And he knows why he has it: The mountains are full of guerrillas, their rifles loaded and trained. They've killed his father, and now they will kill him.

Rodrigo bends down and picks up his rifle, but when he looks in front of him, he sees no guerrillas, only an old woman. Her pink güipil has been sliced down the middle and both of her breasts are exposed. They are small and wrinkled and as brown as dirt. "Why do you hesitate?" she asks. "I am ready."

Rodrigo begins to speak, and when he does, he wakes up. Clara is awake, too, holding him, urging him to be quiet, to go back to sleep.

— 12 —

There are eight men in a circle, and the man in the chair next to Mateo Rey's says, "I could see I was about to die. I could feel death with every drink I had. I could feel death burn in my stomach, in my intestines, in my liver. And I was afraid. I was very afraid, but I couldn't stop. It seemed death was calling me. It didn't matter where I was. I could be with my wife and my mother, eating dinner, and yet I could hear death call me."

The back room of the Elim is lit by a corner lamp, covered with an old shade spotted with dirt. In the light, the men's faces look yellow. Mateo Rey is wearing a crisp white shirt and black pants.

The man, who must be no older than Rodrigo, begins to cry.

"Does death still call you?" Mateo asks.

"Yes," the man acknowledges. He holds his face in his palms, and he is sobbing now. His shadow on the back wall is enormous. "But I have resisted. All this week and last, I resisted."

"You are alive," Mateo says.

"I am alive," the man says.

"You are alive," Mateo says, and the man repeats "I am alive" several times, his words punctuated by sobs.

"Death will come, but only when God deems it, not when the devil deems it. We must be strong. We have mothers and wives and brothers and sisters and sons and daughters. For them, we must be strong. For ourselves, we must be strong. For God, we must be strong, and God will make us strong. Jesus will make us strong." Mateo looks at Rodrigo and nods. "This is why we are here. To find strength together."

When Mateo came to pick up Rodrigo, he was sleeping on the couch in Clara's front room. He had forgotten about the meeting and he'd drunk a bottle of rum. He told Mateo he wasn't feeling well enough to go, but Mateo helped him to his feet. When he left with Mateo, Clara stood in the doorway, her face bright and hopeful. She thanked Mateo, thanked him again and again.

Putting a hand on Rodrigo's shoulder, Mateo says, "I know brother Rodrigo wants to be strong with us. I know he wants to find the light." He squeezes Rodrigo's shoulder. "Am I right, brother?"

Slowly, Rodrigo nods.

"We will help. We are your brothers."

"Brothers!" reply the other men.

Mateo opens the Bible on his lap and begins to read: "'Simon, Simon, behold, Satan demanded to have you, that he might sift you like wheat, but I have prayed for you that your faith may not fail.'"

At the end of the meeting, Rodrigo shakes the hands of all the men. He and Mateo step outside. The night is cool and sweet smelling, the way Cobán usually is after a rain. The streetlights cast bright spots of white onto the wet streets. "There are no more busses tonight to Santa Cruz," Mateo says. "You will, of course, sleep in my house."

Mateo lives in a block house near the public hospital. After Mateo opens the wooden gate, they walk down a path lined with bougainvillea. Mateo opens the metal door with a key, and Rodrigo steps into the house. Mateo shows him to a large, brown sofa in the corner of the living room, and they sit down.

In the room is a bookshelf with Mateo's soccer trophies. On the walls are photographs of all the teams Mateo has been on. Rodrigo finds a photograph of his Imperials team, sees himself standing straight and proud in the back row. A minute later, Mateo's wife brings coffee and sweet bread, and Rodrigo eats hungrily. Mateo tells him he has made a good decision in coming to the meeting; all of the men, he says, were on the brink of self-destruction before they came. "We have lost only one man," Mateo says, and Rodrigo is curious about what happened to him, but he doesn't ask.

When they have finished the sweet bread, Mateo's wife brings sheets and a wool blanket and makes up the couch as a bed. "I have practice at six in the morning," Mateo says. "I won't wake you. My wife will make you breakfast before you go." He reaches out his hand, and Rodrigo shakes it. They say goodnight.

A light from outside the house shines into the window above the couch and strikes Mateo's soccer trophies; one of them, a gold statuette of a soccer player about to kick a ball, is at least three feet tall. Rodrigo tries to sleep, but he keeps opening his eyes and staring at the trophies. He finds he is wide awake, and he keeps thinking about the next morning, when he is sure he will hear Mateo leave for practice.

For Rodrigo, it was easy, always, to rise on the mornings he was going to practice or a game. He would rise with the first cock crow; sometimes he would rise before his mother rose, but she would always be awake soon after he was. She would make him coffee and eggs, and she would warm tortillas and place them in a basket in front of him. He rarely tasted the food she made because he was eager to go, and when he stepped outside, the morning air was pure and he breathed it deeply. He would wait in the park for the bus and it would never be crowded and he would sit in the back by an open window and allow the cool air to rush over him. On the field in Cobán, he would stretch over the dew-dampened grass, and the sun would rise and the heat would grow and soon he would be running faster than anyone, his passes purer than anyone's, his kicks hard and headed exactly where he wanted them to go.

He cannot bear the thought of waking up to find Mateo before him, his red and black Imperials bag around his shoulder, about to step into a morning Rodrigo doesn't know anymore but misses, misses more than he misses his father, misses more, even, than he misses Julia.

Slowly and with as little noise as possible, Rodrigo dresses, opens the door and returns to the night.

— 13 —

Often as she is lying in bed, unable to sleep, Julia thinks of the hotel in Puerto Barrios. She asked Oscar to describe it, and he did the best he could, but she had to use her imagination where his memory failed. This is what she sees: a four-story hotel made of old, dark wood—mahogany or oak or cherry or ceiba, she doesn't know, but she knows it's elegant and durable. There is a large dining room with a two-story ceiling, and on three sides of it are windows offering views of the Caribbean Sea. A few of the waiters worked in the restaurant when Puerto Barrios, booming from the banana trade, was the country's largest port, Guatemala's opening to the world, and have served ship captains from around the globe. They wear black ties and white suit coats at every meal.

The hotel has thirty-two rooms, each with a pair of queen-sized beds and spacious baños with deep bathtubs, and six suites with three bedrooms each and balconies overlooking the sea. Between the hotel and the sea is a long, thin swimming pool and surrounding it are white chairs beneath yellow umbrellas. Below the pool is a smooth sand beach, an easy entrance to the rich blue waters of the Caribbean.

She wants to stand behind the mahogany counter in the reception area and greet tourists from Germany and Argentina and the United States. She wants to keep the hotel books and make the improvements Oscar says the hotel will need: new table cloths and chandeliers in the dining room; new sofas and brighter artwork in the reception area; a snack bar beside the pool. She wants the hotel to be the place sea captains come again after their long journeys hauling bananas and coffee and carda-mom across the ocean. She wants to sit with them and Oscar in the dining room past closing time and listen to their stories.

Her dream of owning the hotel is more fantasy now than ever. Oscar's father decided he didn't want to open a Burger King in Puerto Barrios and, over Oscar's objections, sold his Burger King in Quetzaltenango. "Our orchards," he told Oscar, "are our empire."

But the more unlikely the fulfillment of her dream, the more she desires it, and one morning after she and Oscar have finished breakfast in the sunroom, she asks Oscar again about the hotel. He says, "I have also been thinking about it," and he looks at her with a warmth and comradeship she feels from him only rarely but craves. Seeing her opportunity, she presses him, reminding him of the war's immi-nent end—the government and guerrillas are again meeting in Mexico and reports on their talks have been more hopeful than ever—and the boom in tourism sure to follow.

Oscar nods and, in a sign of his animation, stands up. She likes him when he is like this, ambitious and vibrant. She likes it when she can dream with him.

"You need to test yourself apart from your father," Julia says. "You need to see what you can build alone." At fifty-three, Don Ricardo is healthy, strong and as in-volved as ever in his business. He is likely to live another thirty years, and Oscar knows this.

Sometimes she can feel the warm breeze off the Caribbean. She can taste the salt in the air.

"He wants me to look into buying a couple of orchards in San Marcos," Oscar says. "His plan is to become the only grower of apples in Guatemala." He shakes his head, laughing. "Apples, apples, apples. He thinks the people in this country are as fascinated with apples as Adam and Eve." He claps his hands and holds them together. "When the war is over, we will be part of the world again and we will need to welcome the world, won't we?"

"Yes," Julia says, standing and moving toward him.

"I'll do what he asks. I'll go to San Marcos and I'll see about buying the orchards. But when I'm done, I'll come to him again with our plan and this time, I won't back down."

"Our plan," Julia repeats. Impulsively, she wraps her arms around him, and he responds, clutching her back. This is, she suspects, what she wanted all along; it is what she found in her friendship with Alejandra and Lilian. She wanted an invitation to be more than what she was; she wanted a passport to the wonders of the world.

— 14 —

When teams begin to form for a local soccer tournament, all the team captains want Rodrigo on their side. He weighs forty pounds more than he did when he was a professional, but this doesn't deter them. They say they're sure to win with him, and he believes them.

He chooses to play for the youngest team, composed of students from El Instituto Básico. Although the team has a coach, the school's tall, shy physical education teacher, it is Rodrigo who leads the team in warm-up exercises, organizes the drills and divides the players for scrimmages. The players know Rodrigo's history, and they listen to him deferentially and show off in his presence. They call him Don Rodrigo.

In a few scrimmages, he plays halfback, but he finds even this tiring, and eventually he moves to the goalie box. Here he can survey the entire field; he can shout instructions to his teammates.

At the end of the last practice before the tournament starts, Rodrigo sits in the stands above the field. Six players have joined him. One of the boys, Pepe, has bought them all strawberry helados. The boys discuss the girls they know in school, but without passion. It is as if they are waiting to hear something better, and Rodrigo knows he should be telling them stories about his days with the Imperials. He wishes one of the boys would initiate a conversation, ask him a question.

At last, Pepe turns to him. "When you are a professional player, all the girls love you—right, Don Rodrigo?"

He knows what answer they expect, and it is not an untruthful answer. Frederico Briones, the goalie who wanted to be a merengue singer, used to sit in the last seat on the team bus and tell one story after another about the women who waited for him outside the gates of stadiums in every town they visited. Each of the women would bring him, as a gift and a bribe, some distinct item from her town, so in Livingston it was a bag of coconut bread and in Momostenango it was a wool hat and in Purulhá it was the feather of a quetzal.

To Pepe, Rodrigo answers, "Girls would crowd outside the gates where the players left."

"And you could pick whichever one you wanted?" another boy asks.

"You could pick them all," Rodrigo says, and this draws approving laughter.

Rodrigo doesn't remember noticing the women. He wishes he had. If he had known what would happen between him and Julia, he would have gone with other women: a tall woman, the green-eyed daughter of a German coffee finquero; a short woman with skin as dark and smooth as black jade.

"And you had many women, Don Rodrigo?" Pepe asks.

He begins to tell a lie, invoking his imaginary German's daughter and jade-skinned woman, but he quickly loses interest in what he's inventing. Instead, he tells a story about when he was in the army. He and the other soldiers and the lieutenant were riding in a covered truck, going from one part of the jungle into another. To pass the time, the lieutenant devised a game. He was going to start with the letter A, he said, and he would list all the women's names he could think of that began with that letter. When the lieutenant mentioned the name of a woman one of the soldiers had been with, the soldier was supposed to say what he'd done with her and where.

The game, Rodrigo soon realized, was an excuse for the lieutenant to brag. It seemed he'd been with a woman from all over the alphabet; he'd been with an Alicia and a Bibiana and three Cecilias. When the lieutenant said the name "Julia," Rodrigo opened his mouth, but a soldier next to him boasted of going to a whorehouse to sleep with a Julia on a bed next to a second-story window overlooking the market below. "I could hear a vendor shouting, 'Helados! Helados de coco!'" he said. "But I was already having my dessert." At the end of the game, Rodrigo was called a hueco and a virgin because he'd told no story.

In the midst of his reverie, Rodrigo has stopped talking. He looks at the boys; they sit around him, expectant and concerned. He wonders where he stopped his story and how long he has been silent. He opens his mouth again and tastes how dry it is.

The boys change the topic, talking about the upcoming tournament, but they don't talk long. Soon they shake his hand and leave him sitting in the stands as daylight disappears. He knows he should move, but he is too tired, and he lingers past dusk. Stars appear above him, lonely and bright, the way he'd seen them in the war.

— 15 —

Dreaming of Puerto Barrios, Julia sits down in her sunroom to write a letter she has wanted to write for half a decade. The sky today is a vivid blue; it is so blue, so beautiful, that everything under it seems lovely and rich. The apples on the trees in the orchard are a bold, delicious red, and in the mountains beyond them Julia sees patches of spruce trees she hadn't noticed before, growing tall and hopeful beneath the brown, barren peaks.

She's writing to Alejandra, although she knows it is probably futile. She is sure Alejandra returned to the United States a long time ago, but even if she did, she hopes the organization she worked for, Casas Para El Pueblo, which is based in Puerto Barrios, will forward the letter to her.

In her letter, she asks Alejandra if she remembers her and reminds her about their first encounter in the calvario. She tells her that, even now, she thinks about how the two of them sat in Alejandra's room in Doña Flor's house, drinking coffee and listening to her music. She tells her how close she felt to her, even in the short time they knew each other, and how she was grateful to have her friendship.

Julia hesitates before writing this: "My father was one of the men who came to your room to talk with you and who scared you into leaving Santa Cruz. I wanted to warn you he was coming, but during the feria, I couldn't leave my house and when I did come to see you, it was too late. I know my father to be a more reasonable man than the angry man he must have been in your room. I think he must have acted out of fear and ignorance because he didn't know you or your goodness. I hope you can forgive him. I hope you can forgive me."

She tells Alejandra about what she has done since she last saw her, about Rodrigo, about Oscar, about Georgina.

She finishes her letter by writing, "I am hoping to live in Puerto Barrios one day soon. If I ever hear from you, I will tell you about what I hope will happen in my life."

— 16 —

Rodrigo feels the alcohol burn inside him. It spreads from his gut to his chest and legs, hot and nauseating. Inside him there is beer and boh and whiskey. He drinks another glass of boh, distilled until all the sweetness has been replaced by harshness. It's good. Yes, it's good, although he has ceased to taste it, ceased to feel it rush down his throat. He might as well be drinking water. He drinks quickly, the motion of lifting the glass to his lips as regular and natural as breathing.

On his left is Don Hector, on his right Don Adolfo, and they are laughing. Rodrigo thinks they are laughing at him. He wonders if he should be angry—he thinks he probably should be, he should say something to them, curse them, tell them to go to the devil. Instead, he grins, pleased with his own floating nausea. It carries him beyond bitterness, reproach, jealousy.

But it can't carry him beyond memory because Julia comes again, curly-haired and smiling, to tease him. He knows she's an illusion, but she speaks to him from a time she was real. Once she was close enough for him to kiss. This, and not the beer, not the boh, not the whiskey, makes him stand in the near-empty cantina and howl with rage and tears: "How can this be gone?"

Don Hector and Don Adolfo stand, step back and recede into the blur of bottles on the shelf behind the bar. Rodrigo is alone now. And the cantina is as black and still as night. He's outside, he must be outside, and Julia is calling him, and it's the simplest request.

"Rodrigo," she says, "will you walk me home?"

— 17 —

Rodrigo pushes Clara toward the bed in the corner of the room. He's drunk after too much beer and boh in the wake of his team's loss in the first round of the Santa Cruz campionata. He played goalie and allowed three goals. The alcohol hasn't numbed him as much as he'd like. His muscles ache, as if ropes are tied around his calves and thighs. His stomach feels tight, too, and he's amazed to see it hanging generously over his jeans. He tugs at Clara's dress. "Careful," she half whispers, half hisses. She sits on the bed and lowers her hand over her shoulder to unzip her dress.

Clara's face seems too large. Her cheeks puff like rain-swollen clouds. Even her eyes seem grotesquely wide, wide but unwelcome. He wants her small and manageable, yet she seems to be expanding before him.

She releases her dress and it falls into her lap. Frowning, she unhooks her bra. Her breasts sink halfway to her stomach. This time, he doesn't promise to marry her. He's tired of the charade, speaking the lie, the password to her sex. He'll never marry her.

He kneels and reaches on either side of her waist to take hold of her dress. He pulls it from her waist. He sees the rich black crest of her pubic hair and what it promises excites him, makes him murmur kindly in anticipation of his release. In a moment, he will be inside her, in her warmth, and he will lose himself inside her and, afterwards, he will sleep. He'll have the peace of his sleep. He pulls down his jeans and finds himself only half hard. He pulls on his penis, willing it to stiffen.

Clara's daughter screams. She is in her bed in the next room, but her scream is so ferocious it seems she is next to them. He closes his eyes, but he can't escape her scream. Her scream radiates against his eyes like the sun. It makes his brain throb.

Rodrigo feels Clara push his hands from her. If he'd lied, asked her to marry him, she would have let the child cry. He hears her footsteps as she goes to the other room. Even with eyes closed, he knows what Clara is doing. She's lifting her daughter to her breast, offering comfort for her night terrors.

Rodrigo opens his eyes and stares at the vacated bed. "Puta," he says, the word thick and slow out of his mouth. "Puta," he says again, and although he tries to speak loudly, quickly, violently, the word is clumsy, as if foreign to his lips. What comes next surprises him: from his throat, a prolonged, nauseous cough, then another. He closes his eyes again and sees the universe go dark, and he is the lone planet, the lone star. He wishes Clara would return. He would be gentle. He would touch her shoulder with one finger, lightly, as if she were sleeping and he didn't wish to wake her.

He hears nursing sounds. *She's not my daughter*, he thinks. He opens his eyes. He looks at the bed, the bottom sheet and blanket bunched at the end. The sponge mattress has holes where mice have eaten it.

This isn't my bed.

He looks at the room, its white walls stained with spots of mold.

This isn't my room.

He pulls on his jeans, walks through the front room, opens the door and steps into the night, thinking: *This is not my house. This is not my house. This is not my house.*

The sky is thick with clouds. The moon is buried. Rodrigo limps toward El Dragón. Pedro greets him at the door, smiling, his new silver tooth reflecting the cantina's orange lights. "Where are you going, vos?"

Rodrigo doesn't respond but merely curls his fingers and tips them to his mouth to indicate his intention to drink. Pedro grins and places his hand on Rodrigo's shoulder. "Do you want to come with me to San Cristóbal?"

Rodrigo gazes past Pedro into the empty cantina. On the shelf against the back wall, he sees dark brown bottles of Gallo beer. Rodrigo wonders what he wants more, a woman or another drink. He remembers Clara on the bed, her dress in her lap, her breasts tired but tender. He knows Pedro will pay, as he always does. "Let's go," Rodrigo says, cocking his head to the west.

They get into a pick-up truck, which Pedro is allowed to use because he's the new manager of Finca Santa Elena, a coffee plantation five kilometers south of town. They don't talk on their drive to San Cristóbal. Instead, Pedro sings a song popular on the radio about a woman left alone to raise her child after her lover leaves. Rodrigo wonders if Pedro is mocking him and Clara. He thinks of telling him to shut up, but instead he closes his eyes and wanders into the stars in his head as into a field of flowers.

They park in front of the whorehouse's iron gates, a pair of birds—hawks or vultures, Rodrigo can't be sure—adorning them. Always on entering a whorehouse, Rodrigo feels a stab of guilt. It's an instinctual reaction, a remnant of a time when he loved someone. But he can't betray Julia any longer.

The proprietess seats them in the center of a red-lighted room. A large-breasted girl wearing a blue dress and blue lipstick comes and sits on Pedro's lap. Pedro whispers in her ear. The girl giggles and whispers back. Pedro grins and whispers again. "En serio?" the girl asks. Pedro nods. The girl looks at Rodrigo, then turns again to whisper in Pedro's ear.

Rodrigo senses something sinister about to happen, but he's too tired and drunk to inquire or object. The girl with the blue dress and blue lipstick leaves Pedro's lap and converses with the proprietess in a corner of the room. Rodrigo and Pedro are the only customers, and the place is quiet. Rodrigo can hear a breeze lick the lake a block below the whorehouse.

When they are done talking, the blue girl and the proprietess walk to where Rodrigo and Pedro are sitting. The blue girl sits on Pedro's lap. Gingerly, the proprietess sits on Rodrigo's. The proprietess is skinny and small, with lines in her brown skin. Rodrigo guesses she is over fifty years old, and he is startled to have her suddenly on his lap, caressing his hair.

"She doesn't come cheap, vos, so enjoy yourself," Pedro says as he and the blue girl stand and disappear.

Rodrigo doesn't know what to say to the proprietess. He's furious at Pedro for playing this trick on him. But it's too late to protest, and when the proprietess takes his hand, he follows her out of the red-lighted room and into an adjacent bedroom with soft yellow light. *She's older than my mother.*

Rodrigo sits in a chair near the door. His eyes feel heavy, and as the proprietess removes her blouse he's comforted by the thought that no matter what happens between them he'll soon be asleep.

The proprietess wears no bra; her breasts are tiny, hardly more than nipples. She removes her skirt and underwear. Presently, she stands naked in front of him, her feet spread generously, as if she were trying to keep balanced against a strong wind. She has a forest of hair below her belly button. It trickles across her thighs, falls full between her legs. Rodrigo steps toward her but stumbles and slides to his knees. The room recedes and returns.

"Do you remember me?" he says to her small feet. He looks up. "We met at the Santa Cruz *feria*. I had a *novia*, but I betrayed her with you. I told myself I would follow you until I loved you and you loved me." Darkness crowds the corners of his eyes. "Is it too late?" His head collapses against her belly, but presently she steps back and he is falling. The darkness expands to catch him.

He wakes in the back of Pedro's pickup truck, dew on his face and the sun a desperate light behind a gray curtain of sky.

— 18 —

Julia is surprised when, two weeks after she wrote to Alejandra, she receives a reply postmarked from Puerto Barrios. Alejandra's letter is written on lined school paper in black ink. Her script is like her eyes, large and round, and even before she reads the letter, she feels a rush of joy. *It's you.*

Alejandra's letter begins, "Of course I remember you, Julia. You were the best friend I had in Santa Cruz. And if I do not remember everything about my time in Santa Cruz fondly, I will always be glad to have met you.

"After I left Santa Cruz, I stayed with Ben for a few months before returning to Ohio. Soon afterwards, he, too, returned to the States. We moved together to Chicago, but we found we didn't like our lives nearly as much as we did in Guatemala. Perhaps you will be surprised to hear this, but we found people in Guatemala—at least the people in Puerto Barrios—to be much more understanding of our relationship than people in the United States. Our parents did not welcome our relationship at all. This made it hard for me and Ben to be with them and even to be together.

"Both Ben and I decided we wanted to come back to Guatemala, and we were both hired again by Casas Para El Pueblo. Our commitment this time is for more than a year. In fact, we both have five-year contracts. We wish they were for twenty years!

"I am glad you told me about your father. I do not think he and the men he was with wanted to harm me physically, but I understood they didn't want me in Santa Cruz anymore. Even so, I thought about staying, but when I contacted my supervisor at Casas Para El Pueblo, she told me to leave immediately. As you know, other Americans have on occasion been mistreated—or worse—in Guatemala by people who didn't understand why they were here. And, to be fair, some Americans, a small minority, have behaved badly in this country. I, however, only wanted to do good in Santa Cruz. I think you know this.

"I realize I may have crossed a certain cultural line when I gave condoms to one young woman who asked me for them, but I am not sure I would act any differently now. In Puerto Barrios, I don't have to. This is still a town of sailors and prostitutes, a town of people who are very much in danger of becoming infected with the AIDS virus, and most people here are aware of the danger and are looking to prevent a catastrophe. I have had some success with a project I've started to combat the spread of AIDS and other sexually transmitted diseases. I work two afternoons a week in a centro de salud, and I give lectures in colegios around town. Our latest effort is to put up AIDS awareness posters in the bathrooms of the dozens of bars around town. We are planning a visit to all the houses of prostitution. With hard work, we will be able to contain the spread of this disease and perhaps spare Guatemala from what other countries, including my own, are suffering.

"I offer warm congratulations on your marriage and the birth of your daughter. You don't know how hard it is for me to picture you, so young, as a mother, but I know you are a good mother, Julia. You must come with your family to visit me in Puerto Barrios, and when you do, I will do my best to persuade you to live here.

"And, Julia, you do not need my forgiveness for what happened to me in Santa Cruz. I have long ago forgiven your father and the men he was with. There is too much misunderstanding in this world, and if we confront our misunderstandings with fear and accusation, we will never see each other as anything but strangers. The only way to defeat our fear of each other is by meeting and talking and listening in good faith.

"You and I are religious people, Julia, but even as we find in our hearts forgiveness for the wrongs done to us, we must find with our intellects and courage a way to help people everywhere receive a fair place in the communities they live in, a fair place in their countries and, yes, a fair place in the world.

"Am I sounding like a priest? Do you know I wanted to be a priest when I was girl? I was heartbroken when my mother said only men could be priests. And, as then, I ask, 'Why?'

"Julia, it was wonderful to hear from you. You are now, as always, in my thoughts. I am awaiting the day when we again are able to sit over coffee and you surprise me with one of your jokes."

Julia reads the letter a second and third time. When, at last, she puts it down, she thinks: *I'll see her again. Maybe I'll even help her with her work. Yes, wouldn't it be nice to help her? But, at last, I'll see her. Thank God. I'll see her.*

FIVE

— 1 —

Pedro's voice seems to Rodrigo deep and resonant, but distant, as if he were speaking to him from the back of a cave. "Put down the drink, Rodrigo. Come on, hombre. You've had enough. You'll kill your liver. We'll go home."

I am home, Rodrigo thinks. The blackness is spread out in front of him as far as he can see, and this is where he has learned to feel comfortable. This is where he is at peace.

"Home," Pedro says.

"I am home," Rodrigo says or thinks he says. He feels himself reaching for Pedro, to clasp him, to say thank you. Weak beyond sickness, he wants to tell Pedro how much he has meant to him, how lost he'd be without him.

*Pedro, you have been like my...*But he knows he isn't speaking, isn't able to speak.

Pedro? he tries again, but it's as if he's calling only to himself, his voice echoing along the cave walls of his head. The darkness expands and pulls him in further.

— 2 —

He looks, Julia thinks with shock, repulsion and grief, like a toad. Shivering, she turns her head and prays. She would like to feel hopeful; this is why she has come to Cobán, to see if she can help him live. But less than a minute into her visit, she realizes the enterprise will be fruitless. He is dying in his gray hospital bed. She would have known he was dying even if his mother hadn't told her about his liver and the doctor hadn't confirmed it. "I see this with bolos all the time," the doctor, a woman, said. "It's called alcohol poisoning, and with the wrong kind of liquor, it can happen quickly. They drink until their livers shut down. It's only a matter of time before the rest of their organs follow."

Rodrigo's head moves back and forth as if it is being gently rocked by a pair of invisible hands. His eyes are open wide, as blank and eerie as a toad's eyes, and he is sweating like she has never seen anyone sweat. It is thick, oily sweat. She wonders if his inner juices, whatever lubricates his heart and muscles, are abandoning him, leaving his insides to dry up. His mother, sitting at his side, dabs his face with a damp towel. She seems to have shrunk in the years since Julia saw her last, as if living had stripped her of all but bone and skin and her dark, sad eyes.

Julia came because her mother told her about Rodrigo and because Oscar was again on an extended trip, to San Marcos, west of Quetzaltenango, and because she had, in the last two months, learned how to drive. Oscar had wanted to buy her a new American car—a station wagon, he thought, would be best—but she preferred a Toyota Corolla painted midnight blue, and this is what she'd driven the eight hours from Quetzaltenango. Georgina, nine months old now, had ridden in a car seat, sleeping most of the way. Instead of bringing Veronica, Julia had asked Octavia to come with her and help her look after Georgina.

Rodrigo's bed is in a large room on the first floor of the Cobán Hospital Público. Of the nineteen other beds in the room, a dozen are occupied, two by men who seem to be in the same delirious state as Rodrigo. They, however, have no one by their side, and Julia stops to look at them as she walks down the aisle toward the broad window at the end of the room. One is gray-haired, an indígena farmer, Julia guesses. With his gaunt body, he looks as if he has lived off boh for years. The other man is heavy, with a robust, black mustache. Even in his delirium, he looks familiar. He might have been a bus driver or a tienda owner she encountered somewhere, sometime.

Julia reaches the window, which opens onto a grassy courtyard. It is raining, a chipi-chipi. Even so, Julia can see patches of sunlight on the grass. She looks toward the sky, thinking she might glimpse a rainbow, but she sees only the gray walls of the hospital and, above them, clouds.

She takes a deep breath before returning to Rodrigo's side. In her plastic chair beside the bed, Rodrigo's mother seems to be sleeping. The patient next to Rodrigo, a boy of perhaps ten with burns on his face and neck, is asleep, an I.V. attached to his arm. Julia takes Rodrigo's left hand, finding it both cold and wet. She feels his pulse; every few seconds, his fingers squeeze her, and she looks to see if this is intentional, but she is always met by Rodrigo's toad-eyed stare.

When she was driving from Quetzaltenago, she imagined their reunion differently. She imagined that, upon seeing her, he would rise up in his bed and talk to her the way he used to, in hopeful pictures of what the future would be. She thought she would inspire him to heal. Instead, she holds a cold, damp hand, wishing she had come later, when he was dead, so she could have held on to a purer memory of him.

—

Julia is beside his hospital bed. He thinks. He wants to believe.

Qué bueno. Qué fantastico. Qué maravilloso. You have come. You are with me. At last.

He knows what is important to say to her—to beg forgiveness for his long-ago betrayal, to beg another chance—but first he wants to praise her.

Tu eres una rosa.

Tu eres una mariposa.

He wants to call her every sweet living thing. He wants to compare her to rivers and oceans and mountains under pure blue skies.

Tu eres el sol.

Tu eres la luna.

He wants to call her all the planets and all the stars. He doesn't care if this takes him the rest of his life. This will be his celebration and his penance.

Julia looks at him as if she wants to cry.

No, Julia, don't cry.

Tu no eres La Llorona.

He thinks of the fable his mother told him long ago. La Llorona searches all night for her lost child, her dead child, crying. She haunts men with her sorrow. With her tears and her unbearable pain, she reminds mothers of what they could lose at any moment. She scares children with her anger and her sorrow and her eagerness to grab hold of them in her careless search for what she'll never find.

"Her tears were a river," his mother said. "Her tears flowed into the sky and returned to the earth as rain."

His mother told him La Llorona's story with tears in her eyes, and he wondered if his mother's tears, like La Llorona's, would float toward the sky. But he decided the ceiling would stop them, and he would jump and scoop them into his palms. He would return her tears to her eyes and say, "See, Mother, you have un-cried and now you must be the reverse of sad."

———

Rodrigo's mother asked Julia to speak to him, in hopes her voice would wake him from his trance, and Julia intends to keep her promise. But each time she opens her mouth, she feels Rodrigo's fingers clutch her hand and she keeps silent. At the end of the room, she sees the light growing fainter. She hears someone cough from a nearby bed. A nurse steps into the room, looks around and disappears.

"I have a little girl now, Rodrigo," she says. "Her name is Georgina." She is speaking in a whisper, and she doubts he can hear her. But even if he could, would he want to know about her daughter? She pulls in a deep breath. She squeezes his hand. "I remember when we used to go to the soccer field in Chixajau," she says. "You were a boy and I was a girl and we were free and we had dreams the size of the sky. Do you remember the time you led me under the avocado tree and how close we came"—her voice is less than a whisper now—"to being real lovers? I guess God didn't want us to be together because the soldiers came, but Rodrigo, with you sometimes I was willing to do what God didn't want."

She isn't looking at him. She can't look at him and speak the words she is speaking. She tries not to feel his palm in hers, its cold dampness. She is talking to the Rodrigo who once was, only a short time ago, when he was a boy who smelled like grass and who made her heart dance with the depth and sureness of his voice. "I'm sorry, Rodrigo," she says in a louder voice. "I'm sorry for failing you. You always had more faith than I did. Forgive me." She sees a pair of heads in beds to her right lift from their pillows and look at her.

Rodrigo moans, something grotesque, like a captive animal. She releases her grip and steps back, frightened, disgusted. Rodrigo's mother is at his side now, patting his forehead again with the damp towel. To Julia, the room seems suddenly hot. The window at the end of the room is flushed with sunlight.

Rodrigo's mother whispers into his ear as Julia retreats from the room. She takes one look back and sees Rodrigo's mother standing next to his bed, her head bowed over her son like a supplicant's over an altar. Her blue dress looks large and billowy around her. In the vastness of the sick room, she seems like only another of its maimed and diseased, holding on to whatever remains of life.

———

Julia is gone, if she was ever here. But in the chair below his bed, Rodrigo sees another woman, sleeping. His mother? Sleeping. Or crying? Crying?

Dry your face, Mother. I don't want you to cry.

The darkness swells.

He hears his mother say, "La Llorona looks for her child even when there is no moon to light her way. She looks every night because as long as she is looking for him, there is hope she will find him."

Don't cry, Mother, he wants to say.

His mouth is numb.

He sees the darkness engulf his mother. She is only shadow, an outline of black against black.

It isn't Julia he has betrayed. It never was.

———

Outside the hospital, Julia is surprised to step into a day stunning in its brightness. The sun blazes between great white pillows of clouds. She finds herself walking in swift retreat from the dying she has witnessed, and she reaches the black gates of El Estadio Imperial. The Imperials' season is long over, but the field is occupied by a handful of boys playing soccer, their shirts thrown down as goal markers.

With difficulty, Julia maneuvers her slim body into a gap in the gates and walks onto the grass. The boys look at her with concern, doubtless afraid she'll order them off the field.

The teams are unfairly divided, six against five. When the ball trickles out of bounds toward her, she picks it up. "I'll play on this team," she says, gesturing to her right. The boys, who must be no older than twelve, say nothing until a boy to her right, standing between the shirts, declares, "Okay, but you have to play goalie."

"Sorry," Julia says. "I'm not a goalie."

The boy shrugs his acquiescence. To fit in with the other players, Julia removes her shoes. The damp grass embraces her feet.

The boys on her team are reluctant to pass to her, and she finds herself jogging up and down the field parallel to where the ball is. She begins to sweat, and her breathing deepens. At first she feels both sluggish and light-headed, but as she continues to move, a kind of exhilaration fills her.

A boy sends a pass to her. She kicks the ball down the sideline. As she is pursuing it, she feels the wind rush onto her face and the grass caress her feet. She knows again in a flash, and painfully, why Rodrigo loved to play. She traps the ball, side-steps one boy and finds herself face to face with the goaltender, who crouches in anticipation of her shot. She brings her foot hard into the ball. At the same time the ball leaves her foot, she finds herself slipping, sliding. A moment later, she is on her back. Her teammates shout in celebration; she has scored.

She remains where she is, the grass soft around her. Clouds shimmer in the sun and she listens to herself breath, heavy breaths of exertion and triumph, and she feels the coolness of the grass on her arms and neck and ankles. She pictures Rodrigo as he was, with agile feet and swift, powerful legs. Add the crowds. Add their adoration. Add her, Julia, and whatever he loved best about her—her hair, her jokes and her laughter—and how could he have been content with any other life?

———

In his dream, the field in Chixajau is damp from dew. Clouds hang low in the sky, and a swath of mist sits above the field. In the center of the field, Rodrigo sees a dozen men chasing a soccer ball. Like him, they wear no shoes. It isn't yet dawn. Or if it is, the sun is hidden behind the mountains in the distance.

As he approaches the men, he wonders if they'll stop the game to acknowledge him. They are intent on chasing after the ball, however, and he jogs to keep up with them. "Let me play!" he shouts, but they don't turn around. "Let me play!" he shouts again, and after a moment, a tall man turns and waves him on.

Rodrigo runs and feels no pain. His bare feet spring off the short, dry grass. It's as if the grass is helping him run faster, pushing him forward. In moments, he has caught up to the men. There are more of them than he first counted, perhaps twenty or thirty. The tall man who invited him into the game is dribbling the ball. Rodrigo runs beside him. He wants to ask him where he's going—Rodrigo sees no goalpost, only a long stretch of field—but the man kicks the ball ahead of them. From instinct, from desire, Rodrigo leaves the tall man in pursuit of the ball, his feet flying off the grass.

The ball rolls into a pentagon of sunlight, and Rodrigo is dazzled by its brightness. He's never seen a soccer ball quite so white. He wonders what it will be like to touch it with his bare foot, wonders if it will sting. Or will it feel like something he's never felt before, something soft, pliable, as weightless as air?

With fear, with exhilaration, with his last breath, Rodrigo steps toward it and kicks.

— 3 —

The morning of Rodrigo's funeral is cool and full of sunlight. It is the kind of morning on which Rodrigo, the Rodrigo Julia loved, would have been on the soccer field, dribbling up and down the sidelines, firing shots at an untended goal. It is a brilliant morning, but the good weather alone doesn't explain the size of the crowd, the hundreds of people who have joined the procession.

The priest, a norteamericano with gray-brown eyes and thin gray hair, says a prayer over Rodrigo's casket before being startled by a sound above him. All eyes follow his, and a flock of parakeets, chirping riotously, swoops over the cemetery and flutters toward the mountains to the south. Julia finds a place to stand to the left of Rodrigo's crypt. His mother is next to the priest, and Clara, Rodrigo's novia, stands behind her. Clara's daughter sits in the dirt in front of her mother, playing with a plastic doll.

Behind her, Julia hears a soft whistle and she turns to find Pedro, dressed in black pants and a black, button-down shirt, standing against an aqua-colored crypt. In the years since she has seen him, he hasn't aged. His hair remains black with the same few strands of gray, and his face is unlined. Despite the crowd around her, she feels oddly alone with him, and their proximity sets her heart racing as if she were meeting him at night in a private place. "You look very nice in black," he tells her.

She turns her head quickly and looks again at Rodrigo's casket. Although she is only ten meters from it, she feels she is watching from a greater distance. She looks behind her again, hoping she'll see her mother; but her mother, with Angelica, Georgina and Octavia, must be at the back of the crowd. Her father, meanwhile, refused to miss a day of work to attend the funeral.

Julia sees Hidalia in her green hotel uniform and Rodrigo's friend Galindo, the tallest in the crowd. He is married now, with a baby boy, and is teaching mathematics at El Instituto Básico. Behind Galindo is a dark-skinned woman, and Julia flushes, thinking it's Alejandra. But although the woman appears foreign, she is too short to be Alejandra. Next to the foreign woman is Alma, her former classmate, Don Carlos's daughter. Alma's three-year-old girl fidgets by her side. The child's father, Julia's mother told her, owns a pension in Cobán and is married; he has never acknowledged his daughter.

"He spoke of you often, especially toward the end." Pedro is standing next to Julia now. Although his presence intimidates her, she is drawn to his smell, a smell like aftershave and cherry candy. He smiles. His teeth are magnificent and white save one, capped with silver. "I told him to forget you, but he wouldn't listen."

Julia says, "He had Clara."

Pedro touches her on the shoulder, a tentative touch, as if he were afraid of being burned. She feels how large his hand is. He leaves it on her shoulder, even presses it into her. "He was lonely, and loneliness has its own needs. He couldn't live off his memory of you, although some nights, believe me, he tried."

He withdraws his hand and takes a step back, but she can still smell him. "I told him to forget you," he says, "but I understand why he couldn't."

She glances at him and finds him staring at her with his dark eyes. Quickly, she looks away. A pair of men in work clothes, two of the cemetery's caretakers, slide Rodrigo's casket into a slot in the crypt and begin to cement it shut. Behind Julia, a man shouts, "You should have seen him on the soccer field!"

"I did!" another man replies.

There is a rumbling in the crowd. At first Julia thinks the voices are calls for silence, but she realizes people are recalling the times they, too, watched Rodrigo play. Far from ceasing in the next minutes, their voices increase in number and volume. Even when Rodrigo's mother and brothers turn to follow the priest back to town, people keep talking. Julia hears the names of different teams vanquished by Rodrigo's marvelous feet and powerful shot. She hears her name and the name of Rodrigo's old team, the Imperials.

Don Ofelio, the retired postmaster, stands small and wrinkled against a black iron fence at the cemetery's edge. When Julia moves to walk past him, he holds up his hand to stop her. His wife died long ago and his three sons moved to the capital or to the United States, Julia doesn't remember. He lives by himself in a green block house behind the correos office, drinking more than he should. "I never could go to a game myself," he tells her, "but I always listened on the radio. Every Saturday, I sat in my living room, and if someone came to the door, I invited him to sit with me. You could always tell when Rodrigo had the ball because even before the announcer spoke his name, you could hear the crowd cheer. They always expected something great of him, didn't they? And he was great, wasn't he? You saw him, Julia. You saw how great he was, didn't you?"

He fixes his eyes on her, and she sees he wants an answer, as if he distrusts his memory or if some more recent impression of Rodrigo has intruded upon the purity of what he recalls. Or perhaps, she thinks, he isn't asking about Rodrigo, but about one of his sons or himself or the whole town. He seems to want an answer, but Julia, pushed by the crowd, passes him without replying.

— 4 —

It is past ten o'clock at night, and Julia is walking around town in order to ease her restlessness, her insomnia. Georgina and Octavia are asleep in Julia's old bedroom. When Julia returns, she will slip into the same double bed as Octavia. If on their first night in Santa Cruz, Octavia protested this arrangement, saying she would sleep on a petate on the floor, she is used to it now. Octavia's breathing is quieter than Oscar's.

During nights in Santa Cruz, Georgina has slept in a crib next to the bed without waking, and Julia has decided her daughter sleeps better here, in the northern mountains, where the air is richer thanks to the abundance of trees. But the reason for Georgina's tranquil sleep may be simpler. She is older now and may only have become more at ease with herself, with living.

The town is deserted save an occasional truck coming to or from San Cristóbal, a pair of lovers in the park, melted into each other to form one body and a lone man sitting on a stool in front of Tienda Esperanza. Nights in Santa Cruz have never been anything but empty and lonely, she suspects, but confined to her room, propped behind her desk or snuggled in her bed, she never knew them and could only imagine them as exhilarating and alive with promise.

She approaches Tienda Esperanza, intending to turn right and continue home, when the man on the stool turns around. His eyes run twice across her body. She says his name, and when he doesn't reply, she thinks he must be drunk. She is about to continue her walk when he says, "I wouldn't have expected to see you out here at so late an hour, so I thought I was staring at a ghost." Pedro laughs. "A beautiful ghost, but a ghost all the same."

He stands up. "Let me treat you to a drink," he says.

"You know I don't drink."

"I don't mean alcohol." He holds up his half full bottle and shakes it. "What I'm having: a Coke."

She looks up and down Calle Tres de Mayo, wondering who might be watching her. If someone she knew spotted her with Pedro, rumors would begin overnight and grow into something grotesque by morning. She bows her head and walks the twelve steps to the stool next to his and climbs onto it. The boy behind the tienda's counter leaves his plastic chair and asks what she wants.

The Coke bottle is cool around her hand. She presses it against her forehead.

"Headache?" Pedro asks.

"It's nothing," she says.

Pedro turns around to face the street, but Julia remains sitting forward. The boy manning the tienda has returned to his chair and has closed his eyes. A truck passes, although Julia doesn't turn around to look. She hears its engine rumble as it heads toward San Cristóbal.

"So Rodrigo drank a lot toward the end," Julia says.

"Yes, he did."

"Why?"

"Why does anyone drink? To forget his losses."

She turns to him. Although it is a cool night, beads of sweat dampen his upper lip. "What have you lost, Pedro?"

"Today I buried my best friend. This is a loss."

"But you drank long before Rodrigo died."

"I drank to keep other men company, men who had losses. Their losses became mine. I drank to all the losses in the world."

She looks to see if he is smiling one of his sardonic smiles, but he is only looking down the neck of his Coke bottle. He catches her eye. "Do you think I'm responsible for Rodrigo drinking himself to death?"

"I have heard some people blame you," she says.

"Do you blame me?"

She shrugs. "I could as easily blame myself."

"Or your father."

She stares at him suspiciously. "I couldn't blame him."

"No?" Pedro curls his lips into a provocative smile.

"Why would he be to blame?"

Pedro shrugs.

"Why, Pedro?"

He looks at her before looking away. "I have heard he ordered the soldiers to go to Finca Mundial the day Rodrigo was captured."

Julia waves her hand dismissively. "How could he order them? He isn't in the army."

"But Carlos Sierra is a former army lieutenant, and your father works with him, doesn't he? Your father knew you still planned to marry Rodrigo, even after he forbid it."

Julia puts her bottle down on the tienda's counter. She sees the pair of lovers cross the street and stand under the roof of the municipalidad before splitting, the boy heading east, the girl west.

Julia says, "I am sure my father didn't want me to marry Rodrigo. But I am also sure he didn't ask Don Carlos to send soldiers to Finca Mundial."

Pedro shrugs. "It doesn't matter now."

Although there is nothing left in his bottle, Pedro brings it to his lips. She watches him sip the air inside.

"Do you believe my father is this cruel?" she asks him.

Pedro gazes at her for a long time. "I think your father would do anything to protect you. And I don't blame him. You are worth more than anything he has." He opens his right hand and sweeps it in front of him. "To him, you're worth more than this whole town."

In Pedro's look there is something hungry and covetous, and she is half afraid of his look and half drawn to it.

"I am leaving for Mexico tomorrow," he says. "I have friends in the capital city. Eventually, we will all go to the United States." He pauses. "I, too, am worth more than this town." He gives her a smile, and it's this smile she most associates with Pedro, a confident, arrogant smile.

"You are brave to leave your country."

"Come with me." He stares at her, his gaze unblinking.

"I think you're playing a joke on me. Or are you being disrespectful?"

"No," he says, and she feels his hand on her shoulder. His touch is almost shocking. "I am serious," he says with urgency. "I know you are unhappy. You don't want to go back to your husband and you can't stay here. So I am giving you a third choice. If you think about it, it's the best of the three."

"I have a daughter."

"She would come."

Julia laughs. "And the first time she cried—or perhaps the second—you and your friends would throw us onto the side of the highway."

"You underestimate me."

Julia feels a strange thrill. It is late, and the streets are empty and she and Pedro could be any man and any woman sitting on these stools, any couple with any history. He might be as handsome as he is, but a far better man, and she might be a woman without a child and without a husband; she might have the same wild ambition to see what lies beyond the borders of her country.

"I never realized how romantico you are," she says.

"There's more you don't know about me." He squeezes her shoulder. "You would be surprised." She lets his hand linger on her.

"I know why Rodrigo liked you," she says.

"Why?"

"Because you are a dreamer." She removes his hand from her shoulder and thanks him for the Coke and says goodnight.

She walks home, knowing she won't be able to sleep, knowing she'll remain awake, wondering, wondering.

— 5 —

Julia wakes before her mother, and when her mother finds her in the dark of the kitchen, she turns on the light. The room appears, its walls smoke-singed from when her mother used fire and wood to cook. Her mother doesn't seem surprised to see her sitting on the bench in the corner. Her mother steps up to the stove in the other corner and turns the gas burner on under the kettle. It clicks three times before igniting, sending a blue flame around the kettle. She goes to the refrigerator and pulls a half-full can of beans from it and scoops the contents into a pot. "Will you eat breakfast with your father?"

"No, thank you. I'm not hungry."

"But you will sit with him?"

"Yes."

From the refrigerator, her mother also removes two eggs, which she breaks into a bowl. "You came in late last night."

"You were awake?"

"I can never sleep until my children are asleep."

"Even now?"

"Especially now."

"What are you worried about?"

"What I always worry about. Thieves. Ghosts."

When Julia's father comes into the kitchen, he is dressed in black slacks and a short-sleeved blue shirt. His black shoes are shined. He pauses a moment when he sees Julia at the table, then sits down across from her. "Buenos días," he says.

"Buenos días."

A few moments later, Julia's mother puts his breakfast in front of him. "Tortillas?" he asks her.

"I forgot to buy them from Doña Vidaluz yesterday."

He shrugs. "No bread?"

Julia's mother reaches into a shelf next to the refrigerator and pulls down a covered basket, which she puts on the table. Julia's father reaches into the basket and removes a piece of pan francés. After biting into it, he says, "Stale." He dips it into his coffee and eats it this way. He looks at Julia. Looks away. Looks at her again. In the years since she has lived away from home, his face has grown thinner; his eyes have receded more. "You look unhappy," he tells Julia. "Are you?"

She looks at him, wondering if she'll be able to see the cruelty in him. But she does not look long before, afraid, she turns her head.

"You didn't answer me," he says.

"I can't answer you."

"Why?"

"Because I don't know the answer."

"Should I tell you the answer?"

She looks at him again, half curious, half wary.

"You are unhappy because you have stepped into a place of unhappiness. I know you came because of Rodrigo. You and your mother tried to pretend otherwise, but it was obvious. You thought you could save Rodrigo, but nothing can save a drunk except God and a strong liver."

"Oh, Papá."

"Do you think I speak too crudely? You didn't see him the past few months curled up in doorways, flies crowded around his mouth and eyes."

"Please, Papá."

She turns to look at her mother, but her mother has left the kitchen. She hears her mother turn the faucet of the pila in the courtyard. She hears the rush of the pila's water into the basin. Speaking to the ground, Julia asks, "Papá, did you talk to Don Carlos about sending soldiers to Finca Mundial when Rodrigo was picking coffee there?"

Julia counts the seconds of silence. One, two, three, four. Five.

"Where did you hear this?"

"From people."

"What people?"

"Papá, I wouldn't ask you this, you know I wouldn't, if I didn't feel..." She looks up at him now. Her eyes are irritated, as if the smoke that once filled the kitchen at mealtimes was still in the air. "I didn't believe the rumors, but last night I couldn't sleep, couldn't sleep at all, and I knew I would have to ask you." She holds her look on him. "Did you, Papá? Did you?"

She is expecting him to upbraid her over her rudeness, but he is smiling, a soft, sad smile. He lets a few moments pass before he speaks, his words and his cadence like a preacher's: "It would be nice to imagine I had the power to control the actions of armies. It would be even nicer, I think, to imagine that my love and concern for my daughter were such that I would call on battalions to defend her future."

He pauses, shaking his head, his eyes focused on his half-eaten breakfast. He lifts his head, and he is looking at her with what seems like great seriousness, even sorrow. "I knew you planned to marry Rodrigo against my wishes," he says. "And, yes, I planned to stop it. But my plan involved no armies. It involved no one but myself."

She says softly, "What did you plan, Papá?"

"I planned to take you away. I had even put in for a vacation at work. I planned to take you to places I had seen only in posters, places you never would have seen if you were Rodrigo's wife."

"And if, even then, I loved him?"

He doesn't answer. He doesn't have to.

She listens to the water fall into the pila's deep basin. And she hears an even quieter sound, so quiet her father can't hear: her mother, weeping.

— 6 —

It begins to rain as soon as Julia leaves the calvario. She has been sitting in front of the familiar altar, praying and wondering and thinking. Unlike her previous moments in this place of icons and dying flowers, she didn't care if she was seen by spying eyes. She believes in these moments by herself, with her God, as much as she believes in what the Evangelical preachers say with furious conviction. If this makes her Catholic, she is Catholic.

She has decided this, too: She wants a different country, a different world, where men and boys do not have to decide which side of a war to fight on and if they survive the war, to come home haunted. She wants a world where conversation precedes action, where kindness is offered and offered again and offered a third time before violence or the threat of violence is. She wants a world where fathers protect their daughters by allowing them to grow in the same soil, with the same fertilizer and rain, as their sons. She thinks of Georgina and wonders what world she will know in twenty years.

She doesn't know if she can help Georgina's world be more prosperous, peaceful and good. After Rodrigo's death, she feels more powerless than ever to change what should be changed. But she remembers what Lilian once told her, about how she intended to work to change the wrongs around her, little wrong or large wrongs, it didn't matter. They might be wrongs only she saw, but if she was silent in their presence they would remain wrong and the world would remain the same. The first step, Lilian said, was to speak the wrong aloud. A small revolution, she called it.

From the top of the calvario steps, Julia can see her entire town, including the new Oro Verde development to the east. But even in its expansion, its slow, persistent growth into the mountains, Santa Cruz is the same town she knew as a girl.

She knows the curves of its roads and the chattering calls of its birds, and she will grow old with it, however far from it she lives, because she will always return to it, in memory as much as in fact, and its sorrows will line her face. And, gradually, she will grow more at ease with its ghosts.

She makes the long descent on the concrete stairs, avoiding the toads who have come from the weeds as if to greet her, their swollen eyes giving them the look of old, crying men. As she walks down Calle Principal, a red car pulls beside her. The tinted driver's window comes down, and she sees Pedro inside. He is only a few steps from her, but, with his hand, he beckons her closer. "I was serious, Julia. I want you to come with me."

"When are you leaving?"

"Now."

She takes another step toward his car, and she feels herself opening the back door, like a passenger in a taxi, and settling into the deep, plush seat. The journey is all ahead of her, and it is thrilling.

When Pedro drives off and she sees the red glow of his taillights grow dim and disappear, when she turns west, toward her house and her child and the packing she must do to return to Quetzaltenango, where she will talk with Oscar again, definitively, about moving to Puerto Barrios, she feels the loss of both what once was and what could have been. They are buried together with Rodrigo in his crypt. But even weighted with bereavement, she lifts her head, and on her face she feels the pleasant fall of chipi-chipi. The indígena women returning from market with their unsold vegetables stop in front of her, pausing in their hurry toward home and chores to say "Buenas tardes" and smile and await her reply.

Biography:

Mark Brazaitis is the author of five books of fiction, including *The Incurables: Stories*, winner of the 2012 Richard Sullivan Prize, from the University of Notre Dame Press. He is also the author of a book of poems, *The Other Language*, winner of the 2008 ABZ Poetry Prize. A former Peace Corps Volunteer and technical trainer, he is a professor of English at West Virginia University.

Books from Gival Press—Fiction & Nonfiction

Boys, Lost and Found by Charles Casillo

The Cannibal of Guadalajara by David Winner

A Change of Heart by David Garrett Izzo

The Day Rider and Other Stories by J. E. Robinson

Dead Time / Tiempo muerto by Carlos Rubio

Dreams and Other Ailments / Sueños y otros achaques by Teresa Bevin

The Gay Herman Melville Reader edited by Ken Schellenberg

Gone by Sundown by Peter Leach

An Interdisciplinary Introduction to Women's Studies
        edited by Brianne Friel and Robert L. Giron

Julia & Rodrigo by Mark Brazaitis

The Last Day of Paradise by Kiki Denis

Literatures of the African Diaspora by Yemi D. Ogunyemi

Lockjaw: Collected Appalachian Stories by Holly Farris

Maximus in Catland by David Garrett Izzo

Middlebrow Annoyances: American Drama in the 21st Century by Myles Weber

The Pleasuring of Men by Clifford H. Browder

Riverton Noir by Perry Glasser

Second Acts by Tim W. Brown

Secret Memories / Recuerdos secretos by Carlos Rubio

Show Up, Look Good by Mark Wisniewski

The Smoke Week: Sept. 11-21. 2001 by Ellis Avery

The Spanish Teacher by Barbara de la Cuesta

That Demon Life by Lowell Mick White

Tina Springs into Summer / Tina se lanza al verano by Teresa Bevin

The Tomb on the Periphery by John Domini

Twelve Rivers of the Body by Elizabeth Oness

For a complete list of Gival Press titles, visit: *www.givalpress.com*.
Books available from Follett, your local bookstore, your favorite internet bookseller,
or directly from Gival Press.

    Gival Press, LLC
    PO Box 3812
    Arlington, VA 22203
    givalpress@yahoo.com
    703.351.0079

Made in the USA
San Bernardino, CA
12 September 2014